ODD TIMES FOR SOPHIE FEEGLE

GWEN DEMARCO

CHAPTER 1

The woman in the sharp suit looked over the men and women sitting around the conference table, contempt on her face. Clicking on her tablet, she made a note to fire Cortez. 'Useless' she wrote next to his name.

Standing up, she leaned her hands on the table, looming over those sitting. Her brow dropped into a disappointed frown.

"Has anyone looked at the numbers for this quarter?" she asked.

Everyone stared at the tabletop, too scared to meet her eyes.

"Hmm? Nobody? Nobody here has seen the numbers? Or are you all too chickenshit to speak up?" she taunted.

"The market has been on a downward trend. I believe that all our competitors are in the same—"

Holding up her hand to shut up the sniveling peon, she focused her attention just over their heads, at the far side of the room. Slowly turning, she looked like she was searching for something. Whipping her head to the right, she locked onto her target.

"Hey..." she said, a slow grin spreading across her face. "Who are you two?"

Rubbing her eyes, Sophie reached for her dream journal. "That was a weird one." She hated dreams where she saw herself in the third person. It was too much like her dreams of her sister Ruby.

An arm slipped around her waist, trying to tug her back under the sheets.

"Come back to bed, Soph," Mac muttered with a groan.

"I will in a sec. I just need to write this down before I forget it."

She opened the journal and grabbed her fluffy pen when a buzz from her phone interrupted her writing. *Who would be texting at this hour?* Sighing with annoyance, Sophie tucked the pen back into the pages of her journal and grabbed the phone. A message from Ruby waited for her, lighting the screen up.

I just had the weirdest dream!

Sophie made a strangled noise. *What the hell does that mean?*

She just couldn't deal with this right now. Ruby sent her texts almost every day, despite the radio silence from Sophie's end. Ruby was not getting the memo that Sophie was not interested in a relationship with her psychotic, murderous twin sister. The cheerful, emoji-filled messages were starting to wear on Sophie's nerves. Whenever her phone buzzed in her pocket, she felt her stress levels rise.

With an aggravated huff, she decided that she would deal with it once the sun was up and not a moment sooner. Quickly jotting down the dream, Sophie tossed her journal on the nightstand and slid back into Mac's arms. She glanced at the clock and calculated how much more sleep she could get if she fell asleep immediately.

∼

The room had brightened with enough pre-dawn light that Sophie could make out Mac at her bedroom door, heading out.

"Hey," she called. "Heading to work already?"

2

Mac turned back and sat on the edge of the mattress, leaning over to give Sophie a soft good-morning kiss.

"Sorry if I woke you. You're out of coffee." Mac shushed Sophie when she tried to apologize. "I'm going to go pick us up some coffees before I head to work."

"And a chocolate croissant."

"And a chocolate croissant," Mac confirmed with a chuckle.

With a final kiss, he strode out of the room to fetch Sophie her coffee.

Snuggling back into her pillow, the noise of early morning traffic lulled her back to sleep. It felt like barely five minutes had passed before the creak of her wooden floor let her know Mac had returned.

"That was fast," Sophie said. Rolling onto her side, she saw Mac standing in the doorway to her bedroom, the shadows hiding his face from her view.

A rumbling growl came from Mac, the warning in his tone clear.

"Mac?"

The strobe of a notification on Sophie's phone lit up the room. Glancing at the phone, Sophie saw the words *GET OUT* emblazoned across the screen.

The figure stepped closer, and she instinctively knew that whoever was in her bedroom was not Mac. He had the body of a man, but his face was all wolf. The wolf shifter gave her a grin displaying a row of sharp, gleaming teeth.

"Shit," Sophie yelped, scrambling across her mattress to put the bed between her and the intruder.

Sophie tried to leap to the left, hoping to get out of her bedroom, but the wolf shifter countered her move, cutting her off. Looking around, Sophie realized there was no escape unless she wanted to leap out a third-floor window.

"Mac!" Sophie bellowed.

"The fox is gone. It's just you and me now." The shifter gave a long sniff, his snout pointed up, but his eyes never left Sophie's face. "I can smell your fear."

In the hopes of stalling the shifter, Sophie asked, "What do you want?"

Instead of answering, the wolfman leaped onto the mattress, backing Sophie into the corner of her bedroom. With her night-stand pressing into the back of her thigh, Sophie reached a hand back, scrambling her fingers over the surface, searching for something she could use as a weapon.

The wolfman loomed closer, giving her a wide canine smile. They were both aware that Sophie would be no match for a wolf shifter in his half-form.

At least he's taking his sweet time, Sophie thought as the man swaggered towards her, waving his wickedly sharp claws at Sophie, clicking the pointed tips against one another. He stepped down off the mattress and faced her with another grin. *Dramatic asshole.*

Finally, Sophie's fingers wrapped around the base of the lamp she'd found at a flea market. Back then, she'd bought it because the body was made of antique green Depression glass, but now its best feature was its heavy brass base.

Tightening her grip, Sophie prepared to defend herself with nothing but a damn lamp. At that moment, her phone lit up with another message. When the shifter glanced over his shoulder towards the strobing light, Sophie swung the lamp with all her might. The cord yanked her up short, but she was still able to hit her attacker upside his head. The metal of the lamp made a sick-ening hollow sound as the heavy glass shattered and flew in every direction in a cascade of green shards.

Knowing that wasn't enough to put a shifter down for long, she scrambled over her mattress and out of her bedroom. Her only thought was to get to her taser, which was in her bag by her front door.

The pounding of footsteps thundered behind her, so close

that Sophie could feel the reverberation in her feet. There was no way she would make it to her bag before the shifter reached her. Sophie felt his fingers brush her shoulder as the man tried to snag her by her pajamas. His snatch missed her by a breath as she darted in a new direction. Sophie sprinted towards her kitchen, aiming for the butcher block of knives waiting on the counter.

A rough shove from behind knocked her off her feet and sent her sprawling across her living room floor. Using her hands to cushion the fall, she could feel the burn of the rug's fibers on her palms. In Sophie's head, she could hear her self-defense teacher Paddy bellowing to never let them get you on the ground. She could almost hear his voice with its thick Irish accent telling her to get off her "arse" and fight.

Flipping over so that her back was no longer turned to the assailant, Sophie scrambled back like a terrified crab. Scooting on her ass, she bumped against the wall next to her kitchen entrance. Hopping to her feet, she fell back into the fighting stance Paddy taught her. She tucked her chin toward her chest, staggered to her feet, and lifted her fists to protect her face. A line of blood trickled down the side of her attacker's canine-like face from where Sophie had hit him with the lamp, but the shifter didn't even seem to notice it. She'd shattered a lamp against his skull, and it had barely slowed him down. Sophie had no idea how she would make it out of this one.

The sneer on his furry face solidified her resolve. It looked bleak, but whatever happened, Sophie would go down fighting. This asshole might win the fight, but she would ensure he earned it first. She shifted her weight to the balls of her feet and took a deep breath. *Let's make this count.*

"Not so tough now when you don't have a gun, huh? You can't shoot me like you did to Alphonse. I'm gonna enjoy this," the shifter said, cracking his knuckles and taking a menacing step closer.

"You stupid mutt, I didn't shoot Alphonse!"

"No, that was me," a voice said from behind the wolfman.

Before the shifter could turn around, Ruby vaulted onto his back, climbing up his body like a spider monkey. With a flash of silver highlighted in the growing morning light, she plunged a knife into the space between his neck and shoulder. He howled in agony, jerking Ruby off his back and pitching her at Sophie. Ruby landed on Sophie with a thud, and they both hit the ground in an ungainly heap of tangled arms and legs. Sophie's ribs ached like she'd been kicked by a mule. As she groaned and pushed Ruby off, her eyes bulged as Ruby started laughing next to her.

"Did you see that?" Ruby laughed. "Now I know what a dodgeball feels like. I can't believe I missed. I was aiming for his neck."

Sophie's mouth opened, but words wouldn't come out. Her sister was a deranged lunatic. If they both survived this, she would never speak to Ruby again.

"I'll kill you both," the man screeched, panting in rage and pain with the knife sticking out of his shoulder. Blood coated his shoulder and was quickly spreading across his shirt. The look on his face spelled death for both Sophie and her sister.

When he yanked the knife out of his shoulder, Sophie winced. *You're supposed to leave it in so you don't bleed out.*

Scrambling over a still-giggling Ruby, Sophie clambered into her kitchen. As she yanked a knife from her butcher block, the crack of splintering wood came from her front door. With a resounding crash, Sophie's door snapped open, crashing into the wall.

"FREEZE!" Mac bellowed. "Hands in the air."

The wolf shifter snarled at Mac, then cut his eyes towards Ruby, who was still sitting against the wall. So quickly that Sophie could barely follow his movements, the shifter turned and leaped at Ruby, the knife in his hand aiming right for her.

Sophie had hardly taken a step towards the intruder with her knife at the ready before a gunshot rang out, deafening in the small apartment. The man crashed to the floor like a marionette with its strings cut, landing at Ruby's feet. Kicking the knife out of the man's hand, Ruby leaped up from the floor and crowded next to Sophie in the kitchen's entrance. Together they watched as Mac rolled the man to his back and checked his pulse. Sophie knew before Mac pressed his fingers to the shifter's neck. A sense of death had already begun to fill Sophie's small apartment. The man's face had started to slip back into its human form, further confirming the shifter's death.

Shoving past Ruby, Sophie joined Mac, staring at the man's face.

"Does he look familiar to you?" he asked.

Sophie leaned over to look closer and gave Mac a shrug. "I don't think I've seen him before." Now that he had morphed back to his human form, the man looked to be in his late forties, had dark hair with a sprinkling of gray, and a swarthy complexion. There was nothing remarkable about him. He looked like the type of guy you forget about five minutes after meeting.

"Oh yeah, I know him," Ruby said directly behind Sophie's shoulder. Sophie pressed closer to Mac, creeped out that she hadn't noticed Ruby sneak up behind her. "When tracking Alphonse, I saw this guy with him several times. Do you know him, Mac?"

Mac nodded sharply, starting to respond, but an alarmed voice interrupted him.

"Sophie? Is everyone okay? I called the police."

"Birdie!" Sophie exclaimed, striding over to her ruined front door to keep her neighbor from coming inside and seeing the dead man lying in a pool of blood on her living room floor. "We're all okay. Someone broke in, but Mac stopped them."

With a gentle tug, Sophie steered Birdie back to her apartment, assuring her several times that she was perfectly unharmed. "Stay in here with your door locked. I'll get you once the police arrive. I'm sure they'll want to talk to you. Can you do that for me?"

With fear etched across her face, Birdie clung to Sophie's hand for a moment before reluctantly going inside her apartment. Sophie waited until she heard the click of her deadbolt before heading back to her place. When Sophie returned to the apartment, Mac was busy on his phone, and Ruby was sitting on her couch, casually thumbing through the stack of novels on a side table.

"No romance, huh? Color me unsurprised." Ruby restacked the books back on the table with a disappointed sigh.

"How did you get into my apartment?" Sophie demanded, ignoring the dig at her choice of reading material.

Before Ruby could answer, "POLICE! Hands in the air!" boomed from her front entryway.

An entire SWAT team, armed to the teeth, swarmed through Sophie's apartment as Mac explained that he was an officer while Sophie and Ruby froze with their hands raised. Once they had secured her apartment, which only took a minute, they had Sophie and Ruby park their butts on the couch while they secured the scene.

While keeping an eye on Mac as he made calls and directed everyone around them, Sophie answered a few questions from an indifferent officer about what had happened. Sophie's stomach started to rumble, and she wondered if it would be inappropriate to ask about her croissant.

Suddenly, Sophie could hear her landlord's voice out in the hallway. "What's going on here? What did she do now? I'm so sick of her bullshit. If she gets arrested, I'll finally be able to evict her annoying ass."

"Sir, you can't go in there. It's a crime scene. You need to leave. NOW."

Sophie bit her lips as she listened to Moe's sputtered protests. He'd wanted to push her out of Brown Betty for a while, and she knew Moe would use the break-in to press his advantage. Mac's head swiveled away from the officer he was in a quiet discussion with, staring out into the hallway. A predator peeked out of his blue eyes.

The icy look on Mac's face filled Sophie with warm fuzzies as he stalked out her busted apartment door. Mac's murder face shouldn't do such things to her insides, but they just did. She almost felt bad for Moe. Almost.

Tenants' rights were pretty good in San Francisco, so Moe would have one hell of a time kicking her out. And Sophie would happily fight him tooth and nail before she let him kick her out of the first place that felt like home. They'd only be able to pry her away from Brown Betty and Birdie with a crowbar and maybe some dynamite.

Sophie didn't know what Mac did, but she could hear Moe's loud protests die a quick death from her perch on the sofa.

"Who's that?" Ruby asked.

"My landlord." Sophie gave her a what-can-you-do shrug. Ruby wrinkled her nose in sympathy.

A minute later, Mac strode back into her apartment, Moe nowhere to be seen, with murder still in his eyes. After a quick word with the officer-in-charge, he headed in their direction, but a call on his phone stopped him. Looking at the screen, Sophie watched his shoulders drop. Only the Chief of Police, Wilford Dunham, could put that look on Mac's face.

Sophie wished she could read lips as she watched Mac murmur into his phone. The call didn't take long, but she didn't like the look on Mac's face – a combination of frustration and resignation. Hanging up the call and shoving the phone into his pocket, Mac looked like he wanted to break something.

"Is he always so cranky?" Ruby asked, watching Mac's ire with bemusement.

"Yeah." Sophie could hear the warmth in her voice, but she

couldn't help it. Ruby looked like she thought Sophie had lost all her marbles.

"Everything okay?" Sophie asked when Mac stopped in front of them.

Mac shrugged. "The chief wants us all to come to the station right now. He says it's non-negotiable. I wanted you guys to get checked out by a paramedic, but he says we must go now because Marcella wants to see you both. I told him I wasn't risking your health for a meeting, so he's gonna wait. I don't give a shit."

Both sisters assured him that they were uninjured at Mac's skeptical look. Sophie decided not to mention her sore ribs. They were only bruised anyhow. Nothing a couple of days of rest wouldn't fix.

After changing out of her pajamas, Sophie followed Mac alongside Ruby. In the shabby hallway, Birdie was talking to an officer. She looked frightened and frail, clutching her floral housecoat's lapels to keep it closed over her nightgown. Guilt swirled in Sophie's belly. She'd brought this to Birdie's door. What if something had happened to her? Sophie would have never forgiven herself.

"Sophie," Birdie exclaimed when she spotted them. "Are you okay?"

"I'm fine. Someone broke in and attacked me, but Mac and Ruby helped fight him off."

Birdie's eyes widened so much that a small piece of Sophie was amused despite the circumstances. Then she noticed Ruby standing just behind Sophie and looked like she was going to faint.

"Wow. You said she was your twin, but she's an exact copy." Birdie leaned closer, staring at Ruby as if she couldn't believe her eyes.

"Yeah," Sophie replied, saturating her voice with as much disappointment as possible. Ruby thumped her between her shoulder blades in retaliation, making a tiny grin break out on her face. "Birdie, this is my sister Ruby Rivers. Ruby, this is my neighbor and best friend, Birdie."

Ruby shouldered past Sophie, pulling Birdie into a surprise hug.

"Oh my gosh! It's so nice to meet you." Birdie gave Mac and Sophie a save-me look as she gently patted Ruby's back like she was a lost child.

"You seem very sweet for a… what did you call her, Sophie? Oh, that's right. A sociopathic murderer."

"I prefer vigilante," Ruby corrected, Birdie's sarcasm flying right over her head. Ruby pulled back from the hug, slipping her hands into Birdie's. "We should exchange numbers. Any friend of Sophie's is a friend of mine."

"Uh…" Birdie gave Sophie another pleading look.

"Nope," Sophie interrupted. "Not happening. I don't even like that you have *my* number."

"We need to go," Mac reminded everyone, nudging the group towards the stairs.

Sophie noted that Birdie seemed so shocked and possibly off-put by Ruby's psycho cheerleader personality that she didn't even flirt with Mac like usual.

As they walked through the tiny lobby, Moe stuck his head out his first-floor apartment door to stare at Sophie with his lip curled in disgust. The strobing lights of a squad car sitting out front lit his face in garish bursts, distorting his features into a grotesque mask. Sophie returned his sneer with one of her own, but Mac's low growl had Moe jerking back into his apartment and slamming the door shut.

"I don't like him," Mac grumbled, glaring at the closed door.

"Nobody likes him. Just ignore him like I do," Sophie advised, tugging Mac through the lobby and out the front door.

Mac's gray sedan was parked in its usual spot next to Brown Betty. When Ruby tried to get in the front passenger seat, Sophie checked her with a hip, forcing her away from the front passenger door.

"But I called shotgun!" Ruby complained, giving Sophie an exaggerated pout.

"Girlfriend privileges. I get shotgun for life. So, sit your ass in the backseat and shut up."

Ruby huffed an annoyed breath but got into the backseat without further complaints. Reaching across the center console, Mac threaded his fingers with Sophie's, giving her hand a squeeze.

"Are you really okay?" When Sophie assured him she was unharmed, he looked into the rearview mirror at Ruby humming in the backseat. "Thank you, Ruby. I might have been too late if you hadn't gotten there before me."

"Aww, you're welcome."

"How did you get into my apartment?" Sophie asked again. It couldn't have been through the front door because Mac was always vigilant about safety since Sophie lived in the Tenderloin. There was always enough street crime that he insisted that Sophie take proper precautions, like always keeping the front door bolted.

"Through your bedroom window again. You really should keep it locked."

"I live on the third floor," Sophie stated flatly. There wasn't anything nearby that Ruby could have used to access her apartment; she would have had to climb up a flat surface to make it to her window.

"How'd you know Sophie was in trouble?" Mac asked, diverting Sophie's train of thought.

"Oh, that's easy. I dreamed that you'd just woken up and thought Mac was in your doorway. Then that werewolf came into the room, all growly and scary. I woke up and sent Sophie a text telling her to run."

"Wolf shifter," Sophie corrected absently. "They don't like to be called werewolves."

"That makes sense," Mac replied. "Either way – thank you, Ruby. I owe you."

Sophie was also about to begrudgingly thank Ruby when a thought popped into her head. "Hold up," Sophie said, her brows dropped in confusion. "How'd you get to my place so fast? If you were dreaming about me, that meant you were asleep. It couldn't have been more than a few minutes from your text to when you were stabbing the shifter."

Sophie turned and stared down at her sister, who looked sheepish. She looked like she was trying to shrink down into her seat.

"Explain," Sophie demanded when Ruby didn't answer her immediately.

"Well… When Marcella offered me the job, it included living expenses. I requested that I live near you. I told her that we wanted to live near each other to get to know one another better."

"Near me? You were there in barely five minutes. Where *exactly* do you live?"

"Um, across the street."

For a moment, Sophie just stared at her sister. At a complete loss of words, Sophie blinked, trying to figure out how to explain to Ruby how unacceptable and frankly stalkerish it was of her to purposefully move into a place right across the street.

"You need to move. Immediately."

An outraged silence from the back seat filled the vehicle before Ruby made a noise of anger.

"Rude much? Where's my 'Thanks for saving my life, Ruby,' huh? Where's my 'What's happening in your life? How's the new job going?'" Ruby snarked in a weird squeaky voice. "Thanks for asking, Sophie. I'm doing good besides having a super ungrateful sister. The job's mostly boring. You should be *glad* I live nearby. If

I hadn't been so close, that shifter dude probably would have killed you."

"I do not sound like that," Sophie growled before blowing out a calming breath. Getting Ruby to act like a normal human being was going to be an exercise in restraint and patience. "I'm *so* sorry, Ruby," Sophie simpered. "Thank you for coming to my rescue and stabbing that guy. How are you? I'm glad you're doing well. Sorry to hear that the new job is boring."

"Ugh, this is the first time we finally get to hang out, and now you're just being—"

"Ruby!" Sophie interrupted. "I said thank you. But you need to understand that I don't want you elbowing your way into my life."

"I am *not* elbowing my way in. I'm allowed to move wherever I want. You don't own this city."

Sophie growled with frustration.

"Good lord, you two really *are* sisters," Mac whispered in mock horror. He gave an exaggerated shudder that earned him a middle finger from Sophie.

Ruby's sense of self-preservation finally kicked in because she was thankfully quiet for the rest of the ride to the police head-quarters.

CHAPTER 2

*A*fter arriving at the police station, Mac led them to a conference room on the floor dedicated to the Mythical division of the force. He left the sisters alone to go locate Dunham and Marcella. Ruby was still quietly pouting, so the only noise in the unremarkable room was the ticking of a clock.

"What exactly do you do for Marcella?" Sophie finally asked, unable to stand the quiet for a minute longer.

"Not much. I pretend to be her assistant and shake as many hands as possible. Then if I pull a vision from anyone, I tell Marcella about the murder that person committed. Or murders, really. Some of these guys have been busy. Then she decides what to do about them. That's it."

"No one questions why a Fae like Marcella has a human working for her? You know she's in charge of the Conclave, right? The super-secret society in charge of all the Mythicals in San Francisco?"

"She has some sort of initiative, trying to bring humans into the 'fold'. It's like an outreach program. Everyone treats me like a none-too-bright pet. I get a lot of head pats, like they think I'm a puppy or something. Mythicals are weird."

Hello kettle, meet pot.

A quick knock on the conference room door cut off any more questions Sophie had. Knowing Marcella, she was using Ruby's ability to see if people committed murders as a way to build more power through blackmail and bribery.

Larry Turner popped his head into the room, tipping his fedora at them like some old-timey gentleman from a black-and-white film. Larry was a warlock Sophie had met recently when trying to stop her sister's murder spree. He was a charming chatterbox, so it was no surprise to Sophie when he looked pleased to see them.

"Hey, look, it's the chaos sisters! Didn't think I'd see you two in here again so soon."

"Hey," Ruby said, twirling a lock of hair, batting her eyes at an amused Larry. "Remember me?"

"How could I forget?" Larry replied, making Ruby titter. "If you wanted to see me so bad, I'm happy to give you my number. You don't need to get into trouble as an excuse to visit."

Ugh, barf.

"I don't know if I got your name, Mr. Lie Detector Man."

"I'm Detective Larry Turner, Warlock Extraordinaire," Larry replied, whipping off his hat with a flourish and bowing to Ruby. Sophie's groan of agony was drowned out by her sister's inane giggling.

"A warlock? Does that mean you can cast a love spell on me?"

Larry looked momentarily tempted before glancing at his watch. "Marcella and Dunham are on their way and will be here in a few minutes. I brought you guys some coffee and donuts since I thought you might be hungry."

"You're officially my favorite warlock, Larry," Sophie praised, no longer annoyed by his presence.

"How many warlocks do you know?" Larry teased.

"Just you. But that doesn't change the fact that you're my favorite."

"They're stale," Larry warned, sliding the box of donuts closer to Sophie.

"Don't care." Sophie snagged the only chocolate frosted donut left. Ruby gave her an annoyed look when she saw that all that remained were some jelly-filled ones. *You snooze, you lose.* Sophie took a huge bite of her breakfast, giving an exaggerated 'mmmm' at the taste. With a scoff, Ruby turned her back on Sophie, ignoring the mostly empty donut box.

"We need to stop meeting like this," Ruby cooed at Larry.

"You keep ending up here at the station, and we'll have to get you your own desk."

"I could just share yours," Ruby offered with an exaggerated eye flutter, her voice dripping with innuendo.

"I do have a pretty big… desk we could share."

Sophie rolled her eyes at the two of them. Their flirting would have put her off her breakfast if she hadn't been starving. "Sweet Jesus, make it stop," Sophie prayed, making both idiots in the room cackle.

A throat clearing from behind Larry had him straightening up, his face dropping into an expression of placid professionalism. Backing up, Larry held the door open as Dunham, Marcella, and Mac entered the room. He then left without another word.

"Hey, boss lady," Ruby greeted the Fae leader of the Conclave. Marcella had a face of long-suffering that made Sophie want to smirk at her. She couldn't drum up a single drop of sympathy for Marcella. If she'd wanted to use Ruby's gift so bad that she broke her out of jail, then Marcella deserved every annoying second she had to spend with her.

"Good morning, Ruby. And Sophie. I'm glad to see you're both okay. I'm sorry we keep meeting under such circumstances. It's unacceptable that you were attacked in your home. We're already looking into this matter and will take any necessary steps to ensure it doesn't happen again. We're trying to determine why you were targeted."

Turning in his seat, Mac gave Marcella an incredulous look. "Are you serious? It's obvious why Sophie was targeted. That was Thomas Castillo from the Sunset District pack. He was in Alphonse's inner circle. He was clearly sent by Antonio to kill Sophie in retaliation for his brother's death. Thomas was waiting for me to leave before sneaking into Sophie's apartment. Everyone knows Antonio has blamed Sophie and Ruby for Alphonse's murder."

"I agree. But we don't have any concrete proof that Antonio was behind this attack, and I need more than speculation," Dunham argued.

Mac scoffed. "What did Antonio say when you questioned him?"

"He has refused to come in," Marcella explained, waving a dismissive hand when Mac made a sound of outrage.

"As is his right," Dunham loudly stated when Mac started to rise from his chair. "Sit down. We can't force Antonio to come here unless we have real evidence that he was behind this attack. However, I managed to get him on the phone. I can't say I'm surprised, but he stated that he had nothing to do with the shifter that attacked Sophie. He denies all knowledge and responsibility. He claims that it was a lone shifter overcome by his grief who decided to attack Sophie on his own."

"Bullshit. There's no way that one of his pack members attacked a civilian without his explicit command."

"Until we have proof, we must take him at his word. Antonio says Thomas went rogue and that he was lost to his sorrow over the death of his alpha. And unless we have a way to prove Antonio's involvement, my hands are tied. The Conclave will issue a formal warning, but that's all we can do," Marcella explained.

A whole committee of powerful magical beings, and the best they can do is a warning? It's such weak sauce, Sophie thought.

"We're watching Antonio. If he puts one toe out of line, we'll remove him from his pack," Marcella assured them.

"That's unacceptable. He will keep sending wolves after Sophie and Ruby until one of them is finally successful. A 'warning' from the Conclave won't slow him down for a minute. At the very least, I think they both need better security. Spells and wards on their apartments and places of work. Maybe even a security detail for them both," Mac demanded.

"Whoa. Wait a minute now," Sophie started to protest.

Marcella cleared her throat and gave Mac a quelling look. "Actually... an opportunity has presented itself that will get both Sophie and Ruby out of town and away from any immediate danger while we deal with the repercussions of Alphonse's death. I can exert more pressure on the pack while they are out of the way. Hopefully, it will give Antonio enough time to recover from his loss and see reason."

Mac rolled his eyes at that.

"What opportunity?" Sophie asked.

"I was already going to assign Ruby and Detective Volpes to this mission, but this will be a good chance to get all three of you out of town. Based on latest developments, it turns out that Sophie's gift will probably be the most helpful. It seems like serendipity."

"Wait... What assignment? Why is the first I've heard of it?" Mac demanded.

"I only put the request through Dunham a few days ago."

Sophie could see Mac building up a head of steam, so she cut in. "What's the assignment?"

"Have you heard of Cascadia?" Marcella asked.

Before Sophie could respond that she had not, Mac straightened up even further in his chair, leaning across the surface. "Cascadia?" he repeated. "Is something happening in Cascadia? Does my father know?"

"He specifically requested you."

"Of course he did."

"What's the assignment?" Sophie demanded, aggravated by being ignored.

"There's been some strange occurrences in Cascadia, specifically in the town of Murias. It's the first settlement created specifically for humans and Mythicals to co-exist peacefully, each completely aware of the existence of the other. It is the model I hope the rest of the world can someday adopt. It's my initiative and my reputation at stake if Murias fails. Its way of living must prove successful."

In the modern world of cellphones, facial recognition, and constant surveillance, Sophie had wondered on more than one occasion how Mythicals had remained hidden for so long. It seemed to her that it was just a matter of time before Mythicals got outed. Burg told her that humans would ignore what they didn't understand, but she thought they underestimated the danger. Sophie could only imagine the reaction of humankind if they all found out that the creatures that go bump in the night were real. If Mythicals were creating models to co-exist peacefully, maybe she wasn't the only one who had thought the same thing – that it was just a matter of time before the existence of Mythicals became common knowledge.

"There's been a few unidentified bodies that have turned up recently. Nothing terribly unusual about a few deaths, but they haven't been able to uncover who they were – which *is* strange. I want Ruby and Sophie to head to Murias and use their gifts to see if they can find the murderer. Or murderers, I suppose. Ruby can touch any suspects, and Sophie can pull death visions from the bodies in the morgue. And as a detective, you can discreetly investigate what's happening in town, Mac."

"How many bodies?" Mac asked.

"Two for certain. Maybe more."

"It's a Mythical town. Two deaths? That doesn't warrant a call from my dad."

"It does when we can't figure out exactly how they were killed or who they were. Neither person was in any database, not even the Mythical one." That made Mac's eyebrows rise slightly.

"The first unclaimed body was a Fae that looked like he'd been tortured," Marcella explained. Mac still mainly looked unconvinced, but Sophie could see he was getting intrigued. "But the newest death prompted a call from the sheriff. Apparently, there is something very wrong with the body. He said the body looked like a Picasso painting."

"Ew," Ruby piped up, wrinkling her nose.

"Your cover story is that you all are in town to visit your father with your girlfriend and her sister and to experience the Hunter's Moon festival. There will be a lot of tourists in town, so your presence won't seem out of place. The influx of visitors to the area should allow you to blend in," Dunham explained.

"This is a chance to prove you can work as a team and that your skills are worth the time and effort I've invested in you," Marcella added. "It's perfect because it gets you out of town and out of the reach of the Sunset District pack. Plus, if you fail there, it won't reflect on me. Show me you've got the skills to be a part of the team."

Team? What is she talking about? She hasn't invested any time in me, Sophie thought. She assumed Marcella was mainly referring to Ruby because Sophie had already proven her value a dozen times. All the murder cases she helped solve spoke for themselves. And honestly, she couldn't care less if Marcella thought she was "worthy".

Looking at the glow in Ruby's face, Sophie realized that Marcella's little speech had lit a fire in her sister. Sophie had nothing to prove, but it looked like Ruby didn't feel the same.

"When do we need to leave?" Mac asked.

"Today, if possible. I want you on-site and working on this case as soon as possible. Your father is expecting you."

"Your open cases will be reassigned. This is your top priority," Dunham informed Mac. Mac didn't say anything, but Sophie could see the flexing of his jaw muscle as he clenched his teeth. An outraged silence was the only response he could seem to muster for his boss. Dunham didn't seem to be put out by Mac's aggravated stare.

It looked like asking them to take the assignment was just a formality. Was saying no even an option? *Probably not*, Sophie decided.

"What about Sophie's apartment? Her front door is destroyed, and there's the postmortem clean-up to make her place livable once more. And what about her job?" Mac asked.

"I'll have someone out today to take care of her apartment. And I'll have a security system installed, both magical and mundane. I'll also have her absence cleared with the morgue. I'm certain the Chief Medical Examiner will understand that I require your help." Marcella said, dismissing Mac's concerns with a nonchalant shrug.

"I want a security system installed on my neighbor's apartment, too," Sophie demanded, wanting Birdie to get that same level of safety. "If you want my help with whatever is happening in Cascadia while things die down with the wolf shifters, then I want my neighbor Alberta Gafferty protected."

"Deal," Marcella immediately confirmed. "I'll make sure it happens."

"I guess we're headed to Murias," Mac said.

CHAPTER 3

*S*itting in the front seat of Mac's car, Sophie watched him pace back and forth in front of the bumper, cell phone pressed to his ear. She wished she could hear what he was saying but decided that whatever conversation Mac was having with his father was private – unless he chose to share any details with her.

Ending the call and shoving his phone in his pocket, Mac looked through the windshield at Sophie for a minute. He rolled his head like he sometimes did to loosen the tension from his shoulders before sliding into the driver's seat with a sigh. "Dad says he's getting us some rooms at the local inn, so we should be all set for a place to stay."

"Your dad's the sheriff?" Sophie confirmed as Mac pulled into traffic.

"Yeah. After my mom died, he didn't want to be alpha anymore. He said his drive for it died with her. He headed to Cascadia to retire after he stepped down, leaving my sister behind to run the pack. It didn't take the Conclave long to ask him to be sheriff of Murias. He was perfect for the job. He had the most experience in the area, and the Conclave had a vested interest in making Cascadia a success. He'd been the Civitas sheriff for years and is a tough old alpha shifter. If anyone can wrangle a town of misfit Mythicals, it's the man who kept an unruly fox family under control for thirty years."

"He's okay with us coming to town?"

"Yeah. I haven't seen him since Easter, so he's happy to catch up. And he's looking forward to meeting you. Mostly he just wants to apprehend this murderer that's 'messing around in his town'. He says he sent the Conclave a request last week for me to come and investigate. Marcella called him and suggested her new 'consultant' could also help."

"Does he know what we can do?" Sophie asked.

"Not specifically. He knows you have some magic that can help. I told him we met through work, so he knows you have previously worked on cases with me. I wanted to leave it up to you to decide how much he should know. He's been running a Mythical town for years, so I doubt he'd even bat an eye if he knew about your ability. And he won't tell a soul," Mac promised.

Sophie didn't know how to feel. She'd never been brought home to 'meet the family' before. It made her stomach squirm to think about it.

The relationship between Mac and her was only a few months old. It felt like too big of a step that Sophie wasn't remotely ready for. It made her feel faintly nauseous to think about meeting Mac's family. She wasn't the kind of person someone would want to 'bring home'. Saying that Sophie was a bit rough around the edges would be an understatement. Although, admittedly, Mac wasn't bringing her home just to meet the family. She was being assigned a case that happened to be in the town where Mac's father was sheriff.

However, it didn't change the fact that she was going to meet Mac's dad. Even though they'd be in Murias on a case, she wanted his family to like her. They either liked her or they didn't.

Sophie was who she was, and she couldn't change that, wouldn't change that – not even for the guy she was falling for.

A chime from Mac's phone broke Sophie from her thoughts that were chasing one another like a dog with its tail.

"Oh good," Mac said, glancing at the screen. "Larry's going to meet us at your place so he can set up a perimeter ward while you pack."

"How much should I pack?"

"Hmm. I'd say at least five days' worth. Even if we solve the crimes on the first day, we should stay through the last day of the Hunter's Moon festival. Cascadia is famous for it."

"Is Cascadia a county or a town or something? Where is it exactly?" Sophie asked, wracking her brain to remember if she'd ever heard of this place.

"It's sort of a made-up country," Mac said with a shrug.

"What? A made-up country? Is it Narnia or something?" Sophie snarked, making Mac chuckle.

"Okay, so Cascadia covers most of the Pacific Northwest, mostly Oregon, Washington, and part of British Columbia. It extends along the coastline from northern California to southern Alaska. It's named after the Cascade Mountain Range. It's filled with off-grid wackos, eco-warriors, timber companies, and a whole lotta Mythicals – especially shifters who practically run feral through the forests. There's been a small push to make the area into its own country for several decades. Most people believe this is a movement by conservationists and extreme environmentalists, but, in reality, it's a group of Mythicals trying to create the first nation for humans and Mythicals to live together in 'perfect harmony'." Mac's tone expressed what he thought about that.

"You don't think it's possible? For humans and Mythicals to live together?" Ruby asked from the backseat. She'd been so quiet that Sophie had almost forgotten she was still in the car.

"In small batches, like in Murias, I think it can work. But

when you ask all of humanity – en masse – to accept Mythicals…
I think it would lead to panic and possibly mass slaughter. I don't
trust humans to act rationally. There are too many nutjobs out
there."

"Do you think Mythicals can stay hidden forever? You don't
think it's inevitable that you guys will eventually get outed?"
Sophie argued.

When they pulled up to Brown Betty, the squad cruiser was
still out front, but at least the lights weren't flashing anymore.
Behind the police car was the Medical Examiner's transport van.
Sophie watched some of the morgue's day crew load a gurney
sporting a familiar black body bag into the vehicle.

An officer stopped them with a raised hand before they could
enter the lobby of Brown Betty. He explained that he needed to
keep people out of a crime scene, that only authorized personnel
and approved residents were allowed past the front door. He
seemed pretty puffed up and proud of that fact. He abruptly
stopped talking once Mac showed him his badge. As Mac spoke
to the officer in a low voice, Larry strolled into the lobby, his
loafers squeaking against the worn tile entrance.

"You're here," Mac said to Larry. "Good. Take Ruby to her
place so she can pack. While you're there, set up some basic security so we'll know if anyone uninvited tries to get in."

Turning his back on the cowed officer, Mac gave Larry some
quietly worded instructions before he and Ruby headed back out
the front door. Sophie felt her eyebrows crawl towards her hairline as she watched Ruby enter the building directly across the
street from Brown Betty. *How unobservant am I? Good lord, I have
the survival instincts of a lemming*, Sophie thought in dismay. She
hadn't even realized Ruby was within spitting distance.

Turning, Sophie watched as Mac talked with the young police
officer standing guard in her lobby.

"We'll let you know when we're done at the crime scene.

Detective Turner should be joining us shortly to help wrap up," Mac explained to the man.

"Yes, sir," the man replied. "Here are the keys for the new door."

"Good job," Mac said, accepting the keys and clapping the man on the shoulder before heading up the stairs with an amused Sophie in tow.

"Look at you... turning into a big ol' softie." Sophie poked her fingers into Mac's side, trying to locate a bit of softness to prove her point. Not that she found any – Mac caught her fingers quick as lightning. Screeching and laughing, Sophie tried to tug her hand away as he retaliated against her teasing by pretending to nip at her fingertips. Hauling her to his side, he gave her laughing mouth a kiss. Mac gave her a long, penetrating look, brushing back a black lock of hair that had fallen in her eyes.

"You scared me, Soph. When I heard all that screaming and roaring in your apartment, I thought I was too late."

"It scared me too. Can't believe I have to thank Ruby for saving my life. Again," Sophie complained, making Mac shake his head in commiseration.

"Come on, hellraiser. Let's get this done," Mac said but didn't make a move to head towards her apartment door. Sophie dropped her head to his shoulder and wrapped her arms around his waist. She hadn't even realized how badly she needed a hug until she felt his arms cocooning her.

The feeling of being watched finally pulled Sophie out of the hug. Looking over Mac's shoulder, Sophie spotted the crack in Birdie's front door. Sophie gave that crack a hard stare.

"Birdie," Sophie said, a warning in her tone when her toughest glower proved ineffective against her nosy neighbor.

"Either give me something worth watching or come and explain what the hell happened this morning," Birdie demanded, opening her door with a huff. Sophie was glad to see the scared look on Birdie's face was gone, replaced with her typical naughty expression.

Birdie was one of only a handful of people who knew Sophie could see the last minutes of a person's life by touching their dead body. And she was undoubtedly the only human who knew – well, outside of Ruby, who didn't really count. Sophie had occasionally wondered if it was a bad idea for Birdie to have this information – could it put her in the path of danger? However, Birdie was her best friend. She couldn't imagine hiding something this big from her. Birdie had a way of ferreting out every secret Sophie had ever tried to keep. She'd known something was going on with Mac practically before Sophie did. That old bird was just too observant.

They quickly explained about the shifter attack, letting Birdie know that they were sure that Antonio was behind the incident. Birdie kept giving Sophie increasingly worried looks until they warned her they were both leaving town. She seemed relieved that Sophie would be far away from San Francisco and the Sunset District pack.

Larry and Ruby came around the corner as Birdie was trying to weasel her way into the trip. Thankfully, Larry was enough of a distraction that they didn't need to push back very hard. Based on the amount of flirting Birdie leveled at Larry, she'd already forgotten about trying to join the trip. Sophie was assured that she'd made a full recovery from that morning's fright.

"Does Milton know that you flirt with every man you meet?" Sophie taunted.

"Milton and I have an open relationship," Birdie archly informed Sophie, making Larry laugh out loud.

"I really wish that was information I didn't have," Sophie replied with an exaggerated grimace.

As usual, Birdie accused Sophie of being a prude. Which, in turn, caused Sophie to call Birdie a dirty old lady. It felt good to reclaim a sense of normality in the face of all the craziness in her life.

"That's enough, you two. Sophie needs to pack, and Larry needs to set some wards in Birdie's apartment," Mac interrupted, herding Sophie away and towards her apartment.

"Come with me, Miss Birdie. You'll be as safe as a clam by the time I'm done," Larry said, ushering Birdie back to her place.

After Mac unlocked her new, scuff-free front door, Sophie headed to her tiny hall closet to grab her biggest duffle bag while Ruby followed them inside but headed to the kitchen. Sophie watched her open the fridge door and examine the contents inside with a disappointed look on her face. Sophie didn't have anything yummy for Ruby to steal this time.

"I need to call Reggie and let him know that I won't be coming into work," Sophie announced, pulling her phone out of her back pocket.

Like her, Reggie worked a graveyard shift at the morgue, so Sophie knew he was probably asleep. But this call couldn't wait.

"'Lo?" a sleepy voice answered on the third ring.

"Hey, Reggie. It's me."

"Soph? Is everything okay?"

Tossing her bag on the mattress, Sophie recapped her morning as she stuffed her toiletries into a side pocket.

"Marcella has requested that Mac, Ruby, and I head to Cascadia and investigate these murders and missing people. I won't be able to come to work tonight and probably not for the rest of the week. I'm sorry."

"Don't be sorry. I'm just glad you're all alright. Besides, it's not like you can tell the Conclave no when they send you on assignment."

"I know, but I feel bad. Are you guys going to be okay at work?"

"Don't worry about us. We'll be fine. You just be careful in Cascadia and keep us posted. I'll let the others know what's happening," Reggie replied. Sophie didn't understand how she'd gotten so lucky to have such a good friend and boss in Reggie.

After promising to call him daily to keep him updated on the assignment, Sophie hung up and pulled open a drawer in her dresser. Sophie stared at the haphazard contents in consternation. She'd never worried much about other people's thoughts about how she looked or dressed. She wore what she liked and didn't give a shit about anyone else's opinion of her style. But she'd never been brought home to the parents before. Not that this was *quite* that kind of situation. But still, Sophie was about to meet Mac's father. It made flop sweat gather in her armpits when she thought about it. If Mac's dad didn't like her, would that change how Mac felt about her? Mac didn't seem the type to be easily swayed by other people's opinions. But this was his dad... Besides, she should probably look like a professional if the people of Murias were supposed to take her seriously.

"If I'm supposed to be a 'consultant', should I dress up?" Sophie asked, raising her voice to reach Mac in her living room. She turned and stared into her closet with a sense of despondency.

"Nah, what you usually wear is fine." Mac entered her room and looked into her mostly empty duffle bag. Sophie gave him a dubious look.

"Really? They'll take me seriously if I'm wearing my usual attire?" Sophie asked, shaking an ancient Fugazi t-shirt at Mac. His chuckle didn't settle her nerves. "Why are you laughing? I'm serious here." Sophie shook the shirt at him again for further emphasis.

"You'll see when we get to Murias. No one will bat an eye at the way you dress. I promise. Plus, to most of the town, we're just going to be tourists."

Fine. If Mac wasn't concerned about her clothes, Sophie wouldn't worry either. Murias would have to learn to deal with her combat boots and concert t-shirts. So would Mac's dad, for that matter.

Stuffing enough clothes to last her for the rest of the week into the bag, Sophie zipped it shut and lugged it into the living room to discover Larry was in her kitchen, waving his hands and muttering incantations at the window over her sink.

Sophie sat next to Ruby on her couch, watching as Larry pulled out a piece of chalk and started writing a string of unfamiliar symbols around the windowsill. He finished with a, "Finio," waving his hands through the air in a complicated motion. A shimmering blue haze flashed over the window like a forcefield. It disappeared just as suddenly as it appeared, fading away with a final sparkle. When the window was once again clear, Sophie realized that the chalk markings around her window had disappeared like they had been used up or absorbed into the building.

"Did you pack some weapons?" Ruby suddenly asked, nodding toward Sophie's luggage next to the front door.

"What? No." Sophie gave Ruby a look to let her know she thought Ruby was nuts.

With a huff of disappointment, Ruby pulled up her pant leg where a knife was strapped to her calf. Removing the knife and sheath, she handed the weapon to Sophie. "Things might have gone easier for you if you'd had this handy this morning. You should always be armed."

Sophie tried to refuse the knife, but Ruby declined to take it back. Ruby gave her ankle a pointed stare until Sophie relented and strapped the knife to her leg and hid it under her jeans.

Trying to ignore how weird it felt to have the weapon's lump under her pants leg, Sophie turned her attention back to Larry.

Looking at her floor, Sophie realized her living room rug was gone. It'd already been in the apartment when she moved in and had seen better days. It wasn't a real loss, but she'd need to find something to cover the room's faded, decades-old carpeting. A distinct square was left on the carpet where the rug used to be. Sophie had thought the carpet was a dreary brown. Based on the newly uncovered portion of her floor, it was taupe with a hint of peach. Sophie would bet the contents of her measly checking account that there was a hardwood floor hiding under the hideous carpet. *Why did people do that in the '80s?*

"Isn't it cool?" Ruby breathlessly whispered to Sophie.

"Huh?" Sophie asked, still distracted by her hideous floor.

"What Larry can do. If anyone with ill intentions enters your place, you'll know it. He was able to set it up just using your aura. How cool is that?"

"Yeah. Magic is awesome."

"Do you know if he's dating anyone?" Ruby asked out of the side of her mouth. Sophie stared at Ruby, then looked at the warlock in her apartment, then looked back at Ruby, who was watching him with stars in her eyes. *Really?*

Larry looked like he should be a lead singer in a ska funk band, not a warlock. Sophie stared back at Ruby with a 'him?' look.

"Hey, Larry!" Sophie yelled, ignoring Ruby as she futilely tried to shush her, slapping her hands away. "You single?"

"Single as a Pringle."

"Yeah, it's a real mystery why," Sophie deadpanned.

"Why do you ask? Are you finally ready to dump that loser fox so you can have me all to yourself?" Larry waggled his eyebrows like a wannabe gigolo.

"I'm standing right here," Mac complained to the air, throwing his hands out in an 'excuse me' gesture.

"Not me," Sophie said, cutting her eyes toward her sister's beet-red face.

"Sophie," Ruby quietly griped. "You suck so much. You're the worst sister ever."

"Sorry," Sophie said, not feeling remotely apologetic. She was immensely enjoying needling her sister. And the smile that spread across Larry's face told Sophie that Ruby wasn't the only one possibly catching feelings.

Sophie wouldn't have pegged Ruby as the shy, retiring type. Too many times she'd had a front row seat to her sister violently murdering someone with a cheerfulness that made Sophie distinctly uncomfortable. This same woman was now too timid to ask out *Larry the Warlock*. Sophie suspected that even if she had a million years to study her sister, she'd still never understand how Ruby's mind worked.

Under other circumstances, Sophie would think it was cute, but this was her long-lost murderous twin. She didn't trust Ruby not to murder Larry if they didn't work out. And Sophie liked Larry.

"If everyone's packed, we need to leave. It's almost a five-hour drive to Murias, and I still need to pack my own bags," Mac suggested. "Let's go."

Sophie popped up from the couch and rushed over to Mac. "Actually… why don't we leave Ruby here to get to know Larry better while we get your stuff? We can pick her up on our way out of town."

"Why? Then we'd need to double back. It'll add almost an hour to our drive. Ruby can manage her love life on her own time. We really need to get going."

"I mean, suuuure we could do that. Drive Ruby over to your house so she can see where you live. She'd probably love that," Sophie whispered furiously to Mac, giving him a hard stare. Mac's eyes widened when Sophie's words finally registered.

"Oh. Yeah. No," Mac stuttered, shaking his head, looking vaguely horrified. "Ruby, you should stay here and keep Larry company. He can tell you more about Cascadia. Or he can show you more of his magic. We'll be back as soon as possible."

"Okay, sounds good, guys. See you in a bit," Ruby said in a distracted, dreamy voice, watching Larry avidly.

"Holy shit, what was I thinking?" Mac exclaimed as they

strode out Brown Betty's front door and onto the sidewalk. "I almost took your crazy-ass sister right to my house. She would've known where I lived."

"Did we just sacrifice Larry?" Sophie asked, glancing back towards her apartment as she got into Mac's car.

"Yes, but I can live with the guilt."

Thankfully the traffic was light, and Mac drove like a bat out of hell. Mac and Sophie walked back into Brown Betty's front door less than an hour later.

As they walked down the hall towards her apartment, Sophie heard giggling coming from the other side of her door.

Knocking loudly, Sophie waited a moment before opening the door. She was unsure what Ruby and Larry might've gotten up to while they were gone, and she had no intention of finding out. She figured it was probably only some light flirting, but she knew better than to mentally scar herself by waltzing in without plenty of warning. There wasn't enough eye bleach in all the world for Sophie to be okay catching her sister and Larry doing anything raunchier than flirting.

Looking around her apartment suspiciously, Sophie couldn't find anything that looked disturbed or out of place. She felt like the parent of a wayward teenager trying to determine if they needed to be grounded or not.

"Let's go. I want to get to Murias before sunset," Mac announced. He gave Larry one of the keys from the keyring and asked him to lock up when he was done warding the space.

A glance at her phone told Sophie that it had only been a few hours since she'd woken up to find an intruder in her apartment, rather than the lifetime it felt like. She could hardly believe that it was still the same day.

Grabbing her bags, Sophie followed Mac out the door.

"Byeee," Ruby called out to Larry, extending the word like an exuberant sorority girl, before following them out.

Larry walked them out the front door, waving as they headed

out, telling them to leave before they caused any more problems. "San Francisco can withstand earthquakes, but I don't think it can survive the two of you. See you guys when you get back."

Sophie gave Larry's joke the response it deserved – a middle finger. His laughter followed them out of the building.

"Road trip!" Ruby yelled, gleefully jumping into the backseat of Mac's sedan while he tossed their bags into his trunk. Sophie paused outside the car, watching Ruby bounce in the back seat like a hyperactive toddler on a sugar high.

"This is gonna suck," Sophie informed the sky above her.

"With stops, it'll be about a five-hour drive," Mac warned Sophie with a look of a condemned man.

CHAPTER 4

An hour outside the Redwood National and State Parks, Mac pulled his car into a gas station that looked like it predated the Great Depression. The attendant inside looked like he was an original fixture as well.

Needing to stretch her legs, Sophie set aside the coursework for the Medical Assistant Certification class she'd be starting in a few weeks. She wanted to read ahead to ensure she wouldn't get overwhelmed in the class. Whatever happened, she was not going to fail. God, she was so scared to go back to school.

She got out of the car, twisting until her back gave a satisfying crack. Gaunt and stooped with age, the man inside the station stared at her with undisguised suspicion. The gas station appeared to be the only thing in the area, sitting on a small road just off the highway, a bleak, faded remanent of a past age, nestled into the shade of tall spindly pines.

Sophie stood under the metal overhang shading the pumps from the late afternoon heat, breathing in the warm, stale air rising from the cracked asphalt.

The only sound was the rustling of the overhead branches in

the breeze and the car's cooling engine pinging. The quiet of the woods surrounded her, cocooning Sophie in silence. The occasional chirp of a bug was the only noise.

Ruby woke up from a nap, looking around blearily. It had been blessedly quiet inside the car for the last hour of driving with her napping in the backseat. She had chattered incessantly for the first couple of hours until Sophie was ready to chew her way out of the car to escape.

After filling the tank, Mac asked them if they wanted any snacks.

"Yeah, can you get me a Slurpee and some gummy bears?" Ruby said. "Oh, and a box of Good & Plenty!"

Mac agreed, but he exchanged a look with Sophie before turning and heading inside the gas station.

"What was that?" Ruby asked. "Why'd he give you that look?"

"Do you get Good & Plenties often?" Sophie asked, disregarding the question for a more pressing concern.

"Yeah, they're my favorite. Why?"

"Because I've been having a lot of dreams about candy recently, especially about Good & Plenties," Sophie replied, thinking about her dream journal. That reminded her of that morning's dream and Ruby's text. "And I despise black licorice."

Popping the trunk, Sophie pawed through her bag until she found her bright pink dream journal. Sophie tossed the journal to Ruby as Mac arrived with an armful of snacks.

"What's this?" Ruby asked, turning the book over in her hands.

"It's my dream journal," Sophie explained, ignoring Ruby's snort. "Take a look through it and let me know if anything is familiar."

Sophie didn't want to share her dreams with Ruby. Dreams ought to enjoy a modicum of privacy – but not for Sophie. She had to hand over her dreams to Mac, who gave them to the Chief of Police of San Francisco. And if Dunham had her dreams, she could safely assume that Marcella was also reading through them. It wasn't out of the realm of possibility that her dreams were shared with the entirety of the Conclave. The thought of the shadowy organization that oversaw all the Mythicals in the city reading her private dreams made her feel twitchy and faintly nauseous.

Looking in the rear-view mirror, Sophie grimaced as Ruby giggled at whatever she was reading. *What's one more person?* Sophie thought with a fatalistic roll of her eyes.

While Ruby munched on her snacks, she flipped through the book. "Oh, this was me."

Glancing over her shoulder, Sophie looked at the entry in the journal that Ruby was pointing at. "Which one?"

"I remember this day. I was stocking up on candy. I like to give myself a reward when I'm after a bad guy. Stakeouts get sooo boring, so I like to have a little treat," Ruby explained. She continued to flip through the journal, occasionally calling out when one of the dreams was about her. She was particularly enthralled with the dream where she'd killed Roger, one of Alphonse's henchmen, in an alley behind a bakery. "I was after Alphonse, but that guy just jumped out from behind the dumpster. What was I supposed to do when he attacked me like that?"

"Oh, I don't know... Not stab him in the throat."

Ruby's laugh let Sophie know her sarcasm went over her sister's head.

The only sound in the car was the zipper-swish of pages turning and the wet chomping of Ruby eating her candy. Sophie was contemplating getting her a muzzle if she couldn't chew with her mouth closed when Ruby made a startled sound.

"What is it?" Sophie asked, turning in her seat.

"I had this dream too. I remember it vividly," Ruby said, pointing to a page filled with Sophie's hastily written notes. "It was in one of those fancy restaurants. You know, the kind where the waiter puts the napkin on your lap for you, and they swirl the wine around the glass. I was trying to impress a potential client or something. The guy was really impressed with the foie gras. The dream stuck with me because I remember how good it tasted. Which is just gross."

"Why's that gross? What exactly is foie gras? I remember eating a weird meat spread, but I didn't know what it was."

"You've never heard of foie gras?" Ruby looked scandalized when Sophie shook her head. "It's super cruel. They force feed the goose until its liver gets enlarged and then slaughter it. I would never eat it."

"Yeah, one of my friends is a snow goose shifter. So, yeah, I'd never eat that." Sophie shuddered at the thought. Her stomach turned at the idea of eating the animal counterpart to one of her shifter friends. It felt somehow like cannibalism.

"I'm surprised we don't share more dreams than this," Ruby said with a thoughtful look.

"It's probably because we're on opposite sleep schedules."

"That's true. I have no idea how you work a graveyard shift. I need my beauty sleep. Oh! I remember this morning." Ruby pointed at the journal entry. "I slept in because I'd had a late night the evening before. I'd been trailing Alphonse and some of his goons when they grabbed a guy right off the street and drove him to Muir Woods. I followed them the whole way and ended up calling the police because there were too many targets for me to deal with. I didn't get home that night until almost 3 in the morning."

"That guy was Derek Gibson. They chased him through the woods and ripped him apart. Just so they could replace him on some land development committee with someone of their choosing," Sophie murmured. Remembering Gibson's horrendous last moments as Alphonse tore into him made Sophie want to find a way to reanimate Alphonse's corpse so Ruby could kill him all over again. Maybe slowly this time.

Sophie stared out the car window. The world had morphed from farmland into a dense forest. Thick redwoods and sequoias crowded close to the US 101 as it gently curved and swooped, winding sinuously through the old-growth forest. The trees outside their windows were getting taller and wider the closer they got to the town of Murias. When Sophie exclaimed in delight over the size of the trees, Mac told her that the road was called the Avenue of the Giants. There was something ancient and intimidating about the trees as if they'd been standing sentinel and watching humans like annoying little ants scurrying past for centuries beneath their primordial notice.

When Sophie asked about Murias, Mac explained that the town was the only entrance into the Mythical-held portion of Cascadia – unless you hiked in on foot. But you'd have to find it first, and only those who knew where to look would ever locate it.

"What about Google Earth?" Ruby questioned. "Can't you just find it online?"

"It's been purposefully wiped from any satellite imagery," Mac explained.

How do you remove an entire town from all satellite imagery? That was some *Big Brother is watching* level of government control.

"Wouldn't it just take one person in a plane with a cell phone to unveil the town?" Sophie argued.

Mac chuckled and told them they'd understand better when they arrived.

Sunlight cut like a knife through the thick canopy surrounding them, lighting up the road as it carved a path through the landscape. A light fog hung in the towering pines' upper boughs, hiding the trees' top canopy from view.

"Anything else familiar in there?" Sophie asked, indicating the journal.

Ruby paged through the book, pointing out when the dream was about her. There were several, but nothing was exciting about them. They were of Ruby doing everyday activities like eating or shopping or doing her laundry. Until Ruby got to that morning's entry. When she got to it, Sophie knew just by the hitch in Ruby's breath.

"Oh yeah. This one," Ruby muttered softly.

"Wait," Sophie commanded, snatching the book from Ruby's hands.

"Heeey!" Ruby complained.

"Alright, tell me about the dream from your perspective before you read mine. I want to hear what you remember."

Ruby gave Sophie a dramatic huff. "Okay fine. I dreamed I was wearing this stuffy suit in a big conference room. Although I did have on these gorgeous stilettos." Sophie raised her eyebrows. She didn't remember any shoes from the dream. "It was like a corporate board meeting or something. I was being a jerk to everyone there, yelling at them about sales numbers or something. I didn't really understand it. I remember I planned to fire this guy. What was his name? Something with a C. Maybe Cruz?"

"Cortez. It was Cortez," Sophie replied, pinching the bridge of her nose. She cringed when Ruby squealed in excitement. Mac gave her a significant look. Sophie watched as a worried frown formed on his face. She hadn't had a chance to tell him about the creepy dream.

"Oh my god! His name *was* Cortez," Ruby said. "We're really dream-sharing. I knew we had a deep connection. This is awesome."

"It's really not. Do you remember how the rest of the dream went?"

"Um, I'm not sure. Let me think." The backseat went silent for a moment before Ruby made a little noise of surprise. "Oh, I remember. I was looking around the conference room, staring into the distance like I was daydreaming when something above my employees' heads caught my attention. It was weird. I said, 'Who are you two?' but no one was there."

"Shit. I had the exact same dream. Ruby, other than the one in the fancy restaurant, have you ever had dreams like that one before? Where you're a businesswoman?"

"Maybe? I'm not sure. I mostly have ones where you're cutting up dead people. I don't remember most of my dreams." Ruby tilted her head, looking lost in thought. "Oh my gosh! Do you think there's another one of us? Like triplets? That would be awesome! Do you think she sensed us? Is that why she said that?"

"That can't be what's happening," Sophie guffawed. "I mean, what're the odds? It's crazy. There must be another explanation." If there was another sister out there, Sophie would pull her own hair out. Frankly, the existing sister was one too many. Sophie racked her brain, trying to come up with any plausible explanation.

"Maybe it's a prophecy! What if we can see into the future? How awesome would that be?" Ruby exclaimed.

"A prophecy. Do you seriously think it's possible that either one of us is going to turn into a cut-throat businesswoman?" Sophie scoffed. Ruby had cut her fair share of throats in a more literal sense. Business wasn't their forte. "Maybe it's just a dream. We're putting too much emphasis on these dreams. Besides, what can we do about it?"

Mac placed his hand over Sophie's, making her aware of how tightly she had gripped her seatbelt as Ruby continued to rattle off more and more outrageous possibilities.

"Why didn't you tell me about this dream?" Mac asked.

"Between being attacked by the shifter this morning and being sent to Cascadia, I completely forgot about the dream."

Mac nodded, accepting that explanation. "How many dreams

do you think you've had where you're a cutthroat businesswoman?"

"Hmm. Only a few and not many recently. I never paid them much mind. They tend to be about boring office stuff. Not like the dreams I had of Snow White," Sophie said, trying to look on the bright side.

"Do you really think there could be another sister?" Mac asked. "Or is it just dreams?"

"I have no idea. All I know is that I don't want there to be another one. What are the odds there are three of us?" Sophie huffed out an aggravated breath. "At this point, nothing would surprise me. It reminds me of when I dreamed of Ruby. Her mind feels different, like how Ruby feels different. It's not proof. But I'm worried. Could there really be three of us?"

Mac shrugged. "Who knows?"

"Has there been any progress in looking into our pasts? Like, have you found adoption papers or anything?" Sophie asked.

"No. Dunham has Larry looking into it using both traditional and magical methods. So far, all your birth certificates, parents, everything looks normal. If there was an adoption, it was extremely well hidden. He's hit nothing but roadblocks. But he's not giving up yet. As far as Larry's research shows, you two aren't even related. But we know that's not true."

Sophie chewed at her thumbnail. "Yeah, DNA doesn't lie."

"Can you remember anything else about this new sister? Where she lives and works? What kind of work she does? Anything that can help narrow the search for a third sister."

"Third sister sounds weird," Sophie grumbled. "We need to give her a name."

"How 'bout Corporate Bitch?" Ruby said with a laugh. "She seemed like a real hard-ass businesswoman in the dream. We're the nice ones!"

Jesus, if we're the nice ones...

"There isn't much we can do about it now," Mac said, interrupting Sophie's morose thoughts. "When we get to Murias, I'll send Larry a text and tell him to start looking for another sister. Speaking of, we're almost there."

Sophie looked around, expecting to see anything other than just more trees. They'd driven for miles without seeing anything but an unbroken expanse of pine-and-redwood forest. There hadn't even been another car in sight for the last half hour.

"Where?" Sophie asked. The only change in the scenery was that the trees had steadily been getting bigger and taller the longer they drove. They stood silent and tall like a battalion of soldiers. Flicking on his blinker and slowing the car, Mac pointed ahead to the right at a small break in the forest. Just past the trunk of a redwood wider than a golfcart was a rutted track that quickly disappeared around another bend of trees. It looked like a long-forgotten logging road, overgrown with ferns and under-brush, the tracks almost lost beneath a blanket of discarded pine needles.

"That can't be right," Sophie protested.

"This is it, I promise. I've been here several times."

"Uh, this isn't even a road. How can it possibly lead to a town?" Ruby asked from behind Sophie, leaning between the front seats to stare out the front windshield, apprehension written across her face.

Grabbing her phone, Sophie tried to open her maps app to check their way. The 'road' they were on didn't even register on the screen. It showed them driving through the middle of a forest.

"Are you sure we're headed the right way? There's nothing here," she stated, worry starting to gnaw at her.

That worry coalesced into annoyance at the smug look on Mac's face.

"We should head back to that gas station and ask them how to get to Murias," Ruby suggested, sounding as concerned as Sophie felt.

"Mac! You're going the wrong way!" Sophie yelled, getting upset and starting to panic.

"Turn around," Ruby pleaded, trying to tug on his arm but only managing to grab his shoulder. He easily shrugged off Ruby's grip.

Sophie was reaching for her door handle, planning to jump out, when the feelings of disorientation and alarm dissipated as quickly as they'd arrived.

"What the hell?" Sophie asked, her hand still frozen on the door handle. She yanked her hand back in horrified shock. *What the hell?*

"It's a ward. It's set up to repel unwanted visitors. It makes you believe that you're lost and going the wrong way. The closer you get to the perimeter, the worse it feels. It keeps people from accidentally wandering into Mythical territory. Once you pass through the ward's outer boundary, the feeling goes away."

"A ward? Like what Larry put on my apartment?" Ruby asked.

"It's similar."

"You could have warned us, you dick," Sophie griped, punching Mac in the shoulder. He gave her a wolfish grin, clearly enjoying riling her up. She silently vowed her revenge.

After ten minutes of bumping along the rutted path, they crested a small hill. The forest opened to a vista that stole her breath. Below them was a valley, nestled bright and glowing among the dark towering sequoias. Down on the right was a viridescent meadow filled with grazing animals. Even squinting her eyes, all Sophie could make out was the brown backs of some large animals weaving their way through the prairie grass. To the left was a town. Sophie watched as details of the town grew clearer as they got closer. It looked cute and quaint, like something from a Norman Rockwell painting. Further to the west, past the town in a dip between bluffs, was a hint of the steel blue Pacific Ocean.

"Are those reindeer?" Ruby asked, delight coloring her voice, pulling Sophie's attention away from Murias and the ocean.

A herd of enormous animals grazed contentedly at the field they were passing. If those were deer, they were the biggest ones Sophie had ever seen. Admittedly, she lived in San Francisco – it's not like there were any deer roaming Union Square for her to compare. However, these made Clydesdales look petite.

"No. Those are Roosevelt elk shifters."

"Shifters! So, they're half human?" Ruby exclaimed, shimmying in her seat so much it made the whole vehicle bounce.

The largest elk standing in the field, an enormous beast with intimidating-looking antlers, glanced up, wildflowers dangling from its mouth, and watched them drive past with a suspicious glare. Staring back at the elk, Sophie could see a shrewd intelligence in its eyes. The rest of the herd was placidly eating, nosing through the underbrush for tender shoots of grass, not even glancing up at the vehicle.

They turned onto the main street of the small town. Murias looked like something frozen and lost in time – a lamppost-lined street crowded with vintage storefronts from a bygone era. The pointed steeple of a distant church overlooked the main drag as cars meandered slowly up and down the road. As they drove through the main square, Sophie took stock of all the colorful stores: a bakery, a pharmacy, an outfitter shop with kayaks stacked inside, a brick pub with stained-glass windows, and so many more.

"A cannabis dispensary?" Sophie questioned, pointing out the store to Mac.

"Marijuana farms are big business in this area. Where do you think San Francisco gets all its pot?" he teased, glancing at the dispensary crammed between a diner and a bookstore.

It was a clean, modern-looking building with a large decal of a pot leaf taking up most of the display window. Next to that was a fussy-looking shop with bunches of hanging dried herbs and flowers decorating the front. It announced Madame Venefica's Spells and Potions in loopy letters across the window.

"Aww, it looks just like Mayberry," Ruby cooed. "Look! A candy shop!" she chirped from the backseat. "Can we stop?"

Sophie had been eyeing a tattoo parlor with some interesting flash in the front window when Ruby's excitement made her look to where she was pointing. At the end of the drag, nestled next to an old-fashioned hardware shop, was a candy shop called Cordelia's Confectionary. Inside the storefront, the walls and counters were jam-packed with dozens of glass jars filled with a rainbow assortment of colorful candy. The outside of the building looked a bit like a gingerbread house like it was edible. The décor made Sophie think of the witch's cottage from Hansel and Gretel.

"They make their own soda!" Ruby exclaimed, all but drooling on the car window she was plastered against.

The street was filled with historic charm, lacy architectural details, and postcard-worthy scenes. But what really held Sophie's attention was the people teeming the sidewalks. All manner of Mythical creatures and monsters mixed with humans strolled past the stores like they didn't have a care in the world. Sophie spotted trolls, an ogre, wolfmen, a gaunt tree-like creature holding hands with a pint-sized woman with gossamer wings, and an actual polar bear so large that people had to press against the buildings' facades as it passed. If she didn't know better, she would've thought she'd stumbled into a cosplay convention. Sophie had never even heard of many of the creatures crowding the sidewalk. They defied description; some were beautiful and ethereal, others pulled straight from humanity's worst nightmares.

Sophie's mouth dropped open when a centaur walked out of a shop clutching a paper grocery bag, ducking their head to make it out the front door.

Twisting in her seat, Sophie tried to keep watching the parade of Mythicals, but Mac turned them off the main drag and down a side street. He drove down a block and pulled into a weed-lined parking lot with crumbling asphalt. Next to the lot was a squat beige building that looked like a poor cousin compared to the colorful plumage of the rest of the town. In bold block letters, it proclaimed to be the Sheriff's Office.

Parking the car, Mac looked over at the building with a sigh. "There he is."

CHAPTER 5

*A*s she stepped out of the car, a warm Indian summer breeze ruffled Sophie's hair. She could detect a hint of ocean brine in the air.

Sophie stared at the man that had Mac sighing like a teenager being scolded about not doing their chores. With hands hooked into the pockets of his worn jeans, the man stared at them with eyes like chips of citrine, golden and bright.

"Hey, Dad, we're here," Mac stated.

"Hey, boy. How was the drive?"

Boy?

"It was fine. Dad, I want you to meet Sophie. Sophie, this is my father and sheriff of Murias, Carson Volpes."

Sophie shook his weathered hand, realizing she was getting a preview of what Mac might look like in thirty years. He was handsome in that unfair way some men age. Father and son were the same height, sported the same scowl, and had the same straight patrician nose and square jaw. They even had the same sandy-colored light brown hair, although much of Carson's had turned gray where it peeked out from under his cowboy hat. Other than differently colored eyes, it was like looking into the future. Sophie briefly wondered if Mac had gotten his bright blue eyes from his mother.

"It's nice to meet you," Sophie said.

"Hi! I'm Ruby, Sophie's twin sister." Ruby butted in, reaching for the sheriff's hand.

"Wait," Mac tried to protest before Ruby grabbed his hand. Carson looked like he couldn't believe how rude Mac was being as Ruby shook his hand with her usual amount of enthusiasm. "Never mind," Mac huffed.

"It's okay. He's never killed anyone who didn't deserve it. Isn't that right, Sheriff Volpes?" Ruby said with a giggle as Carson's eyebrows raised so high, they disappeared under the brim of his hat.

"This is the Conclave's consultant and Sophie's sister, Ruby. When she touches someone, she gets visions if they killed anyone," Mac explained.

"It's true!" Ruby exclaimed at Carson's skeptical look.

"She's also a serial killer that hunts serial killers," Mac explained, looking gleeful at the constipated look on his father's face.

"You know I prefer the term vigilante," Ruby complained.

Carson seemed to digest that for a minute before turning to Sophie. "And what can you do?"

Ruby was delighted to tell him before Sophie could respond. "Sophie can see a person's last minutes when she touches their dead body." Sophie gave Ruby an aggravated stare that bounced right off her sister's enthusiasm.

"Really?" Mac's father asked. Sophie wasn't sure how she felt about the gleam in Carson's eyes, maybe because it reminded her a bit of Marcella. "Do you also hunt serial killers?"

He chuckled when Sophie emphatically shook her head.

"Well, that ability will come in handy," Carson replied. "Let's go down to the bakery. I want to check Abernethy Street. A horde of goblins got into town last night and was causing a ruckus at the pub, so I just want to keep an eye on things. You know how the tourists get during the Hunter's Moon Festival – they all think it's time to run around and puff their chests out and get in touch with their 'animal' side. We arrested a banshee on a drunk and disorderly late last night, and she won't stop caterwauling in there." Carson hooked his thumb at the building behind him. "It gives me an excuse to get a piece of pie while I catch you all up on what's been happening 'round here."

They fell into step next to Carson as he led them back towards the main drag Abernethy Street. Sophie kept glancing at Mac's father. Even though the man was dressed in regular jeans and a button-up shirt, something about him made Sophie think of the Old West and gunslingers. The cowboy hat certainly didn't help.

The festive atmosphere of Abernethy Street pulled Sophie's attention away from Carson Volpes. Her eyes felt like they were going to bug out of her head at the crowded street. It was like a carnival of all that was wild and strange. Laughter, yelling, and peculiar animal-like sounds came at Sophie from every direction. The familiar scents of a carnival floated in the air, from spun sugar and buttery popcorn to the distinct aroma of frying dough.

Terrifying monsters strolled by accompanied by creatures so beautiful they looked unreal, practically floating past on gossamer wings. Some creatures were enormous and lumbering, others barely knee-high, scurrying underfoot, and some Mythicals looked like they'd crawled out from beneath children's beds at night. Mixed in with every creature from myth and legend were regular, normal-looking humans. Or at least Mythicals wearing their human skins. It felt like Sophie had stepped out of the world she knew into a fairy tale.

"Sheriff Carson! Sheriff Carson," a voice called out as they wove their way into the foot traffic on the sidewalk. A wiry woman with gray hair and a scowl flagged down Mac's father. By the stiffening of his shoulders and the small, almost silent sigh the man made, Sophie assumed he wasn't looking forward to this interruption.

"Miss McNamara, what can I do for you?"

"Those Porter boys were messing around in my field again. How many times do I have to complain before they get dealt with? If their good-for-nothing parents won't discipline them, I will—"

"Miss McNamara, *I* will deal with the Porter boys. Not you. Mrs. Porter already came to me this morning and complained that you told the boys that you were gonna send the Lullaby Lady to murder them in their sleep. You cannot say things like that to children – no matter that they damaged your blueberry bushes." Carson tugged Mac forward when Miss McNamara looked like she was gearing up for a second round of complaining. "You remember my son Malcolm? He's in town for the festival."

"It's nice to see you again, Miss McNamara," Mac said like a good little sacrifice. He shook the angry woman's hand, who automatically softened up when he smiled at her.

"Oh yes, I haven't seen you since last summer. How was the drive?"

"It was good. This is my girlfriend, Sophie, and her sister Ruby," Mac introduced them, tugging Sophie to his side.

Sophie and Ruby shook the woman's surprisingly strong hands. Miss McNamara excused herself, giving the sheriff a final reminder to deal with the Porter boys, or she would.

They only made it a few more steps before a green-skinned man with a face that strongly resembled a toad's stopped the sheriff. Carson patiently listened while the man complained about a problem with a piece of cracked sidewalk that he believed was dangerous for pedestrians. Gripping the toad man's hand was a tiny green version of him, wearing a frilly pink dress and holding a balloon. There was something unbearably adorable about the little toad girl as she made the balloon bounce on the end of its string.

"If someone trips outside my store, I could get sued," he warned. When his throat bulged like an agitated frog, Ruby tugged urgently on the back of Sophie's shirt as if she couldn't see it too.

"You need to voice your concerns to the city council. I can't do anything about sidewalks. Do you remember my son Malcolm? He's in town for the festival."

After another round of introductions and handshaking, a scuffle in the middle of the street grabbed their attention. Two men who appeared to be half-human and half-hyena were fighting and wrestling on the asphalt. It might have been frightening if both weren't sporting prodigious beer guts and stumbling around, swinging their clawed hands drunkenly. Both men were grunting and cursing so loudly that they didn't notice as the sheriff marched up to them like a thunderstorm.

Carson grabbed both men by their scruffs, pulling them to their feet, even though they were taller than him, and tossing them in opposite directions. "Save it for your pack lands," he growled. "If I see either of you fighting in my streets again, I'll let you spend a few nights in the drunk tank until you cool off. You understand me?"

Both men nodded before slinking off in opposite directions.

"If idiots could fly, this town would be an airport," Carson complained to Mac.

"Enjoying your retirement, old man?" Mac asked, his grin wide and evil. The way Carson growled in response made Sophie concerned for her boyfriend's long-term health.

"'Old man'? I can still whip your ass, whelp, if you keep giving me lip."

"You can try," Mac taunted, rolling his neck. The glint in his eye made it look like he hoped his dad would make a move.

"Sheriff Carson! Sheriff Carson!" another voice called out, pulling the men from their posturing.

"How do you get anything done?" Sophie asked Carson in mild horror.

"It's not normally this bad. Most are just busybodies who want to see who I'm talking to. Small towns," Carson said, shrugging in a whadda-ya-gonna-do way. "Plus, we have double the normal population in town for the festival."

"What's such a big deal about this festival that it brings so many people to town?" Ruby asked.

"It's the Hunter Moon festival. Every year, Cascadia celebrates the first full moon after the autumnal equinox. The moonrise happens sooner than during summer months, so it's good for hunting. It was traditionally a big night for hunting since prey animals had been fattening themselves up all summer and the full moon made visibility better. Historically, shifters would track and hunt prey by bright moonlight to prepare for the winter. There was usually a big feast after the hunt. It's not nearly so bloody anymore. We still celebrate with a feast, but mostly it's just a regular festival nowadays. Food, games, a baking contest. Then, as a culmination of the event, we trek to Gold Bluffs Beach to do a spectacular moonrise party. The festival is a week long, but most of the events happen on Friday night and Saturday, the finale being the beach party."

Sophie hoped they'd wrapped up the investigation before Saturday so they could enjoy the beach party. It sounded fun.

"You picking anything up? Anyone we should keep an eye on?" Mac asked Ruby after she finished shaking another set of hands.

"No one who fits the profile."

"You haven't touched any murderers yet?" Carson's voice was incredulous.

"Less than I thought there'd be in a town filled with goblins and wolves and sorcerers. And none of them are relevant to the murders we're investigating. Most of what I've seen so far happened years and years ago. Do you want me to tell you about every murder committed by the residents here?" Ruby pointed at the little old lady they'd just finished meeting, who was so tiny and frail she looked like a strong wind would knock her over. "Do you want to know that Miss Greta poisoned her first husband?"

Carson looked back and forth between Miss Greta and Ruby in shock. "Miss Greta?" he repeated. "The town librarian who taught hundreds of children to read murdered her husband?"

"He'd started beating her and their kids."

Before Carson could respond, another resident called his name.

By the time they'd made it to the bakery's front door, Sophie felt like she'd shaken a hundred hands, some with claws, some with thorns, one particularly memorable one covered in emerald scales. Mac explained that the woman was a lamia, a Mythical snake person. It had taken them almost forty-five minutes to walk one block. Sophie was entirely sick of meeting strangers. She'd be amazed if she could remember even five people's names. It was all a blur.

The warm, yeasty, cinnamon smell emanating from the bakery made saliva pool in Sophie's mouth. The snacks from the gas station were a distant memory. Sophie made a slight whining noise when some yelling from around the corner made Mac's dad turn in that direction.

A willow-thin man in faded blue pajamas came shuffling around the corner. He was barefoot, and his silvery-blond hair was an unruly halo around his head. His pale blue eyes were wild and lost. Sophie took one look into his eyes and could tell that the lights were on, but nobody was home.

"Ligatures! And fury! Ligatures and fury!" The disheveled man was calling out, his arms raised imploringly. As people strolled the streets, they made a wide berth around the increasingly frantic man who was becoming more agitated. "Two two one. Hurts."

"Milford, what did I say about yelling at people on the street?" Carson asked, but the man looked through him as if he couldn't see the sheriff. He hugged himself with shaking arms, whimpering quiet words about ligatures and pain.

"Milford Bradley!" Carson stated, his voice firm and loud. The man startled and refocused on the sheriff. "How did you get out of the clinic again?"

"Lingering Ferrari. Two two one. Two two one!" the man named Milford said, reemphasizing the words as if repeating them would help them make sense. "The noise," he whimpered, pointing at his head.

Carson gently grasped the man on his shoulder. "Let's get you back to your caretaker," he suggested, his voice gentle and soothing.

Giving Carson a pleading look, Milford's words fell off into mumbling whispers that made even less sense. A woman in teal scrubs came sprinting around the corner, a look of relief crossing her face when she spotted Milford with Carson.

"Sheriff! Thank you. I don't know how he keeps getting away from us," the harried woman exclaimed. She took Milford by the sleeve and led him back the way he'd come.

"Ligatures?" Sophie questioned. "Did someone tie him up or something?"

"We don't really know what happened to him. He showed up a little over a week ago, filthy and half-starved. Walked right out of the woods, lost as a lamb. He didn't have any identification on him. It took us three days to just get his name from him. We're still not sure if he's Milford Bradley or Bradley Milford. I've sent his information and photo to the Conclave; I'm hoping they'll be able to find them in their database. So far, no luck, though. He's Fae, so the only thing we can think of is that he was practicing magic in the redwood forest and something went wrong. A lot of Mythicals come into the area to use the privacy and our ley line to enhance their magic. He's not the first magic user whose spell backfired and fried their brain. The Hunter's Moon Festival draws all kinds. We're hoping that he'll eventually recover."

Sophie glanced back to watch as the man and his nurse disappeared around the corner.

Carson opened the door to the bakery, waving them in. A chorus of voices called out greetings for the sheriff by the few people at the scattered tables spread around the small shop. Carson raised a hand in greeting.

The bell jingling at the top of the door summoned a rosy-cheeked woman with her hair pulled back into a long brown braid. She came bustling from the kitchen, standing behind a long display of baked goods, dusting flour off her hands. The group went through the familiar dance of 'You remember my son?' introductions.

"I'm Pam," the woman said, shaking Sophie and Ruby's hands. She had a drawl that spoke of Southern roots.

"Hi Pam, it's nice to meet you. Everything looks amazing," Sophie greeted, staring at the glass display of baked goodies with greedy eyes.

"Whadda ya recommend today, Pam?" Carson asked.

"I've been practicing for the pie contest on Saturday. You should try the strawberry rhubarb. It's good enough that I think it might be this year's winner. I'm sick of Cordelia lording over us with her 'world famous' bumbleberry pie. I can't wait to see her face when I win. Everyone knows she cheats and uses magic to get her crust so flaky," Pam said, disgust dripping from her voice. "Bless her heart."

"You think you can beat Cordelia?" Carson said with an expression of glee.

"Yep, she's going down this year."

Ah, the politics of small-town living.

"Is the back terrace still open?"

"I just closed it for the day."

"My son just got into town. You know how everyone is...

We'll never get to have a full conversation – nosy parkers will be interrupting us every thirty seconds. We want some privacy to catch up for a minute. I promise we'll clean up after ourselves," Carson said with a wheedling expression that Sophie found disconcertingly familiar. How many times had that same face worked on her when Mac had made it?

"Oh, alright. Just make sure you don't make a mess," Pam said with a shake of her finger and an indulgent look at the sheriff. It comforted Sophie that she wasn't the only one who fell for that look.

Everyone got a slice of the strawberry rhubarb pie except Ruby, who picked out a cinnamon roll almost as big as her head with globs of white frosting dripping down the sides. Pam even threw in a scoop of vanilla over each slice as a welcome-to-town extra, officially making her Sophie's favorite person in Murias.

Carson led the way through a backdoor to an enclosed patio, surrounded by brick on all sides. The tables and chairs were lattice iron. Potted plants crowded every corner, and ivy dripped from the walls, making the space feel like a secret garden.

Sophie took a bite of the pie and made an inhuman noise of pleasure. Pam had heated up the pie so the sweet tartness of the strawberries and rhubarb met with the creamy sugariness of cold vanilla ice cream. It was so many textures and flavors in her mouth that Sophie's taste buds didn't know what to do with themselves.

"If Pam doesn't win this year's pie contest, I'll eat my hat," Carson said with a groan to match Sophie's.

Carson made some small talk around bites of his dessert. "How's your sister? … She and the kids came up for summer break. … Can't believe how big they're getting. … How was the drive?" Blah blah blah. Sophie started to tune them out as they discussed family members and the weather. Mac put up with the fatherly interrogation for a few minutes before steering Carson back to why they were there as he scraped up the last crumbs of pie and melted ice cream with his fork.

"Alright, Dad, we've heard what Marcella had to say about what's happening here. But I'd like to hear it from you."

"Hikers found what we now suspect was the first body off a rarely used trail in the Redwoods almost two months ago. She was half-buried under some scrub brush. The coroner's report said she looked in her forties, with dark hair and a slim build. He found marks that looked like she had been restrained, plus some bruises and burn marks on her torso. The autopsy said she'd likely died of a heart attack, but the cause was too hard to determine based on the state we found the body. Toxicology came back negative, and we could not ID the body."

"Once I touch her, we'll be able to find out what really happened," Sophie said.

"That won't be possible. Since she wasn't claimed for more than a month, we had her buried last week. However, we have the other two bodies. I can get you access as soon as we're all done. The coroner's office is not far from here."

"We could always dig her up if these other bodies don't turn up any visions," Mac suggested.

"It wouldn't be the first time," Sophie retorted with a grin.

"Ah, yes. Our first date," Mac replied, giving Sophie a flirty look.

Sophie gasped in mock-outrage. "Digging up Zhang Liu was *not* our first date! Our first date was the night of the battle at the top of Coit Tower. Obviously."

Carson looked intrigued and concerned in equal measure but held up his hand to cut off whatever Mac's response would have been. "We still have the first victim's clothing in evidence. Can you get a reading off that?"

"No, I've only been able to pull visions from bodies," Sophie explained with a shrug.

"Alrighty, then. After we finish our pie, I'll take you to see the bodies. Eat up now because after you see them, you won't have an appetite any longer," Carson said, scarfing down the last bite of his pie.

Jeez, that's not ominous at all.

"Marcella only mentioned two bodies. Was the Jane Doe one of them?"

"No, there are two others. They're still at the coroner's office. You'll have full access to them."

"Have you had any other strange deaths or murders around here? Maybe there has been more than two," Sophie suggested, channeling her inner gumshoe detective.

"This is a Mythical town. There are always strange deaths and murders. Last week I had a jaguar shifter and a spectacled bear get into a fight to the death behind the ice cream parlor. The week before that, a witch blew up her entire kitchen. She was lucky she only lost a couple of fingers and most of her hair."

"Tell us about the other two bodies—" Mac started to request, but Carson's cell phone ringing interrupted him.

"I need to take this. It's my emergency line. Volpes here," Carson answered the call. Sophie watched as his eyebrows raised comically high before dropping into a dark frown. "Shit. Where?" he demanded in a gruff voice a moment later. "Okay, I'm on my way now. Have Patel and Fredrickson secure the scene. I want the rest of you combing the woods. I'll be there in fifteen."

Standing up and stuffing his phone into his pocket, he grabbed his dirty dishes. "We've gotta go. We've got another one. They just found a body off Trillium Falls Trail."

Scrambling up from the table, they grabbed their dishes and jogged after Carson.

No one approached them this time as Carson stormed down the street with Mac, Sophie, and Ruby trailing in his wake.

"Some campers staying at Elk Meadows were hiking and heard some yelling followed by two gunshots. They found the body shortly after and called us. They're being questioned now. We'll see what's what when we get there."

"They ran towards the gunshot and not away?" Mac asked, looking vaguely impressed.

"Yeah, pretty brave. Possibly stupid, too, but still brave."

"Did they see the perpetrator?" When Carson shook his head, Mac asked, "Do you think this is related to the other murders?"

Carson nodded. "It's very possible. Donovan mentioned it looked like the body had restraint marks, just like the others."

Carson advised them to follow him in their car once they returned to the police station.

Mac pulled around to the back of the building, where his dad was unlocking his patrol car. Sophie watched as Carson tipped his hat to someone that called out a greeting from the sidewalk before climbing into his police cruiser.

"Your dad is not what I envisioned," Sophie commented as the sheriff turned on his flashing lights and headed down the street.

Pulling his car directly behind the cruiser, Mac scoffed. "Don't be fooled. There was a lot less 'aw shucks' and 'y'all's' coming out of that man when I was growing up."

"Oh yeah? Not the good ol' boy he appears?"

"That man has an advanced degree in criminology from UC San Diego. He was the alpha of the largest fox clan in NorCal and was the sheriff of Civitas for almost twenty years. He uses that whole country-boy shtick to get everybody's defenses down. Don't let him fool you."

"So, he's not as nice as he seems?" Ruby asked, sounding let down.

"Not even close."

"Why can't *you* pretend to be nice?" Sophie teased.

"I'm nice," Mac grumbled, making her laugh.

"Oh my gosh, is that a garden gnome?" Ruby squealed from the back seat.

Sophie looked to where Ruby was pointing. Strolling along

the sidewalk looked like a man from Tolkien's imagination. He was built like a stack of bricks, almost as wide as he was tall, with a bushy white beard that tapered to a point near his belly button. But rather than wearing a leather chest plate over chainmail and vambraces, the squat man was in a pair of frayed denim overalls over a green flannel shirt. However, it was the pointed mustard yellow beanie he was sporting that sent some serious garden-gnome vibes.

"Gnomes are usually much smaller. He could be a kobold or a dwarf. Or even just a human. I'd have to smell him to be sure," Mac replied.

"A dwarf! That's even better than a garden gnome."

Instead of heading to Mordor, the man turned into a flower shop and out of Sophie's view.

"I like it here," Sophie said, grinning at Mac.

CHAPTER 6

The strobing of red and blue lights lit the trunks of the enormous trees lining the road garishly, giving the forest a nightmarish look. As they pulled their car onto the shoulder of the road, right behind Carson's vehicle, a woman dressed in a highway trooper's uniform rushed over, a long blond braid slapping her back.

"Jameson," Carson greeted her. "Tell us what you know so far."

"A group of four hikers were exploring the forest when they heard someone screaming. They said it sounded like a man calling for help. They yelled back, trying to locate him. They started in the direction they thought the sound was coming from – about a hundred yards to the east of the main trail. They called out for the man again, but then they heard a gunshot. Two of the hikers ran in that direction. The other two stayed behind. They said they heard a second shot almost immediately after the first one. Then they thought they heard someone rushing through the woods, making a racket. When they ran in the direction the shots came from, they almost stumbled over the body. The guy was already dead. They called us right away. Patel got here in probably fifteen minutes and radioed it in. It's probably been less than thirty minutes since the initial call."

"Tell me about the victim."

"Male, late fifties, heavyset, hands zip-tied behind his back. Smells like Fae. Shot once in the back – looks like he was trying to run away. Then a second time in the right temple. We found a wheelbarrow and a shovel nearby."

"Make sure to check them both thoroughly for prints. I doubt our killer is so sloppy, but maybe we'll get lucky this time. He did get interrupted by the hikers. Has the coroner been notified?"

"Yes, Grady said he's on his way."

The officer fell silent after that, turning to lead them through the woods.

They walked single file through the quiet forest, the only sound the swish and crunch of their feet through fallen pine needles. It felt somehow sacrilegious to fill the air with the sound of chatter.

The light had become weak and soft as the waning daylight caught in the mist that clung to the upper boughs like a shroud. Cold moisture rose from the ground, soaking through Sophie's sneakers, making her toes clammy and numb.

The soaring sequoias towered overhead, making Sophie strain her neck, trying to see their tops. The way the weak sunlight threaded between the massive trunks of the trees looked like fingers of light reaching for the forest floor leaving soft, golden patches of sunlight on the carpet of ferns and rhododendrons below. Mist danced in the beams of light that penetrated the thick forest canopy.

The pristine beauty of the nature surrounding the hiking trail made Sophie's breath catch. Staring around in awe, the majestic, magical forest washed over her in wonder. It made her want to give thanks and send up a prayer.

They marched past a waterfall that made her fingers itch for a camera. Water burbled over rocks covered in vibrant, dripping moss. Ferns drooped over the churning water, their leaves dancing and bobbing where they touched the surface of the tumbling water. The humidity hovering in the air made curls of her hair stick to her face. Sophie dragged in a deep breath, savoring the hints of pine and eucalyptus. There was a musty undertone of composting leaves and soil in the air.

The forest was so quiet and almost ominous that Sophie could hear low conversation filtering through a thicket of trees long before anyone came into view. Getting on her tiptoes to see over Mac's head, Sophie spotted a couple of officers standing in a small clearing. A sense of wrongness, a discordant note in the silence, hung over the glade. A man's body in dark clothing was crumpled at their feet.

They walked up to the body, following only in the footsteps of Jameson's careful path, making sure to not contaminate the crime scene. Sophie tried to peek at the man, but his face was turned away. He was half on his side, splayed out as if he'd been thrown.

Sophie could feel death hovering over the area. If she stretched out her senses, it almost felt like the cold fingers of death reached back. There was something almost comforting in the cold tendrils. Death had become so much a part of her everyday life that it felt steady and reassuringly familiar. Sucking in a breath, she wrapped her arms around her waist. Giving herself a mental shake, Sophie decided she'd spent too much time in the morgue.

Carson bent over to get a better look at the victim.

"Does he look familiar to you?" Carson asked the woman who guided them in.

She shook her head. Carson gave the dead man another long stare, squinting his eyes. "He's not local, but he looks sorta familiar. Maybe I've seen him around town." He stood up, shaking his head in disappointment. "Have Grady take his picture. Once you get it, circulate it around town. See if anyone recognizes him."

"Who is that?" Sophie overheard someone ask as she leaned closer to get a better look at the victim's face.

"She's from the Medical Examiner's office in San Francisco. She's been called in to help," Mac quietly explained. "Let's give her some room to work."

Mac nudged his dad with a raised eyebrow, cutting his eyes to the hovering officers.

"Officers, recheck the area and see if there's anything we missed."

They reluctantly spread out, checking through the under-brush on the edges of the clearing, looking for any evidence missed in their initial sweep. Sophie could feel them sneaking glances at her, but she ignored them.

Mac stepped around to the other side of the body, effectively blocking Sophie from the other officers' view. He tugged his father and Ruby to stand on either side of him, close enough for them to hear anything Sophie had to say.

Using their bodies as shields, Sophie knelt on the spongy ground, soaking the knees of her jeans. Even the air in the woods was moist, water clinging to every surface. There was already dew beading on the dead man's muddied navy parka.

Scuffs and grooves in the grass around the body showed where the man had tried futilely to escape. His arms were zip-tied behind his back, his hands looking twisted and awkward. They were bone-white from loss of circulation. Breathing out a slow breath, Sophie centered herself and pressed a single finger to the back of one of his hands. The last thing Sophie saw before the vision grabbed her was a clump of muddy grass loosely clutched in his palm. She closed her eyes and concentrated on the picture flaring to life in her mind's eye.

"He wakes up and realizes he's on his back in a wheelbar-row. His feet are hanging over the front. All he sees are the treetops above him. He tries not to move so that the person pushing the wheelbarrow won't realize he's awake. His hands are numb behind him, and his shoulders are aching fiercely. His head is buzzing like he's been drugged. Or maybe it's just adrenaline. He feels like fire is burning in his veins, and his heart is racing like crazy. He leaps out of the wheelbarrow and makes a run for it. He's screaming and hollering for help, running blindly, hoping somebody is nearby. He thinks he hears some voices calling back, so he turns in that direction. A blast hits him in the back, knocking him right on his face, sliding in the mud. He tries to get his knees under him, but he just slips, floundering without the use of his hands. He can't get up fast enough. Shoes come into his vision. He tries to plead for his life, but they shoot him again before he can even get the words out. The last thing he sees is a dark figure running away."

Sophie opened her eyes. Pointing to the right, she said to Mac, "The murderer ran that way. Black sneakers, medium build, I think. Wearing a dark jacket with a hood. It looked like a rain-coat, maybe."

Mac yelled at the two remaining officers to stay and stand guard. "Dad, come on. He went this way. Ruby, stay here."

Mac and Carson took off, followed closely by Jameson, sprinting into the woods in the direction Sophie had pointed. She couldn't believe how quiet they were as they ran full out. Within seconds, they were gone. Ruby huffed in annoyance at being left behind.

The officers left on the scene gave Sophie and Ruby curious looks from under the brims of their hats. Sophie stepped back away from the body and next to her sister. The officers slowly came closer, occasionally giving them searching looks. It wasn't long before they started speculating.

"I think it was a hunter," one suggested.

"A hunter? How would a human hunter get past the ward?"

"It's hard to get past, but not impossible. Especially if you know it's there."

"If there were hunters here, I think we'd have already caught them. They're just humans. There's no way they could evade a bunch of shifters," the second officer scoffed.

"Hunters are known for using wolfsbane to cover their tracks."

"Everyone uses wolfsbane to hide their scent trail," Doubting Thomas retorted, rolling his eyes.

"Okay, smartass. Who do *you* think is committing these murders?"

Sophie also wanted to hear his theory, but before the man could answer, Mac and Carson walked back into the clearing, snapping the two men back to military attention.

"Anything?" Sophie asked.

"Whoever he was got away, but I think we may have found his footprint in the mud. Jameson's going to take a casting of it."

Carson looked somehow simultaneously elated and angry. "We're one step closer to catching this bastard."

Ruby slipped closer to the body and carefully pressed her finger in the same spot Sophie had touched the man.

"What are you doing?" Sophie asked.

"I wanted to know if I would see anything."

"Well?"

"Nope. Nothing." Ruby shrugged, wiping her hand off on her pants.

Carson approached Sophie, a thoughtful look on his face. "Did you see the perpetrator's face?"

"No, it was just a shadowy blur under his jacket."

"What type of magic is this? I've never heard of anything like this. You both smell human."

"We get that a lot. We don't know what we are," Ruby said with cheer while Sophie shrugged. "We're human, but the current theory is that one of our ancestors was Fae, and we're probably long-lost Fae royalty."

"No, we're not," Sophie quickly corrected her. If Ruby started talking about the Russian princess Anastasia again, Sophie was going to stuff a sock in her mouth.

"Uh, well, whatever that was, good job. There's nothing else you can do here, so why don't you guys go get settled at the inn, and we can start fresh in the morning. I'll be stuck here for hours, so you might as well get some rest." The look on Carson's face said he wasn't looking forward to his evening.

"Are you sure, Dad? We can help," Mac offered.

"No, go get these girls some food and sleep." Carson wrapped an arm around Ruby's shoulder, steering her away from the dead body. Mac and Sophie were forced to follow. "You sure you don't want to stay at my place? There's plenty of room."

"We're sure. Besides, your sleeper sofa sucks," Mac replied, making Carson chuckle.

"Be at the coroner's at 9 sharp. You know how I feel about tardiness."

"If you're early, you're on time. If you're on time, you're late," Mac parroted, then rolled his eyes. Sophie had a sudden vision of Mac as a teenager. She almost felt bad for Carson.

The walk back to the road seemed to take a lot longer than the original journey, but maybe that was Sophie's exhaustion finally catching up to her. Finally, the road with its plethora of police cars lined up on the shoulder came into view. As they approached Mac's car, a coroner's van pulled up. A short, spry man with ebony skin and hair cropped so close it wasn't more than a shadowed suggestion hopped out of the driver's seat, giving the group a suspicious look.

"Grady, you remember my son?" Carson greeted. When Grady nodded, Carson continued, "The Conclave sent him up for the investigation. These are some consultants here to help. They'll be by tomorrow morning to view the bodies."

Grady looked vaguely relieved before heading to the van's backdoor to pull out a rolling gurney. Rolling the bouncing gurney down the forest path, Grady was quickly swallowed by the foliage, disappearing from view when he followed a turn in the trail. Finally, even the squeaking wheels of the gurney faded away.

"Despite the circumstances, I'm glad you're in town, son," Carson said to Mac as there was silence once more.

"Me too, Dad. We'll see you in the morning."

Getting into the car, Sophie watched the giant trunks of the trees fly past as Mac drove the vehicle back towards town.

Sophie hadn't even realized that she'd fallen asleep until the jolt of the car turning into a driveway woke her up. Rubbing the sleepiness from her eyes, Sophie stared up at the inn where they were staying. She glanced at Mac, then back at the mansion, wondering if they took a wrong turn.

"Is this our hotel?"

"Whoa!" Ruby exclaimed from the back seat. "It looks like an extra fancy Bates Motel."

The sage green building with dark green trim had a square steep-roofed tower topped with a wind vane of a rearing horse. It was flanked by two smaller matching turrets. Sophie's eyes flitted from the wraparound porch to the multiple gables to all the ornate gingerbread detail dripping from every eve. It looked like someone had taken every Queen Anne and Victorian-style mansion and combined them into one building.

Mac pulled the car around the circular drive and right in front of a sprawling set of stairs. A small sign next to the stairs proclaimed the house to be Colpach Inn. As Sophie and Ruby stood at the foot of the stairs trying to take in all the architectural details of the building, Mac fetched their bags from the trunk.

"Thanks," Sophie said, still distracted, taking her bag from Mac.

As they walked up the stairs, the double front doors swung

open. Standing in the opening was a man. With the light behind him, he was mostly just a silhouette – a very tall silhouette. His head almost brushed the top of the doorframe.

"Welcome to Colpach Inn. I'm Davin Colpach, owner and proprietor. Sheriff Volpes called to let me know you were on your way. Your rooms are ready for you." The man stepped to the side, waving them inside.

Sophie felt like she had to say something. It was clear that the proprietor was very proud of his establishment.

"Your inn is so nice."

"Thank you. It was built in 1884 by my great-great-grandfather Lachlan Colpach. He came to the area during the gold rush but made his fortune as a lumber magnate. Legend has it that he felled the first tree for commercial purposes on the Humboldt Bay."

Stepping inside, Sophie was left with the impression of a place out of time. It felt like a museum for the turn of the century, back when robber barons were crushing their competitors and creating monopolies.

The entire foyer was filled with gleaming intricate woodwork. Any surface that wasn't covered in wood was covered in flowery wallpaper.

The owner, Davin, seemed oversized and lumbering in this delicate, pastoral setting. The group followed him up a set of wide stairs to their rooms. Despite his height, Davin was a reed-thin man with shoulders and hands that seemed too big for his body. His clothes hung on him like a scarecrow but strained across his shoulders.

He warned them they were getting some of the last rooms available in the building.

"The dining room is closed for the night, but I could send up some sandwiches," Davin offered when Mac asked about food.

"That sounds marvelous," Sophie responded before Mac even had a chance to accept the offer. The only things she'd had to eat since breakfast were gas station snacks and a piece of rhubarb pie, and her stomach was hollow and complaining.

Davin was determined to retell the history of each archway and doorknob as he led them to their rooms. Not wanting to annoy the person who promised to bring her food, Sophie made appropriately interested noises as Davin monologued.

As they turned up the stairs to the third floor, an enormous stained-glass window came into view. It was of another horse rearing back on its hind legs, pawing the air in a similar stance to the weathervane on top of the mansion. The horse's mane streamed out behind it, made of hundreds of jewel-like pieces of glass in every shade of emerald and jade.

"The horse is green," Ruby pointed out.

"That's not a horse. It's a kelpie. And my great-great-grandfather Lachlan, actually," Davin replied.

"A kelpie?"

"A shape-shifter water spirit. Also called a water horse. Lachlan brought our entire herd from Scotland. We need to live near water, so this area was perfect for my people. Legends state that kelpies used to pull their victims into the water, drown them and then eat them. But we haven't done that for centuries."

"Coo-ool," Ruby replied, drawing the word out into an extra syllable.

Of course, Ruby would think cannibalistic murder-horses are cool.

Davin showed them the two rooms. Ruby happily accepted the smaller room, leaving the larger one to Sophie and Mac. Confirming when the dining room opened in the morning, Mac thanked Davin for taking them in and wished him goodnight.

Sophie ignored the ornately appointed room and tossed herself onto the bed with a groan.

"So tired," Sophie complained, her voice muffled in a pillow.

"Poor thing," Mac sympathized. Sitting on the end of the bed, Mac tugged off her tennis shoes, tossing them towards the open closet. Sophie didn't trust the tone in his voice, but then he dug his thumbs into her arches, and she decided she didn't care anymore if he was mocking her.

When Mac made his way up to her calves, making the tense muscles in her legs unfurl, Sophie decided maybe she wasn't that tired after all.

CHAPTER 7

he following day, Sophie and Mac found the dining room by following the scent of coffee and bacon. Sophie felt like one of those cartoon mice lured by the smell of cheese, toes dragging across the floor.

A man in his mid-twenties with an uncanny resemblance to Davin but without the willowing height led them to one of the last empty tables in the dining room.

With promises of coffee and orange juice, the young man headed off. A laminated menu sat on the table, laying out the limited options for breakfast.

Sipping her coffee, Sophie started people-watching while they waited for their food. A man sitting at a table in the back corner of the room caught Sophie's eye. The way he had positioned himself, with his back to the corner as he faced the rest of the room, spoke to a distrustful nature. Hunched over his food, the man gave the room's occupants a suspicious glower.

He had tangled, scraggly dirty blonde hair falling past his shoulders with a few black feathers sticking out of it. A string of beads that appeared to be made from human carpal bones hung from his neck. His black button-up shirt had seen better days.

Leaning against the wall within reach was a knobby wooden staff topped with the skull of some sort of small animal.

Sophie nudged Mac and nodded in the man's direction. "He looks like a voodoo witch doctor," she whispered.

Mac looked at the man and gave Sophie a slight shrug. "He very well might be one. He smells Fae, though. Most voodoo practitioners are humans, a variation of a warlock, or, usually, a fraud."

At another table was the tiniest woman Sophie had ever seen. She was sitting on a stack of books, eating a piece of toast, looking like a doll someone had dressed up as a medieval peasant woman and then brought to life.

Mac caught her looking at the pint-sized woman and mouthed the word 'leprechaun'.

At that moment, the waiter dropped off their food, saving Sophie from embarrassing herself by confessing that she thought that leprechauns were all little men with red beards and green suits.

Sophie checked the time on her phone with annoyance. Ruby knew what time they needed to be at the coroner's office. She was going to make them late. They had knocked on her door before heading down, but she hadn't answered. They assumed Ruby was sleeping in.

"If she doesn't come down soon, I say we leave without her," Sophie suggested to Mac. A day away from Ruby sounded lovely. "Maybe we should just send her out to shake hands with the townspeople instead of joining us. It's not like she can help at the morgue."

Just then, Ruby came bustling in through the front door with wind-tossed hair and pink cheeks.

"You're late," Mac stated, the flat look in his eyes conveying his annoyance.

"Pssh, the dead bodies aren't going anywhere. You need to learn to relax. I just wanted to take a walk and see the town."

Sophie stabbed her fork at Ruby's hand when she stole a piece of toast off her plate. When Sophie missed by mere centimeters, Ruby stuffed the entire slice of bread in her mouth with a gleeful grin.

"I spit on that," Sophie said.

Ruby shrugged like she didn't care. Sophie couldn't decide if she was just a disgusting animal who didn't mind eating food with spit on it or if Ruby knew that she was bluffing. Pulling her plate away from where Ruby was sitting, Sophie gave her a warning look.

"We thought that we could split up," Mac said. "Sophie and I can head to the coroner's and check out the victims while you get as many readings as possible around town."

Sophie realized she might love Mac just a little.

"No," Ruby whined. "We're a team. Plus, I touched a bunch of people already on my walk this morning and didn't find a thing. I think I should see these dead people, so I'll recognize them from any visions I pull."

Unable to think of a counterargument, they quickly finished their meal and headed out to the car.

The coroner's office was on the same street as the sheriff's department. The building was a bland white stucco with only a street number on the door and nothing else to indicate what was inside.

Carson was waiting outside, a paper bag clutched in his hands.

Mac got out of the car and gave his dad an up-and-down look. "Nice cowboy boots, dad."

"It helps to look and act the part around here. Plus, as a bonus, it annoys you."

As Mac scoffed, Carson offered the paper bag to Sophie and Ruby.

"Stopped by the bakery this morning and had Pam pack a breakfast for you. They don't have any vegan options. I know how you city folk like your vegan rabbit food."

Mac made a sound of outrage. "City folk? Dad, you were born in Fresno."

"I ate at the inn, thank you," Sophie said when Carson offered her the bag, keeping her amusement at the father-son interaction off her face.

When Carson handed the bag to Ruby, she cheered after glancing inside. "Second breakfast!"

When they entered the building, an older woman with snakes sprouting from her head waved them through from behind a counter wordlessly. Sophie tried to act like she wasn't a tourist and raised a hand in thanks. The woman returned Sophie's smile, showing off a mouthful of fangs. The snakes writhed in a hypnotic rhythm around the woman's head.

Ruby wasn't nearly so composed but managed to hold it together until they were out of earshot. "It was Medusa. But we didn't turn into stone. So cool!"

"Lydia is a Gorgon. Medusa was a person, not a breed of Mythical. Although the real Medusa was also a Gorgon," Carson quietly explained.

They found the man from the night before, his dark skin gleaming under the fluorescent lights, standing in front of a wall of refrigerator cabinets.

"Good morning, Grady. Thank you for making time for us."

"Of course. I'll be a happy man if it means getting these cases solved and out of my office." Turning to the sisters, he noticed the bag in Ruby's hand. His nose twitched in a way that reminded Sophie of a mouse.

"Hi, I'm Ruby. Would you like a bear claw? I have plenty," Ruby offered.

"I'm Dr. Musteli. And thank you, I'd love a bear claw. Is it from Pam's?"

When Ruby nodded, Grady happily grabbed a pastry from the bag and quickly demolished it, eating in a way that made Sophie again think of a rodent. Carson quickly introduced everyone else while Grady finished his food.

Wiping the crumbs off his hands, he turned back to Ruby. "I was told one of you works at the San Francisco ME's office. Do you work with Dr. Didel? Sometimes I send some of our more complicated cases his way. His facility is top of the line."

The envy in Grady's voice made Sophie smile. Raising her hand, she said, "I'm the one that works with Dr. Didel. Ruby works for the Conclave."

Grady shook her hand first, then Ruby's. After Ruby finished with Grady's hand, Sophie raised an eyebrow at her, then subtly cut her eyes toward the coroner. Ruby shook her head, letting Sophie know he wasn't the man they were looking for.

"Did you have a chance to do the autopsy on last night's victim?" Carson asked.

"Yes. And I've even got good news for you. We got a hit when I input this guy's info into the missing person's database." Opening the door to one of the cabinets, he slid out a long steel tray with a naked dead body wrapped in clear plastic lying on its surface. Grady pulled the edges of the plastic open, unveiling the man's upper body. "Meet Rowan Loughty from Vermont."

Grady walked over to a desk and grabbed a sheet of paper, handing it to Carson. Looking at the printout, Carson grunted. "Yep, that's him all right."

After reading over the sheet, he handed it to Mac. Sophie crowded close to read it over his shoulder. According to the document, Rowan was forty-four years old and single. He'd been reported missing by his workplace two weeks earlier.

"Looks like our Rowan here might have been going through a rebellious stage," Mac announced. "It says here that he didn't have any tattoos." Mac pointed at the report in his hand, then at the dead man's displayed torso.

Leaning closer to where Mac was pointing at the man's upper

chest, Sophie looked over the tattoo. "This isn't fresh. It looks slightly faded, so it's older. I'm no expert, so I could be wrong."

"Grady, send a picture of the victim and his tattoo to Blathmac to see if he visited the shop and got his tattoo there. Or maybe Blathmac might recognize the work," Carson said.

"Do you think this is a Fae tattoo?" Grady asked.

"No, but Blathmac does plenty of non-Fae tattoos at his shop. At the very least, he might be able to give us a direction to explore. Did the autopsy turn up anything else unusual?" Carson asked. "Do you think this is related to the others?"

"I'd say no, except for the restraint marks and this," Grady replied, pointing to a large bruise covering most of the man's sternum. "But it's not conclusive."

Grabbing some gloves from a nearby box, Sophie pulled them on. She gently probed around the purpled area. The vision of his death tried to reappear in her mind, but she mentally shut the door on it so she could concentrate. "Could it be from a punch?" Sophie balled up her fist and compared the size and shape of the bruise to her hand.

"If it is, that is one hell of a hit," Carson said with a wince.

"What could have caused this? Do the other bodies have something similar?"

Grady shrugged. "I believe so. With one of the bodies, it's impossible to be sure, but the rest all had a similar hematoma." When Sophie raised an eyebrow at him, he shrugged again. "You'll see."

Gently turning Rowan's head, Sophie looked at the gaping bullet wound in his temple. She confirmed with Grady that the headshot was the cause of death. "Huh. Look. His ears are pierced," Sophie said, pointing to the small holes in the man's ears. "Was he wearing earrings when he was brought in?"

"Yes, he had diamond studs. They were bagged as evidence with the rest of his clothes."

"Rowan must've gone through quite a rebellious phase," Mac

retorted. "It doesn't look like his ears are pierced in this picture. And pierced ears aren't mentioned in the missing person's report."

"Maybe it's an older photo of him. Before he hit his midlife crisis," Ruby suggested, pointing at the printout in Mac's hands. "I wonder what he's been up to since this picture was taken."

Sophie completed her inspection of the body. Nothing else stood out to her, and the cause of death was obvious and somewhat mundane compared to what she saw on an average day in the morgue.

"Did anything unusual show up in the tox screening?" Sophie asked him.

Grady scoffed. "I think you're too used to the city. We don't have the facilities to do a tox screening in-house. We have to send out our tox screenings to a lab in Sausalito. It'll be at least a week before we get anything back. When we get the results back, I'll let you know."

"Did any other deaths come back with anything on their toxicology reports?" Mac asked. Grady shook his head.

Sophie hoped they'd have already solved the crimes long before they needed any reports.

Returning Rowan's body to the fridge, Grady pulled another door open.

"This is where I realized that there might be a pattern. He was found on the 21st of last month," Grady announced, dragging out a new body.

Behind her, Ruby started gagging and quickly ran out of the room. Sophie was used to the smell of decomposing bodies, but the smell made even her hardened stomach try to crawl sideways. She repeatedly blinked, trying to get her watering eyes under control.

Despite the advanced decomposition, Sophie would guess that the man was somewhere between his twenties and thirties. He had thick blond hair, a round face, and was a little pudgy with a stark farmer's tan around his neck and biceps. A bruise bloomed large and dark on his breastbone, almost black against the paler skin of his chest. His wrists and ankles were covered in more bruises and scrapes that looked like rope burns to Sophie's untrained eyes.

"Anything unusual about this one?" Mac asked.

"Other than the fact that he hasn't come up on any databases and was dressed for warm weather in shorts and a tank top? Oh, and that his brain was basically turned into mush. No, other than that, totally normal."

"What is listed as the cause of death?" Mac asked.

"Massive cerebral hemorrhage, coupled with catastrophic head trauma. It was the best way I could figure to explain that every blood vessel in this man's brain basically exploded."

"Was he electrocuted?" Sophie asked.

"No. Look, no burn marks. I'm almost certain that he was killed with magic. No way to know exactly what kind. If there was any residue left, it was gone by the time we found him."

That made Sophie straighten up from her examination of the tattoo. "Magic leaves a residue?"

"Sometimes. Depends on the type of magic. Sometimes they use spells or potions that can leave behind trace elements, and some types of blood or death magic leave a mark or scent."

It was all interesting information but didn't help Sophie solve the murder. She needed to touch the body to do that. She started to reach towards the man's arm, mentally preparing herself to receive a vision, when Mac cleared his throat. Sophie stopped and looked at him expectantly, but he turned to the coroner, who was watching with intense interest.

"Dr. Musteli, as you know, Sophie is employed by the San Francisco Medical Examiner's office, but she also reports directly to the SF Chief of Police and the Conclave. What you are about to witness is considered top secret and is to never leave this room. If you breathe a word about what you're about to witness, I will bring the Conclave down on your head. Understood?"

"Of course." Grady looked suitably cowed, but Sophie idly wondered how long they could keep her power a secret. The more people that knew, the more likely it became impossible to keep it under wraps.

Sophie closed her eyes and laid her gloved hand on the man's forearm. Never had she been so glad that she could get readings through her nitrile gloves. Touching his putrefying flesh made her want to start gagging like Ruby.

"It's dark. Wait. No, he's blindfolded. Damn it. I can't see anything," Sophie complained. "He's tied down to a table or hard surface. He is screaming like a banshee – I can hardly hear a thing."

Tilting her head as if to hear better, Sophie pushed all her concentration into the vision. "I think it's more than one person screaming and crying. Maybe. I'm really not sure, though. Perhaps he's somewhere where it's echo-y. I think I hear chanting. Or whispers? No, it sounds like low chanting, but I can't make out the words over this dude's screeching. Something hard is pressed down onto his chest. He tries to buck it off, but whoever is there just presses it harder into his sternum, pinning him to the table. The chanting is getting louder – it's definitely chanting, but I can't understand any of it. It's repetitive. They're whispering the words; I think it's a different language. I don't know. Someone places their hand on his forehead and—"

"Whoa. Are you okay?"

Sophie realized she had managed to jump back several feet. She'd plowed right into Mac's arms, where he was able to catch and steady her. She hadn't even processed what she'd seen and felt before leaping away like a cat dropped in a bath.

Rubbing her hands together to try and dispel the feeling, Sophie shivered as she tried to concentrate on what she'd just witnessed. "I don't know what just happened. It felt like his brain had been set on fire – or electrocuted. I think it started in his chest but flared hard and bright in his mind. If the person who did this to him made his brain explode like you said, he felt that pain. At least he didn't have to suffer long, I guess. It was over in seconds."

"Did you see anyone or hear anything that could give us a clue who killed him?" Mac asked.

Sophie shook her head. "Not really. There was a bunch of screaming. It was overwhelming. It might have been someone else there with him, or he might have been somewhere that echoed a lot, like a cave or a cement cell. I'm not totally sure. Same for the murderer. The chanting was in a low whispery voice. I think it was one person, a man's voice, but I can't be sure. I can't even say with any certainty if it *was* a man. It was so quiet and hushed that I could barely hear him or her over Rowan's screaming. That was weird."

"You think that one's weird? Wait until you see what's behind door number two," Grady warned, pointing a finger at another of the refrigerator doors.

Sophie was thankful when Grady slid the dead man back into the fridge and sealed the door shut. Grady poked his head out the door and let Ruby know the coast was clear.

He warned the group, "The next one smells normal, but looks horrendous."

Sophie thought to warn Ruby that 'normal' was a relative term when it came to the morgue, but an evil part of her decided to let her find out that fact on her own.

"That was fucking disgusting," Ruby griped, striding back into the room. Sophie's eyebrows raised in surprise. She'd never heard Ruby, who was a weird mix of Disney-PG and psychopathic murderer, cuss before. Ruby's nose wrinkled at the lingering scent, glancing around the room, but she was no longer spewing up her bear claws.

"You see dead bodies all the time. You're usually the cause of their death," Sophie countered. "I can't believe you're so squeamish."

"Okay, there have been a few bodies, but I don't wait for them to start rotting. That smell – completely atrocious. Do you have to deal with stuff like that all the time? I've seen some of your work in my dreams, but thankfully the dreams don't really come with smell-o-vision."

Grady stared at the two sisters in bewildered silence before Mac reminded everyone they were there for a reason.

The silence was immediate and heavy when Grady opened the next refrigerator door and pulled the tray out.

"What the—"

Stepping closer, Sophie tried to make sense of what she was looking at.

"I warned you," Grady reminded them. "This one was found last week in a ravine in Berry Glen."

"Am I looking at conjoined twins?" Sophie asked, turning her head sideways. If she closed one eye and squinted, maybe the body would look vaguely human.

"If it is, they should have died in the womb, forget surviving to adulthood. No, whatever we're looking at was caused by magic. I couldn't even find a single cause of death. I had to put massive bodily trauma on the death certificate."

It was a woman with curly auburn hair. She looked like an amoeba who had gotten caught in the middle of duplicating themselves. Her face looked stretched, like melted taffy – her nose and mouth split and pulled apart into two separate halves, the skin sagging and liquefied in between.

It looked like someone had put a couple of human bodies in a blender and then tried to put them back together while blindfolded. An extra arm protruded from her upper chest, this one without nail polish like her other arms as if it was a new growth. From the pelvis down, the woman looked relatively normal. She even had nail polish on her toes that matched two of her three arms.

Grady gently rolled the body so they could see that she had two spines, one normal and the other twisted and humped out like something from a Victor Hugo novel. Her back was a mass of bruises, but no open wounds or cuts appeared across her stretched, bubbled skin.

"Have you ever seen anything like this in your morgue?" Grady asked Sophie. She was a little flattered that he thought she had enough experience to have seen something he had never witnessed before.

"She looks like a Mr. Potato Head that a toddler put together," Sophie replied, shaking her head. "I've seen some crazy things, but I've never seen anything like this. After I pull a reading, I think we should call Reggie and get his opinion. He's been working at the morgue for years. If anyone has seen anything similar, it would be him."

"Does she have the same bruise on her breastbone as the last guy?" Mac asked.

"There's a bruise," Grady pointed to her sternum. "However, she's covered in numerous bruises."

Bracing herself after the last vision, Sophie put her hand on one of the woman's arms. After a minute, Sophie pulled her hand away and looked at Mac in confusion.

"What is it?" he asked.

"I didn't get a vision. Only the feeling of immense pain and energy."

"Energy?"

"Like adrenaline or – I don't know – how it would feel to touch a live wire. Like an overfilled battery. Just bursting with power." Sophie shook out her hands and blew out a long breath. "I'm going to try again. I've never been blocked from a death vision before."

Sophie put her hand back on the woman. The sense of pain

hit Sophie so hard that she had to grit her teeth to keep from yanking her hand away. She could feel herself start to shake. It was a vortex of agony, energy, and chaos, pulling Sophie under until she had no sense of self left.

The next thing she knew, Mac was pulling her away. "Soph, it's okay. You don't have to keep trying."

"I don't want to give up yet."

"You were standing there for a couple of minutes."

"I was?" It had felt like an eternity, but Sophie would have thought it had only been a few seconds.

"Did you get anything new?" Mac asked.

"No. It was like nothing I've ever felt. I couldn't see *anything* – it was like trying to stare down the sun. I couldn't get a sense of anything but pain and power. It felt like standing in the middle of a tornado made of razor wire and lava. The power was tearing her apart." Sophie looked back at the body. "Maybe literally."

"Did the pain feel similar to what Rowan felt?" Mac asked.

Sophie screwed up her face, trying to decide. "Kinda? The best way I can describe the first guy was that his brain got over-loaded. A circuit blew in his head. The pain was similar but way less intense than hers. But the feeling of power was similar. It all felt... aborted. Like when a breaker flips and the spell gets cut off. With her, the pain was pure agony and *much* worse. And the feeling of energy was way higher. He was like licking a nine-volt battery where she was being hit by a lightning bolt. I can't say with complete certainty, but I'd say these two deaths might be related."

"Reggie's shift ended not that long ago," Mac said. "I'd like to see what he thinks about this." When Sophie agreed, Mac asked Grady if he would be okay with them pulling Reggie in for a consult. He seemed keen to get Reggie's opinion, so Mac sent him a quick text. Barely a minute passed when Mac's phone started to ring.

Giving Sophie a quick grin, Mac answered. Reggie's worried face appeared on the screen. "Hey, Reg."

"Mac! Is everything okay? Is Sophie alright?"

"We're fine. Sophie's right here, and she's fine too. We're calling because we've run into a strange case at the Murias morgue and were hoping to run it past you. Here, I'm going to have Sophie explain it."

Mac handed the phone to Sophie. "Hey, Reggie. Sorry to bug you. I hope we didn't wake you up."

"You're never a bother," Reggie chastised. "I was just finishing up last night's paperwork. I'm still in the office, so you're not bugging me. How's everything going in Cascadia?"

"It's good. It's an interesting place."

Reggie's snort made a quick grin flash across Sophie's face before she remembered why they'd called. Sophie recapped what she'd learned so far and the visions she'd pulled from the bodies.

"With the last body, the one that looks distorted and broken, I couldn't even pull a vision."

An incredulous silence filled the line before Reggie managed to sputter, "Really?"

Sophie had never had that happen before, and she was as stumped as Reggie. "It was strange. All I sensed was pain, fear, and confusion. I couldn't see anything else – not her surroundings or even how she died."

"Strange. Do you think that a spell blocked your vision? Or maybe a geas?"

"I don't think so. I think she was in so much pain that it blocked everything else around her. All she could concentrate on was the pain. But that's just my best guess. And I've never seen a body like this." Just to the left of Mac, Grady was hoping from foot to foot, an excited look on his face. "Reg, I have the coroner here with me. He can probably explain this better than me."

Grady practically snatched the phone from Sophie's hands.

"Dr. Didel, it's an honor. This is Dr. Musteli. If you remember, you consulted with me on that case last year with the yeti?"

"Oh yes, I remember. It's nice to see you again, Dr. Musteli. Sophie says you have another interesting case on your hands."

Grady strode over to the dead woman and showed Reggie her mangled corpse. As they reviewed the autopsy results, Sophie found an empty chair to sit in as she figured the two doctors would be awhile.

"Have you ever seen anything like this?" Grady asked Reggie.

The excited fervor of an unsolved mystery filled both men's voices as Sophie listened to them discuss the autopsy findings.

"Not really," Reggie admitted. "I once had a case where a wizard had tried to clone someone. He accidentally duplicated each organ in that case, but it all stayed within the original body. The victim's cadaver was bloated almost like a tick, and the organs crowded each other. Some of them were even fused together. And the whole body turned a strange shade of yellow. Our findings indicated that it was due to the yarrow root he used in his spell. Did you find any trace of yarrow root?"

"No, the only trace elements we found were things like mushroom spores and pine pollen. Considering where the body was found, the elements were to blame. There were traces of ocean salt on her skin, so I believe she was killed near the Pacific. However, she was found in a ravine in the forest at least twenty miles from the coastline."

"Ocean water has been used in a few harmless spells. I can reach out to a few colleagues and see if they know about any spells that could do this to a person. I'll also send you the case file on the body that the wizard tried to clone so you can compare it to your Jane Doe."

Grady thanked Reggie for his help before handing the phone back to Mac.

"Thanks for taking a look, Reg. We appreciate your help," Mac told Reggie.

"What a fascinating case," Reggie said, his eyes bright with curiosity. "I might want to come to take a look at that body since I've never seen anything like it. But only if that won't be stepping on Dr. Musteli's toes."

"I'd be happy for you to visit, Dr. Didel," Grady called out from across the room.

Mac and Sophie assured Reggie that they would keep him posted on their case before hanging up. Sophie and Mac decided to head outside to get some fresh air, while Carson chose to stay behind to talk with the coroner.

"So, now what do we do?" Ruby asked, joining them.

"Sophie's done all she can for now. Unless Reggie can figure out something that Grady missed, it's your turn," Mac replied.

"So, I just need to touch as many people as possible?" Ruby asked.

"We need a plan," Mac started to say when his father exited the building and joined them.

Ruby gave him a confused look. "A plan? I just need to walk around and touch people."

"We should be methodical. Let's start with Abernethy Street. Start on one end and hit each shop. That way, we can keep track of where we've been. Then once we've finished the main drag, we can start expanding outward. Dad can introduce us to everyone. We'll shake hands and figure out who this asshole is that's killing people."

"That's not gonna work. I've been called in to mediate a property dispute," Carson said, an apology in his eyes.

"Dad, let one of your deputies take care of it. I think a murderer running loose is more important," Mac argued.

"This is a territory dispute between the elk herd and the local wolf pack. It has the potential to turn into a bloodbath. I need to take care of this. I'll be back as soon as I get a handle on the situation."

Carson apologized again before he headed to his patrol car. Blowing out an annoyed breath, Mac headed to his car.

"Is Grady a shifter?" Sophie asked, rushing to catch up to Mac.

"Yep. Wolverine."

"Like in the comic book?" Ruby asked, her eyes wide and excited. She looked like she was about to head back into the morgue.

"No, like the animal. They look a bit like small, stocky bears. They're quite vicious, remarkably tough for their smaller size, and excellent in a fight."

Getting into the driver's seat, Mac turned and looked at Sophie. "Okay, here's what we're going to do. Ruby, touch as many people as possible. If you can find a way to get their name, do so. Sophie, I want you to take notes. Names if we can get them, and if not, a physical description of them. At worst, we can give the list to my father, and he can tell us if we've missed anyone suspicious."

Sophie glanced down the street they were parked on. At the end, she could just make out Abernethy Street. It was packed with people wandering around, shopping, eating, and doing generally touristy stuff. "That's going to take forever."

"We don't have any other choice. I can't think of any other way to do this. These crimes are most likely being committed by a local, so focus on them first. Let's start at the bakery."

"Looks like you're getting a third breakfast," Sophie teased Ruby, who cheered in response.

CHAPTER 8

Two days later, Sophie was wholly sick of playing tourist. They'd canvassed one entire side of Abernethy Street and were halfway through the other side. It had been fun at first, but after trailing behind Ruby while she flirted and talked and flitted from one person to the next, Sophie was over it. It was already Thursday, and they were no closer to solving this mystery than when they'd started. The primary festival day was on Saturday, when there would be games, food, and fun, followed by an all-night full moon beach party. Each day the streets crowded with more and more visitors, meaning Ruby's efforts to methodically touch as many people as possible was getting even more difficult.

They'd started the day by having breakfast at the diner, where Ruby made a fuss about wanting to meet the cook so she could shake their hand in thanks for "the best omelet she'd ever eaten". Then they checked the marijuana dispensary, the hardware store, and the bookstore, where Ruby had played dumb to get several store employees to help her find a book. It gave her an excuse to get them from behind the counter where she'd been able to then touch them. Sophie was begrudgingly impressed at Ruby's ability to find a way to touch people, although she suspected that a number of people in town thought they were both weirdos.

Sophie had heard more than one older person in town muttering about how she always was on her phone – "kids these days" had become a familiar refrain. Little did they know that she was taking notes on each and every one of them. Her thumbs were sore from all the typing she'd done over the last few days.

"What's a dominance fight? I don't get it." Ruby had just pulled another vision of a shifter-on-shifter fight that resulted in a death.

Moving her bag of books to her other shoulder, Sophie wondered if she could get the Conclave to reimburse her for all the purchases she and Ruby had made over the last few days. Playing the tourist wasn't cheap.

Carson cleared his throat. He'd caught up to them after breakfast. He was often called away on sheriff's business, but he tried to join them when he could. "It's not supposed to be to the death, but it happens more often than we'd like. When a shifter, often one of the predator breeds, wants to move up in the pack, they will challenge another shifter for their position. Then they shift to their animal form and fight. The rules of who wins depend on the alpha. For some packs, the fight ends with first drawn blood. For others, it's until someone yields or is knocked unconscious. Alphas aren't supposed to push for matches that end in death because that's how you end up losing numbers, but there're a few that won't intervene when a shifter goes for the kill."

"Did you have to deal with that much as an alpha?"

"Never. Most of my pack consisted of family members, and I was happy to knock some heads together before I let those dummies start getting into dominance fights. Good thing this one has a thick skull." Carson pointed his thumb at Mac. "More

ODD TIMES FOR SOPHIE FEEGLE

than once I thought about dropping him and his sister off a cliff when they were teenagers."

Mac gave Sophie a look of aggravation mixed with a certain fondness for his father.

"Aw, were you an annoying teen?" she teased.

"He's still annoying," Carson interjected. Behind his back, Mac mimed choking his father to death.

Carson opened the door to the next shop. Looking up, Sophie realized it was Madame Venefica's Spells and Potions. She'd been told Madame Venefica, whose real name was Veronica, was a real witch. Sophie sincerely hoped that she made concoctions in a giant bubbling cauldron filled with eye of newt and toe of frog.

Before she could enter the store, Carson stopped her with a hand on her elbow. "I'm not going in. Stay out here and keep me company."

It wasn't really a request, but Sophie nodded in agreement anyhow.

Mac gave his dad a look of warning, but Carson looked unconcerned. "Go, boy, and introduce Ruby to everyone. I want to get to know Sophie better. Besides, all the herbs and spices in there make my sinuses act up."

Sophie gave Mac a nod, letting him know that she was okay. Mac gave his dad one last hard stare before following Ruby into the shop.

Sophie turned and raised a challenging eyebrow at Carson. She'd never experienced the parental interrogation before. She wondered if he planned to ask about her intentions toward his son. Frankly, she was looking forward to it.

"How do you like our little town?" Carson asked.

Huh, setting her up with a soft volley to start. Trying to get her to lower her guard.

"Is that really what you want to talk about?"

"Not really. I just wanted to tell you that I'm glad you and Mac have found one another. You're good for him. He seems much happier and is having fun once again. I had started to worry about Malcolm. For the last few years, he's been consumed with his work, and I think both of us know exactly how grim that can get. You see nothing but the worst of people sometimes. Plus, the shifters in his department didn't make it easy for him. At every step, the apex shifters tried to push him out. Don't get me wrong, I'm proud of his accomplishments – I don't know if anybody else could have pushed through all the bullshit and still thrived. He's made the Mythical division of the police force inclusive for non-apex Mythicals. It's one hell of an achievement. But he was alone, and that kind of pressure would grind down anybody. Even a stubborn, bullheaded block like Mac." Sophie had to bite her lip to keep from laughing. "His mother would've liked you. I wish she could have had a chance to see him get settled down with such a nice girl."

"I'm not really that nice."

"Sure, you are. You might have a smart mouth – much like Mac, I might add – but you're a good person at your core. I've been a sheriff and an alpha long enough to be able to tell."

That wasn't what Sophie had expected to hear at all. She had been prepared to defend their relationship, and instead, Carson was telling her how proud he was of his son and that he was glad they were together. It was the kind of conversation that made her keenly feel the loss of her own parents. Sophie had to blink a couple of times to make sure she didn't spill any tears. If Mac came out and found her crying, he would probably jump to the worst conclusions.

The door opened, spilling Mac and Ruby onto the sidewalk.

"Everything good?" Mac asked quietly, staring at Sophie.

"Yeah. We're good."

Sophie was looking forward to the next shop. It was the tattoo parlor she'd been eyeing since they'd first arrived. Mac had confirmed that it was a Fae tattoo shop, so they specialized in sigil tattoos. Mac didn't seem very impressed with magic-imbued tattoos, but Sophie couldn't wait to see a few.

A commotion at the end of the road prevented them from entering the shop. The sound of yelling and glass breaking had the group turning as a single entity. At the end of the street, a crowd gathered outside Cordelia's Confectionary.

Without a word, Mac and Carson headed toward the noise, moving with practiced coordination. Sophie and Ruby scurried to catch up. Mac jerked the door to the candy store open and stormed inside while his father pulled his service revolver and covered him from the door.

"Get back," Carson shouted at the crowd gathering on the street behind him. Through the large glass front window, Sophie watched as Mac approached the man – Milford Bradley (or Bradley Milford) from the other day. This time he was in a pair of white striped pajamas. Sophie's mouth gaped as Milford picked up a jar of colorful gumballs and tossed them at a display case. The enormous glass jar shattered into a million pieces when it smashed against the case, shards of glass and gumballs exploding everywhere, joining other spilled candy and broken dishes littering the floor. The man darted towards the register, screaming incoherently, leaving bloody footprints wherever he stepped. Sophie shuddered when she realized he was barefoot, running over broken pieces of glass like they weren't even there.

"Keep everyone else out," Carson commanded Ruby and Sophie before stepping into the shop. "Milford, you're okay. We're here to help," he said in a low, soothing tone, holstering his gun and holding his hands out in a calming gesture.

Sophie and Ruby took a position in the doorway, ensuring no one would try to enter the shop. Sophie kept one eye on the crowd and one on the scene inside.

Behind the counter, she spotted a woman crouched behind a soda machine. All Sophie could see were her eyes and the top of her head. The woman's white bun kept bobbing over the machine's top as she peeked at the chaos.

Mac and Carson approached the man from each side. When Milford realized that he was being corralled, he tried to make a run for it. He barreled straight at Ruby and Sophie, who were blocking the front door, shrieking like a manic banshee. Sophie braced herself for impact, but Mac and Carson managed to snag Milford by the back of his shirt before he reached them.

They each took an arm and lifted Milford off the ground, trying to prevent him from damaging himself worse than he already had. Blood dripped from his feet in a steady stream.

With a whoosh of missing air, Milford suddenly disappeared from their grip and re-appeared a second later in the street outside the shop, smack dab in the middle of the rubbernecking crowd.

When the bloody, bedraggled man re-appeared, blinking into existence in the middle of the crowd, they reacted predictably by screaming, flailing, and attempting to stampede away. Sophie would've thought that Mythicals would be made of tougher stuff, but people were pushing and knocking each other over, trying to escape from the wailing and bloody man in their midst.

"Get out of the way," Sophie bellowed as she and Ruby dove through the panicking crowd. They reached Milford, grabbing him by his flailing arms, at the same time as a man in a long brown robe. He tossed what appeared to be a thick wire around Milford's torso like a cowboy lassoing a steer.

Screeching like he'd been set on fire, Milford dove away from them, dragging the three of them to the ground in a pile. Sophie tried to wrap Milford up like Paddy had shown her during their sparring sessions, but Ruby was in the way, and Milford bucked and flopped like a slippery eel, making it impossible to lock him up. With all his thrashing, he managed to clip Sophie in the jaw with his elbow, making her see stars for a moment.

Finally, Sophie managed to get him into an arm bar. He tried to punch her with his free hand, but the man in the brown robe caught his fist before it could connect. Sophie got into a position where she could dislocate Milford's elbow with a shift of her hips. When he tried to yank away, she exerted the smallest amount of pressure, giving him a hint of pain. Milford cried out but finally went limp. He was still keening like a wounded animal but had finally stopped flailing around.

Mac and Carson sprinted over and pushed through the remaining crowd. As they reached down to grab him, Sophie released Milford from her grip, letting them pull him to his feet, their hold on him vice-tight. Milford sagged in their arms, mumbling and softly crying, the fight draining from him entirely. Carson called his name, but the sad, broken man was unresponsive. Sophie didn't think Milford knew where he was or what was happening. Her heart hurt to see him so shattered. He didn't even seem to notice his numerous injuries. When Carson loudly barked his full name, Milford finally stopped sobbing and looked around in confusion. He stood as mild as a lamb, shivering and silent next to the sheriff.

Mac helped Ruby and Sophie off the ground while their mysterious good Samaritan in the brown cloak waved off Mac's help and got to his feet on his own steam. The man proceeded to nonchalantly dust off his long, monk-like robe.

"Well, that explains how he keeps escaping the care facility. We had no idea he could teleport," Carson said, picking Milford up so his injured feet were off the ground. Milford was so thin and frail that Carson didn't even grunt when he picked him up. Carson cradled him like a child, walking over to one of the few outdoor chairs that hadn't been knocked over in the fracas and gently set him down. He lifted each of Milford's feet to examine the wounds. "We're going to need to take him to the clinic. There's still glass in some of these cuts. I'll have to tell them to put him in one of the iron-warded rooms. That should keep him in place. Good thinking, Morvan, to wrap him in iron."

The brown-cloaked man who had to be Morvan nodded in acknowledgment to Carson. His hood had fallen back, revealing dark hair and equally dark, deep-set eyes. A short black beard graced his face. His long, wild hair was pulled back into a tail at the base of his skull, emphasizing sharp cheekbones and a high forehead. He reminded Sophie of a painting of an ancient Scythian horse archer from the Russian steppes.

"Iron represses Fae magic," Mac explained when Sophie looked at him for an explanation.

She eyed Morvan, giving him a once-over. He looked like a younger, buff Friar Tuck in a monk's habit. He even had the braided rope belt and sandals she expected from that character.

"What is he?" she quietly asked Mac, discreetly pointing toward Morvan.

"He's a druid."

"What exactly are druids? I thought they were monks or something." She thought it might've had something to do with Stonehenge. "Do they have magic?"

"A druid is more like a religious follower than a species of Mythical. Many are human magic users, but they have all kinds in their sect. Although they're all men." When Sophie opened her mouth to complain, Mac raised a hand to stave off her coming rant. "I've heard some East Coast sects are opening their ranks to women."

Sophie glanced back at Morvan, curling her lip in distaste as Ruby and Carson talked to him.

"They were an ancient Celtic sect of priests and prophets. From all accounts, druids reveled in blood and gore. In ancient times they were famous for building wicker men, putting their victims inside them, and setting them on fire. They were known for sacrifices, blood magic, and occasionally cannibalism. Nowadays, they try to project a more monk-like persona – like priests, magicians, and healers."

Carson handed Milford off to one of his deputies that had

finally shown up, commanding them to keep an eye on him while they waited for an ambulance.

The woman with the white bun called out from the store's interior, asking if the coast was clear. When Carson assured her that the situation was under control, she tiptoed her way through the glass and spilled candy to stand in the open door of her shop, looking at the destruction in dismay.

The woman matched her shop with its gingerbread façade. She looked like a plump fairy godmother with her floral dress covered in a frilly apron. Sophie could picture her with a plate of cookies, pinching her grandchildren's cheeks.

"Cordelia, are you okay? Do you have any injuries?" Carson called out to her.

"I'm perfectly fine. Unlike my poor shop. How will I be able to get ready for Saturday's pie contest when I need to take care of this mess?"

Carson promised to send a few deputies to help clean up the mess once they took care of Milford. Cordelia harrumphed but accepted her fate. She headed back into her shop, and Sophie saw her start to sweep up the mess. A few bystanders offered their help, including the voodoo witch doctor they'd seen a few times around the hotel. Cordelia started handing out brooms and dustpans.

"Morvan, thanks for your help," Carson said, clapping the man in the robe on his shoulder. "Once we get Milford secured, I'll return your cable."

"Of course, glad to help, sheriff. No worries about the cable. I have more." The man's voice was deep and low, like he was speaking from the depths of a cavern.

Ruby stumbled over to Morvan, clasping the front of his robe in her hands. "Oh my gosh, thank you so much for helping us. I don't know what we would've done if you hadn't shown up."

Morvan leered down at Ruby, lapping up her flirtatious damsel-in-distress act. His outfit said pious wiseman, but the lecherous look in his eyes told a different story. Sophie nudged Mac and nodded at the pair so he could witness Ruby giving the man's bicep an admiring squeeze. She was utterly shameless in her quest, making Sophie begrudgingly admire her.

With a final bicep squeeze and a flutter of her eyelashes, Ruby turned her back on Morvan and strode to where Sophie waited with Mac. The simpering smile slid off her face to be replaced by grim determination.

"We've got a hit," Ruby whispered, leaning close to Sophie and Mac.

"You mean…?"

"Yep, I think he might be our guy." Ruby looked back at Morvan and gave him a flirty finger wave.

Mac waved his father over. "Is everybody okay?" While his dad walked over, Mac tugged on Sophie's chin, looking at her intently. The clenching of his jaw meant there must be a mark where Milford managed to hit her. She'd probably have a lovely bruise later. Oh, joy.

"I'm fine," Sophie assured the group. "But Ruby thinks that guy Morvan might be our murderer."

Carson raised an eyebrow at Ruby. "How sure are you?"

"Pretty sure. He's killed at least five people, even if he's not our guy. He tied them down to a stone altar and murdered them. He was with a couple of people in matching robes, and they were all chanting. Sound familiar?"

"He's a druid, so that makes sense. Historically they derived their power from human sacrifices and blood magic. Nowadays, they are only supposed to use goats and chickens for their rituals. Mr. Ruith has always seemed like an enterprising type of guy, so I can't say I'm entirely surprised that Morvan is breaking the edict against human sacrifice."

"So, how do you want to do this, Dad?" Mac asked.

Carson rubbed a thumb along his jaw as he thought. "Let me see if I can get Morvan and his brothers to come to the station.

His brothers are probably his accomplices, especially since they all live on the same property together. While I talk to them, I'll send a few deputies down to scope out their property."

"Sophie and I should go with them," Mac said. "If there are any bodies on site, Sophie can get a reading and see if they fit with the other murders. And I'll be there to watch her back."

"What about me? I want to go with you guys." Ruby gave them a pleading look.

"You should go with Dad and see if you can get your hands on Morvan's brothers. Pull readings from them, too. See if they're accomplices like Dad thinks they are."

"I like that plan," Carson agreed. "Let me talk to Morvan and see if I can convince him to come into the station. I'll tell him that after his assistance with Milford, I'd like him and his brothers to lead the procession to Gold Bluffs Beach on Saturday. His ego won't be able to resist that kind of bait."

Without another word, Carson strode back towards Morvan. He called out for him to wait with Ruby hot on his heels.

Before Carson could reach Morvan, an ambulance pulled onto the street, almost jumping the curb in front of the candy shop. Two EMTs spilled out of the vehicle and went to check on Milford before they packed him into the back of the van and drove away. Their lights were flashing, but the siren was silent. Sophie hoped that Milford could get the help he so desperately needed.

All that was left of the scuffle were some overturned chairs and bloody footprints. Sophie could see a few people sweeping up the glass and candy inside the candy shop. Cordelia headed out of the store, clutching a black velvet drawstring bag. Grabbing a pinch from the bag's contents, she sprinkled a little bit of green powder over one of Milford's bloody footprints. Sophie wasn't close enough to hear her, but Cordelia mouthed some words as she waved her fingers over the print. The red blood turned black and burnt up, crumbling into a smudge of black soot. Once she was done, all that was left was a tiny wisp of smoke that was immediately carried away by the wind. Where once blood had been was only pristine, unmarked sidewalk left. Cordelia walked from one footprint to the next, removing them with her magic until the sidewalk looked like Milford had never bled all over it.

"What is that?" Sophie asked Mac.

"Enochian witch magic." *Cordelia is a witch?* It only reinforced Sophie's initial impression of Cordelia and her candy shop as the witch from Hansel and Gretel.

The milling crowd had started to disperse now that the spectacle was over. A couple of deputies that Sophie recognized from the other night in the woods were shooing the looky-loos away.

Carson and Ruby managed to catch up to Morvan, who had waited for the sheriff to briefly talk to the EMTs.

Sophie and Mac surreptitiously watched as Carson talked to Morvan. Whatever spiel Carson had woven appeared to work, based on the smug grin on Morvan's face. After a few minutes, the two men shook hands while Ruby clapped and bounced in place. Morvan turned away and headed up the street at a quick pace.

Carson snagged his deputies and headed back to Mac and Sophie. Pulling them all into a small huddle, he explained their secret mission.

"We believe that Morvan and his brothers have been committing human sacrifices. I want you to take Mac and Sophie to their cabin and check around the area. Park around the corner from their driveway, out of sight. Morvan is heading to pick up his brothers and meet me at the sheriff's office at 3. He thinks they're about to be invited to head the procession through Fern Canyon to the beach party, but that's just an excuse so we can get them out of the way. I will text you once I have the Ruith brothers in my office. Once you get that text, check out the entire area and report back to me. Make sure no one sees any of you. Remember, no one is to know that my son is here for anything other than a visit with his dear old dad. Also, watch out for booby traps. Who knows what these guys have up their sleeves? Especially if they're up to no good." Carson pulled out his phone and started tapping out a quick note. "I'm pulling in the entire force, even the ones off-shift or out of the territory. If we need to arrest four druids powered with sacrificial blood magic, we will need all the fire power we can rustle up. There's no such thing as too careful."

CHAPTER 9

Two hours later, Sophie and Mac found themselves in the back of a squad car, watching as a jeep driven by Morvan pulled out of a rutted driveway. Sophie decided that Ruby was right – stakeouts suck. The air inside the vehicle had become stale, and her legs felt cramped. The sudden appearance of a green jeep in the driveway made Sophie instinctively duck down even though their car was well-hidden behind thick brush and an invisibility spell. Morvan was behind the wheel with three other men who looked strikingly similar. One of the brothers got out of the car to let the jeep through the gate. Once their car had driven out of sight, Jameson pulled the car out from behind the shrub they'd hidden behind.

A rusted sign on the gate warned *No Trespassers* in large, faded letters. Mac got out and propped the gate open so they could drive through. Once Mac returned to the vehicle, they drove down the long, pothole-filled drive. Every few yards, another *No Trespassing* sign would appear nailed to a post. Each sign gave more and more dire warnings about what would happen to unwanted visitors: towed, prosecuted, shot, and finally vaporized. After several hundred yards, a log cabin finally came into view.

The car jolted to a stop in front of the sprawling two-story hunting lodge. Envy filled Sophie at the deep porch running the entire length of the cabin. It was a space where she could easily envision herself enjoying a steaming mug of coffee on a cool mountain morning. Too bad the building had been allowed to molder and deteriorate until it gave off haunted house vibes. With some scrubbing and maintenance, the cabin had the potential to be a stately throwback to when the first trailblazers settled into the wilds of Northern California.

Stepping out of the car, Sophie looked around at the redwood forest crowding around them. The woods buffered and insulated the area from the distant road, so there was no evocation of traffic in the peace and quiet. A light wind rustling the leaves was the only sound besides the pinging of the cooling police car engine.

Sophie tried to turn her attention from the forest to the quiet and dark cabin, but her senses were pulled back to the surrounding woods. That same ominous foreboding she'd felt when they found Rowan's crumpled body lying among the redwoods swamped her. Was her imagination getting away from her with the forest, or was her connection to death deepening?

"You smell that?" Mac asked the deputies, interrupting Sophie's mini freak out. Both officers nodded, their noses wrinkled in distaste. Sophie tried to smell what they were talking about, but she could only detect the usual scents of pine and moist loam.

Mac noticed her trying to figure out what they were smelling. "It smells strongly of blood. Almost overwhelmingly so. Both old and new. And lots of it."

"Coming from where?" Sophie asked, still trying to smell something but only detecting a slightly sickly-sweet scent mixed in with the usual smells of the forest.

"It's all over the place," Mac replied, his eyes steely as he looked at their surroundings. "But it's coming strongest from that direction." Mac pointed towards the cabin.

Sophie started walking, skirting around the side of the building. Following her instincts, she ignored the house for now. She assumed that the brothers weren't sacrificing people inside their home, especially if there was a lot of blood. Although people were weird, you never knew what they would do next.

There had to be somewhere else they were committing their crimes. However, she'd be willing to bet her paycheck that the brothers didn't make their kills inside their cabin. Casting her eyes in every direction, Sophie looked for a likely place to hide a body. Mac and the deputies fell into step behind her. Soon, she found a lead: around the back of the cabin, heading away from the backdoor, was a well-worn footpath.

Sophie couldn't believe that she was purposefully heading into an ominous forest again, this time in search of a sacrificial altar and blood. When this was all over, she needed to demand hazard pay from the Conclave.

Trees and shrubs quickly hid the house as they walked down the path. Returning her attention to the footpath, Sophie was startled when a fly landed on her face, buzzing in her ear. Swatting the pest away, Sophie blew a strand of hair out of her eyes.

Several hundred yards from the cabin, a small shed came into view. Another fly joined its friend, buzzing around Sophie's head as she stared at the building. *My kingdom for a fly swatter.*

The path widened, allowing Mac to catch up and walk at Sophie's side. His jaw was set, and a grim look entered his eyes as he stared at the ramshackle shed. She didn't even need to ask to know that the smell of blood emanated from the little rundown building at the end of the path. It just screamed Murders-R-Us.

At one point, the building looked like it had been painted a pale blue, but all that was left was a faded, dirty gray. The paint was peeling, showing large chunks of the weather-worn wood underneath. The entire structure seemed to lean to the side like a drunk attempting to appear sober.

Hanging from the eaves from long ratty strings were small birds' skulls, swaying gently in the wind. Looking away from the tiny boney heads, Sophie realized that words were written on the front door in brown ink.

Shit, that's not ink. That's old blood.

The lettering was in a messy script, the letters painted on carelessly with long dribbles and splashes dripping from the words. It must have been on the door for a while because the dried blood was starting to flake off.

One Crow for Sorrow
Two Crows for Mirth
Three Crows for a Wedding
Four Crows for a Birth
Five Crows for Silver
Six Crows for Gold
Seven Crows for a Secret, not to be told
Eight Crows for Heaven
Nine Crows for Hell
Ten Crows for the Devil's Own Self

"It's a counting crows' poem. It was historically used in prophecy," Mac explained. "It looks like they modified it. No doubt for nefarious purposes."

Glancing back at the tiny skulls, she counted ten of them. "What the—"

The devil's own self? How lovely. Let's head into the dark, scary death shack dedicated to the devil.

Mac put his nose close to the poem and took several slow, deliberate breaths. "Smells like bird's blood." Mac took another sniff at the door before grimacing. "But I smell human blood on the other side of this door. And it's fresh."

The other two deputies came to the door at Mac's beckoning and agreed with his assessment after smelling the door. Sophie wondered what kind of shifters they were, but it didn't seem like the time to ask.

"Well, let's see what's inside." Mac waved everyone away from the door, in case it was warded or boobytrapped. Sophie backed up to stand next to the deputies while the door swung slowly inwards on creaking hinges. The inside of the shed was shadowed and murky. The light from the door barely penetrated the darkness. All Sophie could see was a large square shape taking up most of the space inside the tiny shack.

After waiting for a long minute, Mac grunted. "Not even warded. How brazen are these guys?"

Mac and Sophie stepped into the doorway together to try and get a better look at whatever they were about to face. As Sophie leaned into the room, a swarm of flies on a billowing gust of fetid, wet air suddenly flew into her face, making her stumble back. Coughing and gasping, Sophie tried waving the insects away, their buzzing loud and angry in her face. She clenched her jaw and breathed carefully through her nose. It would be just her luck to get one in her mouth.

After a moment, the flies dispersed, disappearing into the surrounding forest. Sophie had thought she was immune to the smell of death and rot but had to grit her teeth and repeatedly swallow to keep her breakfast omelet from making a reappearance. But that just might have been the flies. She really didn't like bugs.

"Damn it," Mac muttered. "There *was* a ward. It wasn't set up to keep anyone out but to keep the magic in. Disgusting."

They waited a few minutes for the last of the flies and smell to dissipate somewhat before once again approaching the shanty.

Sophie hesitated in the doorway, letting Mac walk through first this time. When nothing else happened, she followed him into the gloom. Straining her eyes, she could only make out vague shapes in the dim interior. The only sound was the buzzing of an occasional fly as it bumbled around the room, looking for an escape.

"Hold on," Mac said, shuffling around the darkened room. She knew his ability to see in the dark was better than hers by several degrees, so she was happy to let him traverse the space alone. Mac opened a curtain with a rustle, letting light pierce the gloom.

Sophie started to look around, but her attention was grabbed immediately by the enormous stone block in the middle of the room. It took up almost all the available space in the shed.

Splayed on top of the altar was a naked male body. He was tied spreadeagle, hands and ankles attached to deadeye bolts embedded into each corner of the stone altar. The man was cut open from the base of his throat to his groin, the skin peeled open, displaying the entirety of his abdomen's insides. It made Sophie think of a pinned butterfly on display with glistening intestines half-hanging out of his body. Sophie was used to seeing dead bodies cut open because of her morgue assistant job, but this was different. There was a level of savage butchery that turned her stomach. The coppery scent of blood and offal was so thick in the air that Sophie lifted her shirt collar to cover her mouth and nose. Now that Sophie was prepared for the smell, she could keep her gorge down. *Practice makes perfect.*

Walking around the altar, Sophie stared at the man's face. His mouth was frozen in a rictus of agonized pain and horror. One of his eyes was missing from its socket, the wound wet and gaping, but the other eye stared, milky and unseeing, at the ceiling. Someone had carved a series of sharp lines across the man's forehead.

It was one of the worst scenes Sophie had ever witnessed. She hoped Carson made Morvan and his brothers pay dearly for this travesty.

A noise from the doorway made Sophie look up. The two deputies were hovering in the doorway, their jaws set and faces stony. Mac suggested they check around the property to see if there were any other buildings or evidence in the area. The relief was evident on their faces when they turned and trotted away.

Sophie gazed one more time at the dead man's face before looking up at Mac and shaking her head. "This isn't like the other victims at all. None of those guys were cut open." She gave him a worried look. "This doesn't feel right."

Mac nodded. "This victim is also human, not Fae like the others. Either way, I need to let Dad know. He's gonna have a litter of kittens when he finds out that the druids have been sacrificing people right under his nose. He will have to investigate the entire sect in this region to ensure the other members aren't in on this. It's gonna be a shitshow."

While Mac typed a quick message to his father, Sophie walked around the room, careful not to touch or disturb anything. Underneath her feet, the floor was hard-packed dirt, stained black with old blood near the altar. Large, red still-wet drips were on the floor leading from the altar to the far side of the shed. Following the trail of stains, Sophie arrived at a long wooden counter lining one wall. The scarred wood table was covered in various bowls piled high with assorted powders. A few black feathers littered the surface. Next to the bowls was a large mortar and pestle with a residue of black powder in its bottom. The surface of the table was covered in more splattered stains. To the right was a pool of gummy, congealed blood, bright red against the dark wood. Sitting in the middle of the puddle was a bloody dagger with a bejeweled hilt. Next to the weapon was a chalice. In the bottom of the chalice were the dregs of more blood. A couple of neatly tied bundles of branches – covered in green leaves and speckled with white berries – were stacked on the far end of the table. Another large mortar and pestle sat in front of the bundles.

"Do druids drink blood?" Sophie asked, her attention drawn back to the bloody goblet, unable to keep from shuddering in revulsion. The set of Mac's jaw answered the question for her.

Reaching into her bag, Sophie grabbed a pair of gloves. It was amazing that this was her life now, that she carried emergency nitrile gloves with her wherever she went. However, even standing in the middle of this horrific shack, with the stench of death clogging her nose, she wouldn't change it for anything.

"Let's do this," she said, waving away a random fly before placing a hand on the dead man's shoulder. "Okay, the man wakes up and starts struggling when he realizes that he's strapped down. There are four men in the room. I think I recognize Morvan. Morvan approaches the strapped-down man—"

Sophie's words cut off with a ragged gasp. Swallowing thickly, Sophie tried again to tell Mac what she was seeing. "He... He's—"

Sophie fell silent again, the only sound in the room her panting breaths.

"Soph?" Mac asked quietly. Stepping closer, he hesitated to touch her. Small animal-like noises of pain issued from her mouth.

A series of shudders wracked her frame before Sophie finally snatched her hand away from the man's shoulder.

"Fuck! Those fucking—" Sophie whirled away from the body, making an inarticulate noise of rage. She stared unseeingly at the dirty, smeared wall in front of her, trying to get her anger under control.

"Soph?"

"He was awake for all of this," Sophie explained, waving her hand behind her at the man's displayed innards. "They vivisected him, and he was conscious for every moment of it. I don't even know how they kept him alive the whole time. At the very least, he should have died from blood loss or shock long before they were finished. The last thing this man felt, and saw, was Morvan carving out his heart and taking a bite of it like... like it was an apple."

Mac grabbed Sophie by her elbow and gently dragged her out of the shack. Sophie stood on shaky legs, staring out at the vibrant green life of the forest outside, and took grateful breaths of fresh air. It took her a few minutes before she was calm enough to continue.

"These aren't the guys we're looking for. They're murderous pieces of garbage, but unless they drastically changed their methods, they didn't kill those other people."

"How sure are you?"

When Sophie gave him a sharp, annoyed look, Mac shrugged unrepentantly. That took the wind out of Sophie's sails. She realized she was still upset and freaked out by the vision she'd just witnessed and was picking the wrong fight. She rolled her shoulders, trying to dispel the tension.

"I'm pretty sure. The other victims only felt a burning pain in their chests and heads, like electricity or overpowering energy was burning them from the inside out. They didn't have much awareness of what was happening to them, only a sense of power and pain streaming through their bodies. They couldn't see anything. This was entirely different. They pinned this guy down and cut him open slowly. He was aware of every millisecond. They made him watch, and he knew exactly what they were doing to him the whole time. There was so much pain, but it was the kind caused by a knife – no energy or power. Even the chanting was different. These guys sounded like Gregorian monks, you know what I mean? Sort of musical. The chanting in the other vision was more like whispered prayers… more monotonous and quiet."

Disappointment swamped Sophie when she realized they still hadn't cracked the case. At the rate they were going, they might never figure it out. A throat clearing broke Sophie out of her morose thoughts.

"Hey, uh, sorry to interrupt," one of the deputies said. "We found a fire pit behind the building that smells like it's been used for more than just wood."

That's not ominous at all.

"Where's Jameson?" Mac asked the officer.

"She's checking around the house. She's got a better nose than me. I swear wolf shifters can track a butterfly's trail on the wind."

Sophie and Mac followed the deputy around the shed to another footpath leading further into the woods. After a short walk, that path ended at a small clearing. The glade was so perfectly circular with the fire pit in its dead center that it felt unnatural in the middle of the wild forest surrounding it. The fire pit was more than ten feet across. A large, rusted metal tripod perched tall and skeletal over the pit with a long chain that ended in a large hook hanging over the middle of the ring.

Mac thanked the man and asked him to keep checking around the property for anything else out of the ordinary. "Once you're done, meet back up with us. We'll all check the inside of the main cabin together." The officer nodded before turning and heading back along the path.

Sophie found herself staring at the metal contraption. Her mind kept conjuring various horrible images of what that tripod and hook meant. The chain swayed with a rusty creak in the light afternoon breeze, sending a shiver down Sophie's spine. As she stared, a crow landed at the point of the tripod and squawked, staring at her with beady black eyes. The animal radiated a kind of fierce intelligence, turning its head as if to better examine the human below it.

"Mac, is the crow dangerous? Is it a shifter or something?" Sophie asked, alarm rushing through her at the memory of the creepy poem on the shed door.

Mac looked at her, then followed her pointing finger. "No, it's not dangerous. It's just a regular crow. Not a shifter. Crows and ravens are often found with druids. Morvan and his brothers probably fed them to keep them close. They're considered harbingers of good fortune. The druids also use the feathers for some of their rituals. They're associated with Morrigan – one of their goddesses."

Two more crows landed next to the first and cawed loudly, staring Sophie down with intelligent, crafty eyes.

I'm in a staring contest with a murder of crows. Today just keeps getting better and better.

Pointedly looking away from the tripod and the corvids that were still staring intently at her, Sophie gazed into the fire pit's ashes. Walking closer, something in the old ashes caught her attention – a bit of silver glinting in the sunlight.

"I smell human," Mac said, his voice flat, following the direction of Sophie's stare.

With one foot on a rock lining the pit, Sophie leaned over, snagging the item. Shaking off the ash, Sophie held it up for Mac to see. Pinched between Sophie's fingers was a jawbone with one silver-filled tooth. The distinctive shape and omnivorous teeth meant it couldn't be anything other than human. Or Mythical, Sophie silently amended.

"Can you get a reading from a bone?" Mac asked, pointing at the brittle mandible in Sophie's grip.

"I can't pull a reading without a brain," she explained, recollecting her experiments with Reggie and wishing that wasn't the case. Not that she was eager to see any more of Morvan's handiwork.

Reggie had theorized that the brain holds memories, even severely damaged ones. And a body part, such as a bone or an internal organ, can't retain a sensation or memory. One unforgettable night, Reggie had given Sophie a brain without a body to test, and she'd been able to pull the death memory from it.

Carefully returning the bone to the firepit, Sophie followed Mac as they explored the rest of the property, looking for more clues and bodies. If it weren't for the fact that she knew murders had been committed on the property, it would've seemed like a lovely vacation spot – a place to escape from the hustle and bustle of her daily life. Sophie was a confirmed city dweller, but looking around at the quiet greenery, she could see the appeal of living like a hedge witch or a hermit. A small cottage nestled in the woods with no one but Mac for miles sounded heavenly.

An hour later, Sophie was sitting on the broad steps of the porch while Mac and the deputies explored the cabin. She'd started to go in, but one look at the bachelor-pad squalor of the interior, and she had refused to enter the building. Not her circus, not her monkeys. She'd told Mac that unless they found a body for her, she'd just wait outside, thank you very much.

Mac had called her a wuss with a dark chuckle, to which Sophie had happily agreed.

Lounging on the steps, Sophie heard the cry of several sirens before she saw the caravan of police cars pull up to the cabin. She started to call for Mac, but he was already striding down the steps. Carson stepped out of the lead car, looking worse for the wear. His cowboy hat was missing in action, and he had a darkening goose egg on his forehead. His hair stood in wild disarray, and his shirt was half untucked.

Sophie stood up from the step as he strode closer. Behind her, Jameson and the other deputy hovered on the porch just outside the front door. As Carson got close, Sophie realized that one of his sleeves was ripped at the shoulder, and dark smudges and blood splatters decorated his jeans and button-up chambray shirt.

"Are you okay?" Sophie asked.

Carson looked at where Sophie was staring at his shirt. "Ah, I'm fine. It's not my blood."

"What happened?" Mac asked, his voice deceptively light. If someone had hurt his father, they wouldn't be long for this world based on the look in his eyes.

"The Ruith brothers acted predictably when we started to read them their rights. Those dumb assholes tried to escape by creating a magical explosion inside the sheriff's office, which is warded against magical attacks. Most of it recoiled back on them, but they managed to blow out every window in the entire building. When that didn't work, the youngest brother came up with the bright idea to try and take your sister hostage with a dagger he had hidden on him. I'm not saddened to announce that Carrick has shed his mortal coil." His words were clipped like he was biting the air instead of speaking. Carson was a volcano one step away from blowing its top.

"Did you help him on his way?" Mac said, looking at the blood decorating Carson's shirt.

"He wanted to go out in a blaze of glory, and I was more than happy to oblige him," Carson snarked. "Ruby was quite helpful too. She also had a knife hidden on her body. Shocked me silly when she went for his throat. She's pretty damn vicious. I'll tell ya, I almost wish the other brothers had pulled the same shit. I have a lot of aggravation I still need to work out." Sophie could tell; it rolled off Carson in waves. She decided then and there to avoid pissing off Mac's dad – at least until he cooled off some.

"Where's Ruby?" Sophie asked, looking around for her trouble-prone sibling.

"She didn't appear injured, but I insisted she get checked out at the clinic just in case. She made quite a fuss, so I had to put my foot down."

"Did you have to go all alpha on her?" Mac teased.

"No, I pulled the dad-guilt card. You youngsters are suckers for those. I explained how bad I would feel if she had internal bleeding and died on my watch. And I told her that her sister would probably never forgive me, which would negatively affect Sophie's relationship with my only son."

"You're diabolical," Sophie said with a laugh. Mac just looked like he was in pain.

With tires crunching over the gravel, the coroner van pulled past the still-flashing police cars and parked near the group standing at the foot of the steps. Turning to one of the deputies, Carson commanded him to go help the coroner. Grady got out of the car and headed their way. Behind him trailed the Gorgon from the other day, a camera slung over her shoulder.

"What've you got for me?" Grady asked, excitement making his voice vibrate. Mac suggested Grady follow him to find out. Sophie trailed behind the group, watching the gurney bump and jolt along the narrow path.

"Whooaa," Sophie heard Grady's drawn-out exclamation right after he entered the ramshackle shed.

Carson sent half of the group of gathered officers to secure the area and the other half to look for evidence. When Carson peered inside, Sophie could feel the tension vibrate even tighter through his frame. A low, disturbing growl rumbled from his mouth. His teeth had noticeably sharpened and claws had started to extend from his fingertips. He looked like he wanted to tear something apart. *Oh wow, no sign of intelligent life there. Morvan and his brothers better pray that Carson doesn't get a hold of them any time soon.*

Sophie cleared her throat, catching Mac's attention. She nodded at his dad, silently telling him to intervene before Carson blew a gasket, just as Grady popped his head back out of the shed door and beckoned Sophie inside.

Leaving the two men behind, Sophie stepped in. She spotted Lydia taking photos of the corpse, the snakes around her head undulating in agitation. One of them caught Sophie staring and hissed at her. Sophie opened her mouth to start asking invasive questions, but Grady rescued her from herself by grabbing her arm and tugging her over to the body.

"Mac says you got a reading from the body. You saw the sacrificial ritual?" Grady's eyes shone bright and excited at the prospect.

When Sophie nodded, Grady waved an excited hand at the body, telling Sophie to get started. Mac and a much calmer Carson joined them in the now-crowded space.

"Take me through the whole process, step-by-step. Don't leave out a single thing, okay?" Grady said.

Mac offered to record her words on his phone so that Sophie could take that off her plate. She placed her hand back on the body.

Sophie took them through every miserable, excruciating moment of their victim's torture and eventual death: from the first moment he awoke until he took his last breath. She even recounted how the victim felt when Morvan carved lines in his forehead.

"It's not just simple lines," Grady excitedly explained. "It's the word 'Dagda' in the Ogham alphabet. Do you see how all the lines are straight? There are no curves in the Ogham alphabet because it was originally meant to be carved into stones."

"They look like runes," Sophie said.

"No, not like runes," Grady said, looking slightly offended. "Runes are similar in the sense that they are made from straight lines, but it's an entirely different alphabet. Runes were used by the Germanic people in ancient times. Interestingly there's a Norse variant as well. Ogham is a Celtic alphabet."

Sophie looked down at the incomprehensible lines carved into the man's skin. It didn't look like a word to her. It just looked like butchery. She grimaced when a fly landed on the victim's forehead and started picking at one of the wounds and waved it away with a shudder of disgust.

"So, what does Dagda mean?" she asked.

"Not what, but a who. Dagda is the Father God of Ireland. He was one of the Tuatha Dé Danann's kings and was supposed to have immense magical power. That is probably why the Ruith brothers made this sacrifice in his name. It's fascinating stuff. Dagda had a magic club that could both end life and give it. Legends also say he had a cauldron that was bottomless and ever-filled with food. He was married to the goddess Morrigan, and they had a bunch of kids." Grady, who had pulled out a notebook and taken feverish notes during Sophie's reading, was using the pen for emphasis as he talked. He used it to point out a charcoal drawing of a bird on the wall that Sophie hadn't noticed earlier. "That's probably used to worship and honor Morrigan."

"How lovely. A husband-and-wife duo. You know what they say: a family that sacrifices together, stays together."

Clearly not appreciating Sophie's sense of humor, Grady shook his head at her. Using his pen to point back at the body, he indicated that Sophie needed to get back to recounting the murder.

"You seem to know a lot about the druids and their gods and stuff," Sophie commented.

"I've been studying druid and Celtic mythology for decades. I've wanted to visit Ireland and Scotland for years in the hopes of learning more. But you're providing an insight into their rituals I would never get otherwise. The druids are very secretive about their religion and they've put a lot of effort into downplaying their bloody history. Nowadays, they pretend they're all teachers, shamans, priests, and such, projecting this image of nature-loving monks – and many of them are, don't get me wrong – pretending that their sect doesn't have a dark and bloody past. They were famous for trying to divine the future in their victims' entrails and setting people on fire inside giant wicker men. Does that sound very nature-loving to you? They've tried to suppress all knowledge about their past, so we have almost no information on their ceremonial practices. I can't believe I get to learn how they conduct their sacrifices."

"I'm glad you're learning about something you find interesting." That wasn't strictly true, but Sophie decided to ignore her misgivings about how excited Grady was. After working with Reggie, she was used to the single-minded quest for knowledge of a scientific mind. "It's too bad this murder is unrelated to the others we're here to investigate. I was bummed out when I realized we hadn't found the murderer."

Sophie swatted at her arm as another fly tried to land on her. Only a few from the original swarm were still in the room, but even a single fly was one too many, in her opinion. They buzzed lazily around the room, annoying her with their gross crawly feet.

"I could have told you the other murders weren't committed by druids," Grady said with a pointed sniff. He waved a hand toward the bundle of dried branches with the white berries on the long wooden counter. "There was no trace of mistletoe on the other bodies. I don't know much about their rituals, but everyone knows they love mistletoe. Druids use mistletoe in almost all their ceremonies, especially during sacrifices. When I perform the autopsy on this fellow here, there is almost certainly going to be mistletoe pollen in his stomach. And that powder they sprinkled over him...." Grady said, recalling a part of the ritual Sophie recounted, then took a quick sniff over the body. "Definitely powdered mistletoe berries."

"Any idea who this is or where they grabbed him from?" Carson asked.

"My visions don't really work like that," Sophie said. "I only see the final moments of a person's life."

"Did you see the other men assisting Morvan during the sacrifice?"

"There was a total of four men, including Morvan. The other three looked like the guys we saw leaving the property earlier, but they were too far away earlier for me to be completely sure."

"Would you mind looking at their mugshots later?" Carson requested. Sophie was happy to look at the pictures if it kept these assholes in jail.

Finally, Sophie finished describing the rest of the murder for Grady, ending with the grand finale of Morvan munching on a dying man's heart. Grady's notebook looked like it was filled with notes, his chicken-scratch writing filling the pages.

"Did Morvan eat the whole thing himself or share with his brothers?" Grady asked.

"I have no idea. He died before I could see anything else."

"This is great. So exciting. Thank you for sharing."

Peeling off her gloves, Sophie dug the heels of her palms into her eyes until little white lights danced behind her eyelids. Despite her best efforts, she kept seeing the man's death over and over again in her mind.

"I don't think I can help with anything else, so I'm going to head out," Sophie informed Grady.

He gave her a hesitant look. "If I ever get another body that I'm having trouble with or is unusual, do you think I could call you for a consultation?"

"Of course. You'll probably need to clear it with the Conclave and my boss, but I'll always help if I can."

Grady shook her hand with a grateful smile before turning back to the dead man, calling for the Gorgon to help him get the body onto the gurney. Sophie could have offered assistance, but she needed out of the shed, and she'd frankly done enough for the day.

Striding out of the murder-hut, another fly landed on her shoulder. Slapping at and missing, Sophie growled at the disgusting bug.

"That. Is. It," Sophie announced, completely skeeved out from standing in that blood-soaked shed filled with flies. "I've had enough. I want a scalding hot shower, followed by a Manhattan. Made with good whiskey too, none of that cheap shit."

"I think you've earned both those things," Mac said, appearing behind her. "Dad! We're heading out. Give me your keys. I'll leave your cruiser at the sheriff's office and your keys with the front desk."

Carson walked out of the shanty and slapped his keys into Mac's hand. "Yeah, you guys have earned a break. I'll check in with you once we wrap up here. Although that might take forever," Carson complained with a grimace.

Hand in hand, they headed back down the path toward Carson's police cruiser. Relief lightened Sophie's steps the further they got away from the crime scene.

"Oh, wait!" Carson called out. "You guys need to pick up Ruby from the clinic."

"Could we pretend we didn't hear that and leave her there?" Sophie pleaded with Mac, clasping her hands in supplication.

Mac's laughter chased away the rest of Sophie's lingering disquiet.

CHAPTER 10

*A*fter her delicious salmon dinner, Sophie was halfway through a crisp made from a fruit called a marionberry. It looked a lot like blackberry to her untrained eyes. Whatever it was made from, it was delicious. Sophie scooped up another bite and offered it to Mac. He took the bite with a groan that made her squirm in her seat. She was on her second Manhattan, inching her way towards tipsy.

After scrubbing herself to a bright pink, with Mac's assistance, they'd headed to the inn's dining room, and Davin had helpfully found a table in a dark corner of the room. The lighting was low and romantic. The murmur of conversation filled the space, creating a buffer from the outside world.

"Damn it," Mac groaned. Sophie followed Mac's gaze and saw Carson talking to Davin, who was pointing towards where they were sitting.

"We need to find out what happened anyway," Sophie assured Mac.

"You need a break," Mac growled, invisible hackles raised.

"This is what we do." When Mac gave her a skeptical look, she snagged his hand, lacing their fingers together. "It's fine. This was all the break I needed. I promise."

Carson walked over, plopping himself in an empty chair at their table. When the waitress appeared, he told her to bring whatever was fastest to make as he didn't have much time.

Sophie squeezed Mac's fingers as he opened his mouth, no doubt to tell his dad off, but Carson's posture spoke of exhaustion and tension. His hair stood up in tangled tufts the same way Mac's did when he was agitated and repeatedly running his fingers through the strands.

Once the waitress was out of earshot, Carson turned back to Sophie and Mac. "They found two more bodies in the cellar. I'll never look at deep freezers the same way again. There's also evidence of several bodies in their burn pit. Grady has asked if you would come down to the morgue and pull readings from whatever is intact." Carson stretched his neck like he was trying to loosen a crick.

Sophie slid her Manhattan over to him. He sniffed the drink, then tossed back the entire beverage in one swallow. After he finished his alcohol shudder, Carson coughed out a rough thank you to Sophie.

"Dad, you don't drink," Mac said slowly.

"Not normally, but this has been one hell of a day."

As the waitress dropped off Carson's dinner, he pulled out a folder and handed it to Sophie. Inside was a stack of mugshots with some familiar faces. "Were any of those guys in this afternoon's vision?"

Sophie paged through the stack of photos slowly, carefully noting each one. Three mugshots jumped out immediately, but she wanted to be thorough. After flipping through the entire stack, Sophie pulled out three and slid them to Carson. He looked at them and nodded. "There's the Ruith brothers in all their demented glory. Anybody else in there look familiar?"

Sophie shook her head and gave the folder back to Carson,

who was busy shoveling food into his mouth as if he was afraid someone would steal it from him.

"Where's the third Musketeer?" Carson asked after finishing his meal. He looked around the dining room like he expected to spot Ruby lurking nearby.

"She decided to take a nap when we got back to the hotel. Then we invited her to dinner, but she decided to head back out and continue her quest to touch every person in Murias," Sophie explained.

"Interesting woman," Carson commented mildly, making Sophie snort at the understatement. Interesting hardly covered it. "I get the vibe that she's trying very hard to impress you, Sophie."

She didn't know what to do with that information. Ruby didn't care what Sophie thought of her, did she? Ruby was so confident and buoyant and crazy; why would she care what Sophie's opinion of her was? Sophie decided to stick a pin in that idea and think about it later. Probably much, much later. "Do you need me to come in to do a reading on the new bodies?"

"That can wait until tomorrow. The odds are, you're just going to witness the Ruith brothers performing the exact same ritual. We've got them dead to rights, so I'm not worried. Right now, my focus needs to be on investigating the entire OBOD chapter in this area, and it's gonna be a bitch."

"OBOD?"

"The Order of Bards, Ovates & Druids. That's the name of the druid sect. The San Francisco chapter has already caught wind of what happened with the Ruith brothers and is up in arms. They're sending a representative here and are requesting that any grimoires or spell books found at the brother's cabin either be destroyed or returned to their care. It's all to protect their interests and keep their secret rituals from getting out and possibly into the wrong hands, which is rich coming from them considering what I've been dealing with all afternoon. I've had to call the Conclave and demand *they* send a representative to mediate

125

that bullshit. I'm happy to let them duke it out over who gets to keep those books. They're dangerous and should probably be destroyed, in my humble opinion."

Carson wiped his mouth with his napkin, standing up from the table while wishing them a good evening. His phone rang, and he started cussing.

Answering the call, he barked out, "What?! What do you mean they lost him? Did they put Milford in the iron-lined room like I told them to? Fucking morons!" Carson strode out of the dining room, loudly arguing with the person on the other end of the call.

"Sure, Dad, dinner's on me," Mac bellowed at his retreating back. Carson raised his hand in acknowledgment, then turned the corner and disappeared from sight. Mac shook his head, fondness and exasperation fighting for dominance on his face.

Sophie wanted to tease Mac about his dad, but a chime from her phone distracted her. It was Reggie doing his daily check-in. She typed a quick recap of the day. Not a minute after hitting send, her phone rang with 'Boss Man' on her display screen.

"Reggie, hey—"

"Are you okay?" Reggie's worried voice interrupted.

"Yes, I'm totally fine. I promise."

"Druids can be very dangerous, especially if they've done blood magic to enhance their power."

Sophie assured Reggie she was completely unharmed and gave him a recap of the day's events.

"You really saw an entire druid sacrificial ritual?" Reggie asked with a familiar eagerness in his voice. "And you have two more victims you're going to pull visions from tomorrow? Oh, how I would love to see something like that. Did you know that they're very secretive about their ceremonies and rituals? Almost no one who is not a druid knows anything about what goes on inside a sect."

"Yeah, I'd heard something about that," Sophie replied, suppressing the laugh that wanted to bubble up.

"Do you think I could come up and watch one of the readings? It would be invaluable information."

"I wouldn't mind a bit. I'd love to see you. But we should probably clear it with Grady first." Although Sophie suspected that he would be over the moon if Reggie came for a visit.

"I'm going to call him and ask. I hope he's still in his office."

"Grady is probably still there. He mentioned wanting to get the autopsy done today. Plus, he has the two new bodies to deal with. They have a much smaller facility here than we do. And I'm almost positive Grady will be glad to have you witness my next reading."

"Plus, I'd get to come for the Hunter's Moon Festival. I've always wanted to go to one. I've heard they're quite fun."

Reggie hung up after promising to text Sophie when he expected to arrive in town.

The ice cream had melted, turning her crisp into a soggy mess by the time Sophie returned her attention to her dessert. It had been such a long day that she seriously considered forgetting the extra cost and ordering another. Deciding against the frivolous expense, Sophie pushed the plate away.

Mac took one look at the soupy dessert and called Davin over to bring a fresh one and another Manhattan. Sophie knew she was looking at Mac all sappy, but she couldn't help herself. Who knew such a grump could be so caring and thoughtful?

When the fresh dessert arrived, Sophie offered Mac the first bite. Then she kissed him, tasting the sweet tartness of the crisp on his lips.

The screech of a chair against the wooden floor jolted Sophie away from Mac. Despite her annoyed stare, Ruby plopped into Carson's abandoned seat with a dramatic sigh.

"I've had the worst day," Ruby complained, picking up Sophie's fork and taking a bite of her dessert. The growl that issued from Mac's mouth made even Sophie freeze up for a second.

"Get your own dessert." Mac pulled the fork out of Ruby's hand, where it was frozen midway to her mouth, handing it back to Sophie. He slid the plate out of reach from her.

Ruby rolled her eyes. "Whatever. It's not a big deal. We're sisters. Sisters share."

"We barely know each other," Sophie was saying before she could stop herself. "You're hardly more than a stranger." Sophie could see the moment the words registered with Ruby. Hurt swam in her eyes. And, unbelievably, Sophie felt terrible. It was like kicking a puppy.

"Hey, I—" Sophie started to say, but Ruby stood up and left, stalking out of the dining room, her back ramrod straight. "I'm an asshole," Sophie lamented.

"No, you're not," Mac said. "She's asking for a relationship you're not ready for. It's delusional if she thinks it's normal to become best friends this swiftly. She's glommed onto you so quickly that it makes her appear like a stalker. You're right to be cautious."

"I know you're right. It's just… She genuinely wants to be a family. It's me that's hesitating. And I'm not totally sure why. She's loud and overly friendly and doesn't understand boundaries whatsoever, but she's trying, and I keep pushing her away. It's not even the serial-killer thing that bugs me. It's her enthusiasm and clinginess that puts me off. I don't like that I'm being a jerk. And now I've hurt her feelings."

"She'll come around. I know that deep down she understands. She's not stupid. I think she's just so excited that it's getting away from her."

"Damn it. I should go talk to her." Sophie gave her dessert, and her boyfriend, a longing gaze before chasing after Ruby.

She caught up to Ruby as she was leaving the hotel. "Hey, wait! Seriously, Ruby, wait."

Ruby stopped at the edge of the porch steps, turning and giving Sophie an irritated look.

"I'm sorry, okay," Sophie started. "It was a shitty thing for me to say. We're sisters. And I'm happy about that. I'm just having a hard time adjusting. I'm doing my best, but I'll try harder to be nicer to you. You don't deserve my attitude."

"Ugh, you don't have to be perfect all the time."

"I'm not perfect! I'm just trying to be normal. All I want is my boyfriend, my friends, and a job that pays my rent. But no, I keep having visions of these awful things that I can't unsee. And everyone's demanding my help all the time. It sucks."

"Yes, you're right. I wouldn't know *anything* about how that feels."

Sophie winced. If she kept putting her foot in her mouth at the rate she was going, she might start to develop a permanent shoe print on her tongue.

"Alright, you're right. If anyone understands what it feels like, it's you. But it doesn't help that you keep acting like a stalker. You moved across the street from me and didn't tell me."

"It's not that big a deal. You're making more out of it than it deserves. I was just hoping we could become friends. I'm the fun one, and you're a sourpuss, but you've got all these people that come running whenever you call. I don't have any friends, so when I saw that apartment on the list of housing options Marcella offered me, I thought it would be fun to get to know one another. But then you wouldn't answer any of my texts, and I didn't know how to tell you where I lived. I realized you'd be pissed about it, but I'd already pulled all my stuff out of storage. You didn't need to be so standoffish."

"You're a serial killer! My sister kills people by stabbing them in the throat. You don't think that deserves some caution?"

"Kiss my ass. I'm. A. Vigilante." Ruby threw her hands up in the air. "Do you think I like killing people? I'm only doing it because the police didn't help, and I was just trying to save lives.

At least I'm saving people. You can only find out who did it after the fact rather than prevent a death. I don't think you have the right to judge me."

Ruby turned on her heel and started to stalk away. Sophie let fly a few colorful curse words under her breath. This was not how she envisioned this conversation going.

Sophie chased after Ruby again. "Stop running away. I'm trying to apologize here."

"Is that what you're trying to do? You kinda suck at it," Ruby responded matter-of-factly.

"You're right. I do. I don't like saying sorry, and I certainly don't like being wrong. But I'm wrong, and I'm sorry. I don't want to fight with you. I promise to stop being such a jerk to you. I understand that we're both just trying to do our best with our weird powers. You've done your best with some shitty choices. I want to be your sister and I want us to be friends. Can we please, *please* start over?"

Ruby stopped striding away. She paused on the sidewalk, frozen in thought. Sophie decided to shut her mouth for once and let Ruby process the offer.

Turning, Ruby blew out a long breath. "Okay. Let's start fresh. It's not like we have much of a choice. We have to work together while we're here. But. I'll stop trying to be so pushy."

Sophie nodded her acceptance. "And I'll stop being such a bitch."

Ruby scoffed playfully. "Don't make promises you can't keep."

"Ha ha," Sophie snarked, but then she ruined her pretend anger by laughing.

CHAPTER 11

On Friday, Sophie shadowed Ruby as she walked around the less populated side street shops branching off Abernethy. They'd already made their way through the main drag that morning. The entire town seemed to be setting up booths offering fair food, local delicacies, art, crafts, and games.

They had tried to go into several shops, but it was so crowded with tourists that it was a press of bodies on all sides. Ruby had trouble processing all the conflicting readings simultaneously. Sophie had hoped to meet one of the artists in the tattoo shop, but they were booked full, and she quickly left. Within a minute, it had felt too claustrophobic inside the shop, and she felt like she couldn't breathe.

Despite their lack of progress, Ruby was in a cheerful mood. Their fight from the night before was apparently forgotten.

Reggie had texted Sophie and let her know when he expected to arrive in town. She glanced at her phone and was happy to see that he would arrive in less than an hour – unless traffic caused a delay. The plan was to head to the coroner's office to pull the death visions from the druids' sacrifices once Reggie arrived.

They hadn't seen Carson the entire day as he and his people

were busy inspecting every druid-owned piece of property in the county. Mac had decided that morning to accompany his father in case any of the druids chose to put up a fight. He had texted Sophie earlier to tell her how the druids were calling the inspections unlawful. Apparently, they weren't too happy about having trackers sniffing their properties for dead bodies. Sophie's heart went out to them. *Not.*

"Let's try here again. There are some new people inside," Ruby suggested, pointing at a tea shop they had previously visited earlier in the week.

"Ruby!" The tea shop owner cheered when they entered the store like Ruby was one of his regulars. Hiding her amusement, Sophie greeted the shopkeeper once he was done hugging her sister.

"George, do you have any tea that might help with insomnia? I've been having the hardest time with my sleep schedule lately," Ruby asked.

The shop owner hustled from behind his counter to show Ruby some options around his shop to help her with her imaginary sleep troubles. On their way to one of the shelves, she pretended to not see a customer and bumped into them. After apologizing, Ruby introduced herself. When the person gave their name, Ruby scratched her right ear.

They'd devised a hand signal system to get through the town's population more efficiently. If Ruby pulled her right ear, the person had never murdered anyone. If she rubbed her forehead, the person had committed murder, but it was "justified" according to Ruby. If she scratched her chin, the person wasn't their killer but had committed a murder they needed to tell Carson about. If they ever actually found the person they were after, she would cough loudly and say something about her allergies.

Sophie had lost all faith that she'd see that last signal. She wasn't ready to give up, but it had started to feel hopeless.

They now had a comprehensive spreadsheet filled with the names of townspeople and visitors who had never killed, those who committed a "justifiable" murder, and murderers that needed to be arrested. Luckily, they'd only found two people so far worthy of bringing to the sheriff's attention. But it felt like a losing proposition – there were just too many people to keep up with and more kept arriving every hour. Every store and shop was overcrowded and filled with tourists. It was impossible to touch everyone, but they were doing their best.

The tea shop was filled from floor to ceiling with shallow, wooden shelves. Large tins filled every inch of the shelves, each container filled with different types of tea: Oolong, black, Pu-erh, green, yerba mate, herbal…

Sophie's feet slowed and then backtracked. There, in the middle of the herbal selections was catnip tea. Catnip. There was a tin of catnip tea, and her friend Amira was a cat shifter. Sophie had to get her some; it was too funny to resist.

"Hey George, could I get some of this catnip tea?"

"Of course! It's great for anxiety, headaches, and insomnia, or helping to soothe the digestive system. I like it with a squeeze of lemon and honey. The lemon really brings out the minty, citrusy flavor of the leaves."

When Sophie explained it was a gift for a friend, George put it in a cute little bag with a bit of ribbon. The sisters exited the shop, each clutching a bag. If they continued to make so many purchases, Sophie was concerned that she'd have to dip into her meager savings to cover her bills next month. She promised herself to stick to window-shopping only for the rest of the trip.

"Another bust," Ruby complained but didn't sound particularly upset. "Do you want to go grab an early lunch? We could try that seafood joint on Fairfax."

The chime of Sophie's phone sounded before she had a chance to answer. Looking at the message waiting for her, she turned to Ruby, excitement bursting out of her.

"Reggie's here! He's almost to the coroner's office. Let's go meet him there."

Sophie typed out a quick response and then texted Mac to let him know where she'd be. He immediately responded that he needed a break from dealing with the druids, and his father, and would meet them there.

Sophie walked to the coroner's office in record time, practically dragging Ruby behind her. She was so excited to have her friend join them in Murias. Reggie felt like normalcy to her, and his kind and soothing presence would make this whole experience more bearable. Plus, Sophie just plain missed her friend.

As they turned the corner of 5th Street, Sophie spotted a familiar Camry parked next to the coroner's office. Talking to Mac was Reggie. But to Sophie's shock and delight, Ace, Fitz, and Amira were with him.

"Guys! You all came!" she exclaimed.

"When Reggie said he was coming up to see you, we decided to make it a road trip. So, we're here if you need backup. Plus, I've always wanted to visit Cascadia," Amira explained. She pulled Sophie into a quick hug before handing her off to Ace, who skipped the hug with a wrinkled nose and passed Sophie straight to Fitz. Ace wasn't exactly the hugging type. He probably didn't want to ruin his reputation as a sardonic grump.

Reggie pulled her from Fitz's arms and gave her a hug. Pulling back, he gave her a fatherly once-over as if checking for injuries. "Are you okay? Dr. Musteli told me that you did a reading on a druid sacrifice. They're notoriously brutal."

"I'm fine. But yeah, that death was the worst one I've ever witnessed. It was even worse than that rabid vampire last month. But it's part of the job, and I'm glad to help."

Ruby made a noise of skepticism, a small *ahem*. Sophie turned to her, remembering the previous night's fight when she had complained to Ruby about her gift like an ungrateful asshole. "I know what I said last night," Sophie said. "And while it's true that sometimes what we see sucks, I wouldn't get rid of my ability, even if I could. Would you?"

Ruby conceded her point, looking vaguely relieved. When Sophie turned back to Reggie, she realized everyone was now staring at her sister with faces that ranged from concerned to guarded to outright dislike.

Sophie realized that her friends had picked up on and adopted her distrust of Ruby. *Time to fix that.*

Sophie introduced each member of the Odd Ones to Ruby, who enthusiastically shook everyone's hands and treated Reggie like a long-lost friend. Either she didn't have the ability to read a room, or she was just choosing to ignore everyone's distant reception. Sophie suspected Ruby would bulldoze her way into her friends' lives if given half a chance. A week ago, that would've given Sophie a case of the hives.

Desperate to break the lingering tension, Sophie looked around for a distraction. She remembered that she still had the gift bag from the tea shop in her hand. "Oh, Amira, I got you a gift."

She handed the bag to Amira, who looked positively over the moon to receive a present. She pulled the tissue paper out with wild abandon, stuffing the crumpled paper into Ace's hands, then pulled the container of loose tea out of the bag's depths.

"Oh! Oh my," Amira said, quickly dropping the tea back into the bag and shoving the whole thing back into Sophie's hands. Amira's pupils expanded so fast that Sophie worried she'd somehow scared her friend. "If I want to be functional today, you'll need to hold onto that for me. I don't want to get stoned while we have to work." Plugging her nose, Amira took a quick step back from Sophie.

"Stoned?" Sophie and Ruby said at the same time.

"I'm a cat shifter."

"OH. Right." Sophie remembered how Birdie's cat Ginsberg would act when he got a new catnip toy. First, there was dramatic pouncing, followed by rolling around with his four limbs akimbo, ending with him falling into a drooling stupor that could last for hours.

Grady came outside at that moment and saved Sophie from the awkward moment. He hustled over to Reggie to introduce himself, giving his hand a vigorous, enthusiastic shake. "It's so good to meet you in person, Dr. Didel. I'm an admirer of your work on vampirism. Your article on how the composition of vampire red blood cells helps explain the slow aging of the species was inspired. I've always been interested in that area of study, but we have almost no vampires in Cascadia. You know how they tend to stay in urban areas."

Reggie made a humming sigh of sympathy. "If you'd ever like to visit our facility, I'm sure we could spend a day sharing data."

"I'll keep you to that promise," Grady responded, his golden-brown eyes alight with excitement.

"Do you guys want to get started on the readings?" Sophie asked once she realized that Grady and Reggie's Mutual Admiration Society meeting could go on indefinitely if she didn't distract them.

"Yes, I can't wait to see if these other sacrifices followed the same ritual or if there were variations," Grady said. "I'd like to get this done immediately since the SF chapter of OBOD is on their way, and I know they'll try to interfere." Grady turned to Reggie. "I haven't had a chance to start the autopsy on either body. Would you like to attend them once Sophie gets her readings?"

Reggie enthusiastically agreed.

"The San Francisco Mythical community is in a complete uproar that some druids are sacrificing humans," Ace said. "The local druid group is in major hot water because they didn't realize what one of their highest-ranking members was up to. I imagine the Conclave is making their chapter answer some very uncomfortable questions right now." He seemed gleeful at the prospect.

"Then we should hurry," Reggie said. "I've always wanted to learn how druids pull their magical power from their victims. Is it from the blood specifically or from the soul? I can't wait to learn more."

"It's all so exciting!" Grady agreed. "What I couldn't figure out from Sophie's other reading was how they kept the person alive for the entirety of the ritual. The man should have died from blood loss long before the ritual was complete. I'm hoping one of these other two bodies can give us the answer."

With barely repressed impatience, Grady waved everyone inside. Amira, Fitz, and Ace declined to attend. "We're going to split up and scope out the town and see if anything seems off."

"Are you sure?" Sophie asked, feeling guilty that everyone was here because of her.

"Yeah, this is gonna be fun," Fitz assured her. "We're gonna get all the local gossip. Just you wait and see."

"By the way, did you know there will be a pie baking contest tomorrow?" Sophie asked, amused when Fitz's eyes lit up. "The local rumor mill says that Pam from the bakery and Cordelia from the candy shop are the two big contenders." Sophie knew that she'd just thrown a gauntlet at Fitz's feet that he wouldn't be able to resist.

"Oh, really? You mean that they *used* to be the contenders. I'm here now, and I'll have to see if the hotel will let me borrow their kitchen."

Waving them off as they trotted off towards Abernethy Street, Sophie hesitated for a second, soaking in the sunshine. Inhaling a deep cleansing breath to clear out any lingering uncertainty and disquiet, she rolled her shoulders, mentally preparing to watch two people suffer and die. Not that there was truly a way to prepare for something like that.

"Are you okay? You don't have to do this," Mac's voice murmured as Reggie and Grady headed inside the building.

"I'm good. Not exactly looking forward to it. But I already

know what to expect. So, I won't be as caught off guard as I was yesterday."

After her fight with Ruby, Sophie had realized that she was glad she had her ability. She had to believe that it was around for a reason. She refused to hide her head in the sand if she could help prevent more people from being hurt. *No more complaining. It's time to put my bitch face on.*

~

THIRTY MINUTES LATER, SOPHIE HAD FINISHED BOTH READINGS.

When Grady had opened the fridge door and pulled out the tray with the first victim's body, Ruby had taken one look at the carved-up woman and yelled out, "Nope!" She had announced that there was no way she needed to see anything else and that Sophie was crazy going around touching dead people.

"I'm heading to Abernethy Street. Text me when you're done here. And make sure you wash your hands." With a final shudder, Ruby had headed out, muttering darkly under her breath.

The first body was a woman in her mid-sixties. According to Grady, he found a match in the FBI database listing her as a missing woman from Seattle. He said it was a lucky break because she had been homeless, and often displaced people aren't reported as missing. Her murder had been very similar to the other sacrifice. The only difference was that it was performed by one of the other Ruith brothers, not Morvan.

The second victim was a man in his twenties. Based on the track marks on his arms, Grady theorized that he was another homeless person suffering from addiction. He believed the Ruith brothers were grabbing humans that people wouldn't notice were missing.

"A move pulled right from the serial killer handbook," Reggie muttered darkly.

Second verse same as the first, performed by yet another

Ruith brother. Mac suggested that they each took turns performing the rituals in order to get equal power. He said that the brothers aren't talking yet, but the Conclave has people who can force them to answer all their questions.

A few minutes after Grady put away the body, they could hear Carson's voice from the lobby. Sophie gave Mac a sideways glance because he sounded highly pissed off. His voice continued to gain in volume until Sophie could make out the words.

"You people put me in charge of this town, and now you want to get in the way of me doing my job?"

"Sheriff, there is no reason to get angry. You must understand that anything to do with druids needs to be handled delicately," another man's voice responded in a honeyed tone that set Sophie's teeth on edge. She could only imagine how well that went over with Carson and his zero-bullshit tolerance. "It's already been decided by the Conclave, Carson. It's out of both our hands."

Lydia popped her head in the door with an apologetic expression. "Sorry to bother you, Dr. Musteli. There's a man here to see you. I told him that you're in the middle of work, but he insists that he needs to talk to you right now. He says the Conclave sent him."

"No worries, Lydia. Please send him in."

Carson entered the autopsy room, followed closely by a man Sophie had previously seen in the company of Marcella. He was either a member of the Conclave or one of its representatives.

"Ruby, how lovely to see you again," the man said when he spotted Sophie.

"I'm not Ruby. I'm the other sister, Sophie."

"Oh yes, of course," the man responded. "It's nice to finally meet you. I'm Ziad. Quite a mess with this druid business. The Conclave sent me to help clean it all up."

Ziad gave Sophie the impression of a man who viewed other people through a lens of his own puffed-up self-importance.

Sophie's dislike of the man was swift and inexplicable. "Nice to meet you," she said faintly.

"What are you doing here in Cascadia?" Ziad asked.

Looks like you don't know everything, huh? Let's keep it that way.

"Oh, I'm just here on vacation. Mac wanted me to meet his family."

With that explanation, Ziad moved on to talk to Grady. He quickly explained that the bodies in his possession would need to be immediately transferred to the city morgue so their expert could do the autopsies.

Grady exchanged a vaguely amused look with Reggie. "You must understand that we have a very skilled doctor at the Medical Examiner's office who is highly qualified for this type of high-profile case," Ziad explained.

"Do you mean Dr. Didel?" Reggie asked with a small smile.

"Yes. You've heard of him?" Ziad replied.

"A time or two."

"And you are?" Ziad asked, displeasure and annoyance starting to form in his voice.

"Sorry! I'm Dr. Reginald Didel. It's nice to meet you," Reggie replied placidly, holding his hand out for a handshake.

Ziad hesitated for a moment, staring at Reggie's face as if trying to determine if he was joking. "I see. I didn't realize that you were in town."

"I can see how that would be confusing for you. When Dr. Musteli called me for a consultation about the first druid sacrifice, he kindly offered the use of his facility for my convenience."

"Is Magistrate Venturi aware that you're not in the city?" Ziad asked.

"Oh yes, I called Marcella immediately to get approval for this trip."

Both men spoke to each other with such polite, professional tones, but the undercurrent of their conversation was so sharp Sophie was surprised no one got a cut.

A few awkward minutes later, Ziad made a hasty exit, citing that he needed to oversee the questioning of the druid sect members.

"Trumped up, self-important little weasel," Reggie muttered hotly once Ziad was out of earshot.

"Have you had to deal with him before?" Sophie asked.

"No, but Ziad's reputation proceeds him. He would push his own mother in front of an oncoming train if it got him ahead in the Conclave. If you allow him at your back, don't be surprised when you find a knife in it."

Sophie's stomach started rumbling at that moment, and she realized that she'd accidentally skipped lunch.

"You hungry?" Mac asked with a grin at Sophie's loudly gurgling midsection.

He suggested seeing if the rest of the Odd Ones wanted to join them for a meal. Reggie demurred, stating that he'd like to stay for the autopsies.

As Sophie, Mac, and Carson headed out to find the crew and get some food, she looked back and watched as Reggie and Grady bent their heads together, excitedly reviewing some notes on a clipboard.

CHAPTER 12

⚜

C arson managed to sweet talk the owner of Wedderburn's Seafood Grille into merging a couple of tables in a back corner of the busy restaurant for the group. Mac teased his dad that his 'aw shucks' shtick was good for something after all.

Carson was in a particularly jovial mood as the waiters brought platter after platter heaped with seafood. When Sophie questioned him, assuming he would be pissed off about losing jurisdiction over the druids, he shook his head.

"One of my deputies said that after the Conclave took over, the head druid of OBOD showed up and is raising hell," he explained. "He almost got into a fistfight with Ziad over the brothers' grimoires. I was asked to mediate. I made sure to remind that asshole Ziad that he commanded me to stay out of his way. 'This is a situation for professionals who understand the intricacies of Mythical inter-species cooperation.' I hope he's getting the day he deserves."

Well, alrighty then, Carson's suddenly become a real Southern lady.

He snapped a crab leg with a concerning amount of relish, dipped the meat in clarified butter, and tossed it into his mouth with a shit-eating grin.

In the middle of the meal, Reggie and Grady joined the group. They had to shift chairs and plates, but it was a more-the-merrier kind of meal.

Grady had everyone raise their glass for a toast. "May your glass be ever full. May the roof over your head be always strong. And may you be in heaven half an hour before the devil knows you're gone."

Sophie laughed and took a big slurp of her beer. She looked around the table at her friends as they laughed and joked, plowing through a veritable feast. Ace and Amira were bickering and sniping at each other as usual. Fitz was picking over a crab in his usual methodical way, his fingers long and nimble as they teased crab meat out of a claw. Grady was eating his crab cakes in his usual fastidious way. He and Reggie sat beside each other, discussing some new medical research. They had bonded and were becoming fast friends.

"Mom would have loved this," Mac quietly commented to his dad. Sophie looked up from her plate to watch Mac nudge his dad with his shoulder.

"Yeah, she would have."

"And she would have loved this town. To have Mythicals and humans living together in harmony like this? It was everything she ever dreamed of."

"Yeah, I wish she could've seen this." Carson gave Mac a warm smile before returning to his meal.

Even though they still had a case to solve, this break was just what everyone, especially Sophie, needed. The only way it could have been better was if Birdie and Burg were there. Realizing that she hadn't talked to Birdie in a couple of days, Sophie excused herself from the table to give her friend a call.

As she got up, Mac gave her a concerned look, but she waved him off and told him to enjoy his meal.

"I can't eat another bite. I'll be right back. I just want to check in with Birdie. Her soaps just ended for the day, so it's perfect timing."

Finding a bench outside the restaurant shaded by a maple tree, Sophie dialed up Birdie. A few minutes later, she was laughing as her friend described how one of the men at the senior's club was vying for her hand and trying to steal her away from Milton. The front door slamming open jolted her in surprise. Carson came storming out of the restaurant with Mac and Ruby on his heels. Carson and Mac's faces were a combination of anger and determination.

"Hey, Birdie, I need to go. I think something's come up. I'll try to call you tomorrow, okay?" After exchanging goodbyes, Sophie stuffed her phone into her pocket. "What's happened?"

"A body was found in the ocean off Agate Beach."

"Another druid sacrifice?" Sophie asked. Dread started to spread through her stomach. If she never had to see another person vivisected as long as she lived, that'd be just fine.

"No," Mac replied, his blue eyes alight. "But it was reported that the body had a large bruise on their chest."

"Really?" That news made Sophie's heart double in rhythm. Maybe they could finally solve the case.

"Yeah, I thought that might interest you." Mac gave her a teasing nudge, understanding exactly how she felt. The rest of the crew shuffled out of the restaurant, talking in small groups.

Carson ushered Mac, Sophie, and Ruby to his cruiser. Reggie said he'd catch a ride out with Grady, and the rest of the group would stay behind. Fitz, Ace, and Amira would continue to scope out the town, though Sophie hoped that their assistance would become unnecessary once she pulled the death vision from the body. She wasn't superstitious, but she crossed her fingers for luck.

Abernethy Street was blocked off for the festival, so Carson had to take a few side streets before pulling onto Redwood Highway, heading north along the coast.

"What exactly are we heading into, Dad?" Mac asked from the back seat next to Sophie. When Ruby had tried to get in the back seat with her, she'd nudged her into the front passenger seat next to Carson. She'd gone without protest for once. Sophie figured that Ruby was finally feeling more secure in their sisterhood. Maybe something good *had* come out of their fight.

"We'll find out more once we get to Agate Beach, but what I've been told so far is a merman was free diving for abalone – which is completely illegal right now, and I'll be having a word with him – when he found a man's body tangled in the kelp forest. It looks like he'd been in the water for a while. Weights had been wrapped around the victim to keep him from washing ashore."

The road curved closer to the coast, opening to a vista of the Pacific and the rocky northern California coastline. To their left, rocky cliffs soared high above the ocean, dropping into jagged outcroppings with white-capped waves crashing and churning upon their bases. The cobalt blue ocean stretched to the horizon, merging into the distant gloomy fog.

Carson's phone ringing broke Sophie's attention from staring at the breathtaking view. "You got the body? Excellent... Yes, go ahead and conduct a search... Yes, you can tell admin I'm authorizing the overtime."

In the distance, a lone, grand house sat upon a grassy rolling hill overlooking the ocean. The churning gray sky made the bright, colorful house stand out like a gleaming jewel. Sophie could just imagine the view from the widow's walk at the top of the mansion.

"Wow. Look at that place," Sophie said, poking Ruby to show it to her.

Carson glanced over. "That's one of the Butterfat Palaces. That one is owned by Cordelia."

"The candy lady? Wow, I guess the candy business is lucrative!" Ruby said with a giggle.

"Butterfat Palace?" Sophie repeated. "That's a weird name."

"In the late 1800s, several prominent families in this area made their fortunes as dairy farmers. Those farmers built these ornate palaces, just like Cordelia's place. People started calling the houses Butterfat Palaces. You can see a lot more of them if you head down to Ferndale, but we have a couple of them in the area. Cordelia's family has been in Cascadia for generations. One of her ancestors built that house, and she inherited it," Carson explained. The house sat like a vibrant ornament, painted a cheerful blue and yellow. It was nestled on a green meadow like a ring displayed on velvet.

The road curved back to the right, concealing the mansion and the ocean behind a tall stand of redwoods and cypress. The view of the water was quickly hidden by the encroaching forest. The greenery was so thick that Sophie couldn't see a hint of the sky, much less the Pacific through the trees.

They drove past the visitor center, a rustic building covered in cinnamon-colored redwood shingles and dark green trim. Following small signs, Carson pulled into a small gravel lot surrounded by cypress trees bent sideways from the unrelenting wind coming off the ocean. One of Carson's deputies was posted at the entrance to the parking area, barring the way for unauthorized visitors, looking stern and unapproachable.

Getting out of the car, Sophie walked over to the west end of the wooden fence encircling the lot and gazed out. The wind whipped through Sophie's light jacket, trying to freeze her bones and making her shiver in the harsh cold. The space was perched on the edge of a bluff that quickly dropped into a plunging, rock-strewn cliff face. Winding down the side of that bluff, like it had been cut into the rock, was a zigzagging path down to the sandy beach.

Behind her, the crunch of gravel announced Grady, Lydia, and Reggie's arrival. They must have stopped at the coroner's office to pick up the Gorgon. Lydia pulled out a portable body board since a gurney couldn't make it down the rutted, steep path to the shore. Her snakes were wrapped tightly around her head like a strange French twist, likely trying to stay close to the warmth of Lydia's scalp.

Far down on the beach, Sophie could see several uniformed officers – so small in the distance that they reminded her of toys – gathered around a body. One of the officers was off to the side talking to a bare-chested man wearing only a pair of tiny swim trunks. Sophie was already chilled to the bone, and there was a guy in a soaked swimsuit. He clearly wasn't human – probably the merman Carson mentioned in the car. Maybe merpeople were impervious to the cold?

"You ready?" Mac asked, joining her at the fence and handing her a police-issued jacket. Sophie slipped on the oversized coat gratefully and nodded her readiness, flipping up the jacket's collar to cover her freezing ears.

At the entrance to the path, a sign warned visitors against powerful rip currents. Following Carson and Mac down the steep winding trail, the wind tugged and tangled Sophie's hair, making the strands dance on the cold wind. Behind her, Grady and Lydia carried the body board, with Reggie bringing up the rear.

The twisting path narrowed enough that everyone had to walk in a line. Sophie slowly made her way down the steep pebble-strewn path, the loose scree making it slippery. She made sure that each step was settled before taking the next. Holding onto the wooden handrail with a death grip, she made her way down to the sandy beach.

Walking across the wet sand, Sophie kicked a large pebble. The wind kicked up sand in Sophie's face in retaliation as she approached the group near the water's edge.

The beach was an inverted arc, and they were in the middle of the concave bowl of the bay. To the left and right, dark waves crashed against craggy rocks jutting from the water like tiny mountain ranges at the distant edges of the basin. White foam surged violently up the sides of the cliffs. If someone fell into the water at the far ends of the beach, they'd be bashed against the jagged rockface.

Overhead the sky was dark and gray, but no sign of rain was on the wind. Looking away from the gathering, Sophie realized the half-moon bay beach was covered in round, tumbled rocks scattered underfoot. Smooth stones made of agate peppered the sand, along with driftwood and outcroppings of sharp boulders. The agate pebbles came in a multitude of colors, with fine-grained bands of white striping each bright rock.

Bending down, Sophie snagged a shiny, deep-orange stone, the same color as the heart of a campfire, and slipped it into her pocket as a souvenir.

The wind gusted across the beach. Pushing back the loose strands and twisting them into a bun, she saw that Mac had stepped aside to let her approach the corpse. It was mostly covered in a sheet, but when she neared the person's feet, Officer Jameson tugged the sheet off the body so they could see the victim.

"I want to talk to the merman before you start your reading. Do you mind waiting a moment?" Carson asked.

Sophie distractedly nodded, staring at the corpse at her feet. Walking around the body, she stopped near the man's head.

She knelt to get a better look at the victim. Reggie joined her and said, "The cold water has slowed the decomposition."

That made sense to Sophie because the misty breeze felt like icy needles against her face. The ocean had to be an ice bath. The body was bloated, slightly bleached, and wrinkled like her fingers got after a long bath. Patches of the man's skin had begun to blister and turn a greenish-black. It was evident that various sea creatures had made a feast of him. Because of all the soft tissue and no clothing to cover it, very little of his face remained. Sophie couldn't begin to guess the man's age.

"How long do you think he's been in the water?" she asked.

Pulling on a pair of gloves, Reggie said, "Hard to say exactly, but until we can get him into the autopsy room, I'd guess a minimum of ten days. Probably more like two or three weeks. See, look here," Reggie said, gently palpitating the skin on the man's arm. "Adipocere has only just begun to form."

"What's that?"

"It's what happens to bodies submerged in water for a long period – also called grave wax. It's a hard, grayish substance that forms during decomposition. Basically, the fatty tissue beneath the skin begins to turn into soap. This process usually takes a couple of months."

"Soap?" Jameson repeated. "Our fat turns into soap?"

"Only under the right conditions," Reggie assured her. "Did you know that the average adult human body has enough fat to make over seven bars of soap?"

Another officer snorted. "I'd probably make eighteen."

Jameson laughed, teasing the deputy about his love of the local bakery.

Carson approached the group, kicking pebbles and growling under his breath. In his hands was a net bag filled with large, red-shelled mollusks, each almost as big as a dinner plate. Carson handed the bag off to one of his officers and commanded him to return them to where they belonged. He then rejoined the group gathered around the corpse.

"Everything okay, Dad?" Mac asked.

"Poachers piss me off. What does he think? That the Fish and Game Commission enjoys making up arbitrary rules just to rain on his parade? We're trying to preserve an entire species impor-tant to our ecosystem. And he's just pissed off that he can't get his delicacy. Even before the current ban, you could only harvest nine a year. Nine!" He held up nine fingers as if no one knew how to count. "Guess how many red abalones that asshole had in his bag? Eleven! I wrote him a ticket for the maximum fine allowable. If I could haul his ass to jail, I would."

Carson gave a dark look in the direction of where the merman was still arguing with another deputy.

"He was the one who found the body?" Mac asked.

"He was about a hundred yards out, free diving for abalone, when he spotted a body tangled in the kelp on the sea floor. You wouldn't believe how many free divers we would lose every year until the abalone ban went into effect. That's why I have a kelpie and a mermaid on call for this type of retrieval; they brought the body up. I sent them back out to search the area in case there are others. I've got my doubts we'll find anything, but I've got to give it a shot. Frankly, we're lucky there was so much left of this one. There are a lot of scavengers out there," Carson said, waving a hand towards the choppy waves.

When Carson sent the deputies away to give them privacy, Jameson gave Sophie a lingering look of curiosity. It didn't take a genius to realize that Sophie wasn't in town only as Mac's girlfriend. However, she imagined that if she gave Jameson a hundred tries, she'd never guess that Sophie was there to pull death visions from corpses.

Once the deputies were out of earshot, she placed her hand on the man's cold skin.

"He wakes up slowly," Sophie began. "He's groggy and scared. He's blindfolded, tied down, and has no idea how he got wherever he is. He calls out hello. A man responds from his right. The man cries out, asking what is happening. They start talking. Our guy here introduces himself as Michael. The other guy says his name is John. John doesn't know how he got there or who took him. Michael is rubbing his head onto his shoulder, trying to push off his blindfold. He gets it a little loose and can see a little out of the bottom of the cloth. He can't get it any looser; his hair is caught in the knot at the back of his head. Tilting his head up, he can see a little bit of the room. It looks like they might be in a basement – stone walls, damp and stained. Floor joists span across the ceiling. A few bare light bulbs hang at intervals. The room looks like a cross between an old basement and a scientist's lab. There's a table off to the side with beakers and equipment and such. I think there are some large cages in the far corner. That's horrible. He realizes that he's tied to a metal table. He looks to his right; he can see the bottom half of a man tied to a similar table a few feet away. The other man is wearing black jeans and brown loafers and maybe a plain blue t-shirt? He can't see further. I don't have John's hair color, face, or anything."

Sophie took a breath and rolled her shoulders. "There's the sound of a door opening behind and above him. The two men go instantly silent. There are footsteps above his head. It sounds wooden, if that makes sense, like someone is coming down the stairs. There's some low murmuring – like a man's voice. There are sounds of movement behind him, like shuffling papers or something. This new person steps between the tables. Michael can't see much, but the new person is dressed in black. Michael and John both start asking the man what he wants and what is happening. They're begging to be let go, saying they don't have any money. The guy completely ignores them. He starts chanting. It's in another language, and I can't hear him very well. *Priore forma? Eundo ad originem...* Shit, I need this guy to speak up. Wait, he's stepping closer to Michael. He presses something hard into his chest. I can't tell what it is, but it's hard, and I think it might've been green. Michael is trying to buck him off and starts to really yell and scream. Michael's begging him not to hurt him. The man continues to ignore him and chant. Pressure feels like it's building inside Michael's head. The man presses his chest even harder until it feels like he's going to break his sternum. Then he says something – *ligare et furari* – loudly. At least that bit was clear.

"Michael starts screaming in pain. He can still see under his mask, and it looks like white light is entering his body through his chest. It hurts so bad, like he's being electrocuted. Oh shit, something's wrong. He's starting to convulse. There's so much pain. It's like the others, but not as sharp. It keeps building and getting worse, like an overfilled battery, ready to burst. I can hear John screaming as well. The light coming into Michael's body dies off, and he slumps back on the table. John's screams cut off with a gurgle. The man in black yells 'damn it' and throws something across the room. I think it was a book. There's a pause.

"Then he mutters darkly and strides toward where he tossed the book. He picks it up off the ground, near Michael's feet. He's turning around! Holy shit. It's that voodoo guy. We know this guy.

"I think Michael's dying. His nose and ears feel wet, like they're bleeding, and his vision is starting to dim. He's fading fast. There's one last thing he hears the man say: 'Another failure. But it's so close.' And that's it."

Sophie opened her eyes and locked her gaze with Mac. Triumph roared through her body, lighting every nerve ending on fire. "We got him!"

"The voodoo witch doctor – that guy we saw at the inn?" Mac asked, sharing an excited look with Sophie when she nodded.

"You saw him?" Carson asked, reminding Sophie of a hunting dog about to be let off leash.

"Yeah, he's staying at the same inn as us," Mac replied. "He dresses up like a witch doctor – black clothes, a top hat, a necklace with beads made of bones. He has long blond hair. Always carries a wooden staff topped with a goat skull."

"A goat skull? That's gotta be Henri Boudreaux. He's a regular visitor to the area. A warlock, I believe. He's been coming to Murias every couple of months for years. He's never caused a problem or acted suspiciously. Quiet, keeps to himself. I believe he lives in Slidell, Louisiana." Carson gave Mac and Sophie a victorious look.

"Now that I think about it, I don't know why he comes here or what he does when he's in town. As far as I know, he doesn't have any family or business interests here. I say we go talk to Mr. Boudreaux." Carson rubbed his hands together in anticipation.

He got on his phone and yet again started organizing his people for another full-scale operation. He sounded like he was preparing for war. Maybe he was.

As Carson talked into his phone, Mac turned to Ruby. "Did you not get a reading on Boudreaux?"

"I only saw that guy in the hotel once and I never even got close to him," Ruby replied, giving Mac a cross look.

Sophie squashed the urge to defend Ruby from Mac's questioning. No one could argue that Ruby hadn't done her best to touch as many people as possible.

When Grady, Reggie, and Lydia started processing the body and getting ready to take what was left of Michael to the coroner's office, Sophie headed over to help, but they waved her off.

Wandering away, closer to the water's edge, Sophie found a large piece of driftwood, worn smooth from years of waves washing over it, and parked her butt on it. A cold, briny mist sprayed with each wave that crashed on the shore. The dark water and gray skies felt raw and elemental, like an angry god raging.

Sophie felt Mac join her on her piece of driftwood. She knew it was him without having to look. He slipped his arm around her, and together they watched the water.

Over the sound of the wind and the waves, Sophie could just make out Carson's voice as he paced around, gathering his troops.

"Is he dangerous? Boudreaux, I mean," Sophie whispered to Mac. "Like how the Ruith brothers blew up the sheriff's office?"

"Probably," Mac admitted. "Dad will bring plenty of backup with powers strong enough to counteract Boudreaux's. Don't worry. He's been dealing with heavy-hitting Mythicals for as long as I can remember."

Out of the water, a woman's head appeared. Staring in surprise, Sophie watched as the woman stalked through the crashing waves, completely naked, her dark hair streaming down her back. Behind her, an emerald-green horse followed. As the creature came closer, Sophie noticed it had sharp fangs, and its mane wasn't made of hair, but dark green, almost black, seaweed. It was similar enough to the stained-glass window at Colpach Inn that Sophie was certain she was looking at a kelpie in their Mythical form. It was smaller than the average horse and had a delicate, almost dainty appearance. With a shimmer, the kelpie transformed into a naked man – a familiar naked man.

Averting her eyes, Sophie asked, "Doesn't he work at the inn?"

"Yes, I believe that's the owner's nephew. He was at the front desk when we checked in."

"Aren't they cold?" Sophie asked, shivering with sympathy.

"Kelpies and mermaids are made for cold water. It probably feels great to them."

"Well, good for them, but I'm freezing my ass off," Sophie jokingly complained.

"We could go warm up in Dad's car," Mac offered. "Maybe make out in the back seat."

He gave Sophie an exaggerated leer, making her laugh.

"You know what? Yes. I'd like to make out with you in the backseat of your dad's car." Sophie tugged Mac to his feet, heading towards the cliff face and the path back to the parking lot.

"Dad!" Mac bellowed. "Sophie's cold. Give me your keys so she can get out of the weather."

Carson tossed Mac the keys. He was still on his phone, talking urgently to whoever was on the other end, pacing a worn track through the damp sand. Ruby hovered at his elbow, walking one step behind him, like an assistant, or perhaps more aptly, a loyal canine companion, ready to spring into action.

Twenty minutes later, a sharp knock on the cruiser's back window and a loud command to "get a room" interrupted Sophie and Mac's make-out session. Even Carson's disapproving frown didn't bother Sophie after such a delicious snog.

CHAPTER 13

*C*arson waved Mac into the driver's seat to get them back to Murias, saying that he needed to concentrate on coordinating their strategic efforts. The sheriff got into the front passenger seat while distracted on his phone, so with a silent huff, Sophie sat in the back with Ruby. She watched as Grady and Reggie got into the coroner's van to head to the morgue to immediately get started on Michael's autopsy.

"What does *'ligare et furari'* mean?" Ruby quietly asked Sophie.

"Huh?" Sophie responded, distracted by thoughts of the impending arrest. It sounded like they were headed directly to the Colpach Inn, where half of the Cascadian police force would be hiding in the bushes.

"You said that the voodoo man said *'ligare et furari'*. I'm just wondering what it means. That sounds like Italian to me. And what was the rest of it? *Primo* form something? What do you think? It's obviously some kind of spell. But what was the point of it? He was killing people, but I don't think that's what he was going for. You said he was pissed off when Michael and John died. He threw his spell book across the room. I'm just wondering what was so important that he would risk killing a bunch of people."

"I have no idea," Sophie said. "The Ruith brothers were doing it for power. Maybe it was something like that. It's not really my problem anymore."

"Aren't you curious?"

"Not really. I've seen a lot of deaths since I started working at the morgue. People's motivations start to not matter after a while. Discovering how the person died is the only thing I worry about now. It's the police's job to catch the culprit and make sure they pay. But if you are so interested, you can probably find a translation online," Sophie suggested. Reggie had warned Sophie on her first day at the morgue that she'd eventually see enough bodies that she wouldn't care to keep track of them any longer. It had barely taken a month for that prediction to come true. She never forgot a death, but she no longer worried about what happened to the case once she submitted her vision.

Ruby pulled her phone out of her bag and started typing.

"Huh. I think it was Latin," Ruby murmured, staring at her phone. "*Ligare et furari* means 'to bind and steal'. What the hell does that mean?"

"What makes you think I know?" Sophie asked, getting exasperated by all her questions.

"Because you saw it. It's just... do you think the white light was energy entering his body? Or maybe the witch doctor was pulling his soul out of him? Aren't you curious?"

Well, Ruby had her there. Yes, Sophie was indeed just a little bit curious despite her protests saying otherwise.

"My job is to pull the vision. I don't know enough about the Mythical world or magic to even hazard a guess. Honestly, I feel like I've done my part. I'm happy to let the professionals do theirs." Sophie hesitated. She felt like she owed Ruby the truth. "But, yes, I'm a tiny bit curious."

Ruby wiggled in her seat like a happy puppy, making Sophie laugh under her breath.

"Yay! So, tell me... the light... Was it going *into* that guy's body, or was it being pulled out? Oh! And what did the light look like? Because I figure it would look hazy and thin, like a ghost, if it was a soul. Wait. *Do you think ghosts are real?*"

"Is that relevant right now?" Sophie gave Ruby a get-back-on-track look.

"You're right. I'm getting distracted. You said the guy felt like he was being blasted with energy. And I picture that like bright electricity or lightning."

Sophie closed her eyes, trying to remember the scene. "The mask covering his eyes made it hard to see much, but the light was bright – bright enough that it felt like it was burning his retinas. I don't know if there was a direction to the light – if it was going into him or being pulled out – it was too vivid to tell."

They spent the rest of the ride back to Murias letting their imaginations go, spinning up tales and theories about what Boudreaux was doing.

"We should have Reggie send us the recording so we can look up the rest of those Latin words," Ruby exclaimed.

"We can do that. But the Conclave has people who understand this stuff. They'll probably figure it out before we even finish typing it into Google."

Sophie almost felt bad stomping on Ruby's enthusiasm, but she knew that the Conclave had knowledgeable people who specialized in all types of magic and would be able to interpret what Boudreaux was doing. And, honestly, nothing kept Ruby down for long. She probably hadn't even noticed Sophie's sour tone.

"I don't know about that," Carson said, pulling his phone from his ear. "The two of you have solved more murders in a week than most detectives do in a month."

Ruby gave Sophie a smug look.

When they pulled into the long drive of the Colpach Inn, Ruby begged Carson to allow them to witness the arrest.

"Please," she begged, a puppy-dog expression on her face.

"That look doesn't work on me. You forget I had a teenage daughter." Carson held up a quelling hand as Ruby started to pout. "However, you guys have earned the right to watch. Just stay back and out of trouble."

He gave Ruby a fatherly stare down until she meekly agreed.

"Keep an eye on them," Carson commanded Mac, pointing a stern finger at his son.

They followed the sheriff up the grand porch steps and to the check-out desk where Davin Colpach was working on his computer.

Davin took one look at Carson's face and paled. The affable country town sheriff façade had been wiped away, and Sophie could see the recalibration happening in Davin's now-wary eyes as Carson strode up to the counter.

"Davin, is Henri Boudreaux in his room?" Carson asked.

"Um, I believe he checked out this morning," Davin responded. With trembling fingers, he started typing at the desk computer. "Let me double-check that for you."

"Damn it," Carson grumbled when Davin confirmed that Boudreaux had slipped through their fingers.

"I'm so s-sorry. If I had known you wanted to talk to him, I could have delayed him or something," Davin sputtered.

"No need to apologize, Davin. You couldn't have known. I didn't mean to take my frustration out on you. Thank you for your help. However, if you ever see Boudreaux again, I'd appreciate a call."

"Of course," Davin replied, looking relieved.

Carson headed to where Mac, Sophie, and Ruby were waiting for him, shaking his head in disappointment.

"Let's head back to my office. Marcella wanted us to call once we apprehended Boudreaux, so she's expecting my call. Let's break the bad news to her together. She'll want to talk about what Sophie saw today. If Boudreaux has left town, there's not much else I can do about him. I'll put out an APB, but the best course is to let the Conclave take care of him. They've got the reach and the resources."

Carson stalked to the front door and called Jameson over from where she was lingering outside.

"Boudreaux's gone. He's our number one suspect, so this is our top priority. I want you to interview Davin. Find out who Boudreaux associated with. See if he ever mentioned why he came to town, if there was anyone he came to see or places he visited. Check out the room he was in – we might be able to get a tracing spell started if he was stupid enough to leave something personal behind. You're my best tracker, so see if you can sniff him out. I want to know everything about him by the time you're done, from his shoe size to his favorite toothpaste to what he ate for breakfast this morning. Get it all."

"Yes, sir." Jameson turned and hurried into the lobby like Carson had just told her to storm a castle.

As Carson headed down the stairs, he called over one of his deputies and commanded him to get an APB out for Henri Boudreaux. "He is considered very dangerous. If he's still in the borders of Cascadia, I want him found. I'll be at my office – what's left of it. Call me if anything comes up."

The afternoon sun was quickly fading as they drove past Abernethy Street, heading to the sheriff's office. As they drove past, Sophie saw that the street party was getting into full swing. Each end of the street had been cordoned off, and fairy lights were strung over the main drag, giving everything beneath a golden glow. People crowded the area, pressed elbow to elbow, their laughter and conversations a roar of noise. The high squeals of children's laughter rang out over the din. Dozens of children in various costumes wove around adults, playing a game of tag. Tents and tables were filled with food, and the sound of music drifted overhead. It looked like a place where magic and mischief ran rampant.

It was a snapshot of something magical and ethereal. There and gone, disappearing from sight as quickly as it had appeared. Sophie turned in her seat and stared back towards the festival with envy.

The sheriff's department was empty except for one officer at the front desk and phone. The lobby felt dark and cramped with all the boarded-up windows blocking any outside light. The officer manning the desk looked up from his computer and gave the group a curious look as they trudged in.

When Carson unlocked his office, Mac stopped him with a hand on his elbow. "Hey, Dad, we'll be there in a minute."

Carson raised an eyebrow but must've recognized something in Mac's face because he chuckled and shook his head. "Sure thing, boy. We'll make the call once you guys join us."

Without another word, Mac spun from his dad and tugged Sophie back down the hall they'd just traversed. Dragging her after him, Mac jigged each door he passed in the hallway until one gave under his hand.

Sophie glanced around the room, looking at the copier, printer, and shelves with office supplies in confusion. Giving her an evil grin, Mac pulled her into the room and shut the door.

"What—"

As soon as the door clicked shut, Mac scooped Sophie into his arms. She automatically wrapped her legs around his hips as he spun and pressed her against the wall. With another grin, Mac leaned close and gave Sophie a soft, lingering kiss. Pulling back, she stared for a moment at Mac's face. Her eyes traced over his ice blue eyes, up to his perpetually tousled hair, back down to his cheeks that were pinked from all the sun and wind of the last few days. Her gaze fell to his mouth, where he had caught his lip between his teeth. She tunneled her fingers into his dirty blond hair with a soft exhalation and pulled his mouth back to hers.

Mac dove into the kiss, meshing his mouth with hers, becoming more demanding as lust curled its way up Sophie's spine.

A sound of a slamming door in the distance pulled them from the intense moment.

Mac gave her one last, soft kiss before depositing her back on her feet.

"What was that for?" Sophie asked, trying to nonchalantly catch her breath and slow her thudding pulse.

"I just wanted to say congratulations," Mac said with a one-shouldered shrug.

"And you needed to say it with your tongue?" Sophie tried to sound stern, but Mac's unrepentant smirk broke through her ire. "Did you just make everyone postpone an important call so you could make out with me in the supply closet?"

"Yes. I wanted to celebrate. You're the only one who could've solved this case, hellraiser."

Sophie rolled her eyes. "I didn't solve anything. It's not like I figured out the clues and deduced who the murderer was in a blaze of intellectual glory. I watched the bad guy do it the same way someone might watch a movie. It took almost no effort on my part."

"Doesn't matter. You were able to do something other people can't. It doesn't have to be difficult to make it worthy. Plus, I know for a fact that there's effort on your part. What you do isn't easy, and everyone who has witnessed you in action knows exactly how hard it is. What you do is amazing. And when we're done here, we're going to celebrate your success in style. I plan to show you just how impressed I am with your skills."

"Oh yeah? And how are you going to do that?"

Opening the door, Mac reached back and caught her hand in his. Tugging her out of the supply room, he made his eyebrows bounce like a demented Casanova.

"*That's* my reward? I thought I'd earned something impressive."

Sophie saw the moment the insult registered with Mac. Her instincts took over, and she was running away before she'd consciously decided to do so. A growl rolled down the hall, inches behind her, making her yelp and run faster. She ran like the ground was on fire and the devil was riding her coattails.

Arms wrapped around Sophie's waist like a vise, lifting her off her feet. "Kidding! I was kidding," Sophie squealed as Mac swung her around to face him.

"You call my prowess into question?" Mac roared, shaking her in his arms.

Laughing, Sophie choked out, "I would never! Please, O Mighty Lover, shower me with your prowess-ness!"

A door at the end of the hall opened, and Carson stuck his head out, a pained expression on his face. "Are you two quite done yet?"

Not setting Sophie down, Mac carried her like a sack of potatoes into the crowded office and dropped her in an empty chair. Carson was still shaking his head, the look of a weary father exasperated from dealing with recalcitrant children on his face. Mac gave Sophie a wink and a smirk before dropping his face into a serious expression, but she could see a smile tugging on the corners of his mouth.

After making sure everyone was ready, Carson dialed Marcella's number. The phone had barely finished its first ring when a familiar but impatient voice came over the line.

"Sheriff Volpes, you have news?"

"Yes, we've discovered who the murderer is."

"Who—"

"However, he left town this morning before we could apprehend him." Marcella made a noncommittal sound, so Carson continued, "He is a warlock named Henri Boudreaux. He's been a regular visitor to the area for years. We believe he lives in Louisiana."

"Henri Boudreaux, you said?" Marcella's voice murmured something quiet to someone else on her end of the call. "I think I know that name. I believe he is a warlock the Conclave has previously used as a contractor. That should make it easier to track him down. How certain are you that Mr. Boudreaux is the culprit?"

"Very," Carson replied. He then recapped everything that had happened over the previous day.

"Do you know what he was trying to accomplish with the spells?" Ruby asked Marcella once they were done.

"No," Marcella said, "but if you get me a transcript from Miss Feegle's vision, I have some people here that may be able to figure it out."

"Is there anything else you need us to do here?" Mac asked.

"No, my people will take over tracking down Mr. Boudreaux. You've all done as much as you can. I'm pleased with this outcome. I think you work well as a team. If you continue to use your skills to get these kinds of results, you all have a real future with the Conclave."

Marcella thanked everyone for their hard work, signing off by asking Carson to get her a full report as soon as possible. Carson hung up the phone and gave everyone a proud look.

"That's it? We're done now?" Ruby asked. When she looked around at the indifferent faces of the group, she huffed in annoyance. "But… the case isn't over. We don't even know why he was killing people. We should call Larry. He'd know what all those Latin words mean. I have his number."

"You have Larry the Warlock's number?" Sophie asked, giving Ruby a long stare as she dug in her pocket for her phone, watching as her cheeks slowly turned pink.

"I got it the morning that shifter attacked you in your apartment." Ruby shrugged, trying to look nonchalant. "We've been talking a little bit. No biggie."

Sophie resisted the sisterly urge to sing about Larry and Ruby sitting in a tree.

"We've done as much as we need to," Carson said. "You can follow up with your warlock. Be careful, though. Unless he has clearance from Marcella, do not tell him too much. Keep your questions vague and see what he thinks."

Carson's ominous tone caused Ruby to stop and blink up at him. "You don't want Marcella pissed at you," he reminded her.

Ruby chuckled softly. "True. She's scary."

Carson then ushered everyone out of the sheriff's office, stating that he needed to get back to watching over the festival participants. "There's nothing worse than a bunch of drunk Mythical tourists. Just a bunch of morons. I expect to have to break up at least three inter-Mythical incidents before the night's over."

Mac clapped his dad on his shoulder. "Call us if you need us, Dad."

"You need a ride?" Carson offered.

"Nah, thanks. It's a nice night. I think I'd like to walk." Mac stopped and glanced at Sophie. "Is that okay with you?"

Alone with Mac, under the stars on a nice night?

"I'd really like that," she responded, lacing her fingers with Mac's.

Wishing everyone else a good night, Sophie and Mac strolled in the direction of their hotel.

Night had fallen while they'd been on the call with Marcella. The sky was dark as they made their way towards Colpach Inn. The night air was crisp and cold, with only a slight breeze that ruffled Sophie's bangs. In the distance, she could hear the crowd's muted roar, but everything was quiet and still around Sophie and Mac. It felt like everyone in town was on Abernethy Street, and they had the rest of Murias to themselves.

The low-hanging clouds from earlier in the day were gone, and the stars shone bright and clear above their heads.

"I'm hungry," Sophie announced, realizing she'd missed lunch in all the day's drama.

"Oh yeah? What're you in the mood for?"

"Room service."

~

FROM HER OFFICE SHE HAD THE PERFECT VIEW TO OBSERVE ALL HER employees. She'd had a film added to the glass wall separating her office from her underlings so she could watch them but they couldn't see her. She found it provided the perfect amount of 'motivation' to keep her employees hard at work if they never knew when they were being observed.

It also had the added benefit of reducing the inane chatter they all seemed to engage in. 'How was your weekend?' or 'Did you catch the game?'. She'd rather listen to nails on a chalkboard than discuss the weather.

She smirked as she watched Cortez slink off the elevator and quietly sit at his desk. She checked the time on her computer. Perfect. He's late.

Cortez furtively glanced around, looking like he was waiting for the other shoe to drop. When nothing occurred, his shoulders slowly lowered and he turned to his computer, booting up the machine.

Picking up her phone, she called security. "Good morning. I need you to send two security guards up to my office to oversee an employee removal. Thank you."

Hanging up the call, she pressed the button for her assistant's number. As the phone on Julia's desk rang, she enjoyed the way her assistant flinched. Before Julia could greet her, she interrupted. "Julia, please have Mr. Cortez come to my office. Immediately."

"Yes, ma'am," Julia replied, her voice subdued and quiet.

Dropping the receiver back in its cradle, she leaned back in her chair, steepling her fingers under her chin. She attempted to school her face into a look of stern disappointment.

A light knock on her door announced Cortez's arrival.

"Enter."

Cortez slowly opened the door and timidly entered the room.

"Close the door, please," she commanded. She pointed at one of the chairs facing her desk. "Sit."

"You wanted to talk to me?"

"You were late... Again."

"No, I don't think so. I'm pretty sure I was on time."

She gave him an impatient look. "Are you accusing me of not knowing how to read a clock?"

"No, of course—"

"I'm not done talking. Do not interrupt me again."

Cortez opened his mouth to apologize but didn't say anything. She had been hoping he'd fall into the trap of speaking again but he seemed to think better of it. Pity.

"I watched you arrive. You are supposed to be at your desk at nine sharp. What time did you arrive this morning? Do not attempt to lie to me, I specifically checked the time when you finally showed up."

"Um, I arrived at nine ten, ma'am," Cortez responded, looking deliciously downtrodden.

"That's the second time this month. Plus, your sales numbers are not cutting it. I'm sorry to have to do this, but we're going to have to let you go."

His head snapped up to give her an incredulous look. His mouth opened and closed several times as he attempted to formulate a response.

Behind Cortez's head, she saw the elevator doors open, spilling out two black-clad security guards.

Perfect timing.

"Wait. You're firing me!?"

"Just figuring that out are you," she replied with a condescending smirk.

"Fuck you, you bitch. After everything I've done for you! I've worked

late. I've come in early and on the weekends. I picked up your stupid dry cleaning. I went on all those errands to pick up all those weird artifacts for you. And this is how you repay all my hard work?"

"Gabriel," she reprimanded, clucking her tongue. "Calm yourself. It's nothing personal. You just don't have what it takes to thrive in a fast-paced environment like this one. Perhaps you should consider a career change, something more in line with your abilities. I've heard that being a dog walker can be very fulfilling."

She had nothing against dog walkers, but she had happened to over-hear Cortez complaining about being allergic once.

His face turned white and then puce with anger. She ignored him, buzzing Julia again.

"Julia, please send in the security personnel."

Cortez turned in his chair to see the waiting officers, who were looking appropriately menacing. He turned back, giving her a look of loathing. "Is that necessary?" he asked.

The two guards entered the room, looming over Cortez's chair, ready to remove him from the room by force if necessary. She sincerely hoped it would become necessary.

"We've had other employees act inappropriately in this situation. It pays to be cautious. Like I said before, this is not personal."

"Not personal? How's this for not personal? Fuck you. Fuck your company. Everyone here hates you. I hope you get struck by a bus."

She shook her head, a look of disappointment on her face. Waving an imperious hand for the security to remove Cortez, she turned her attention to her computer, effectively dismissing him.

Cortez shoved out of his chair, shrugging off the security guards helping hands. "Do not touch me."

"I wouldn't expect a letter of recommendation if I were you," she gave as one final parting shot as they headed for her office door.

She had hoped that would rile him up more, but Cortez just seemed to deflate. He gave her one final look with hatred in his eyes. "Fuck. You."

She raised one sardonic eyebrow as he left.

She watched the security guards escort him out of her office and over to his cubicle. Turning her attention away from her ex-employee, she buzzed her assistant.

"Julia, I need some chocolate after that spectacle. Go get a bar from that place I like. I want one with toffee in it this time."

"Yes, ma'am. Right away." After she hung up, she watched as Julia heaved a sigh.

She turned and looked out her office window, enjoying her view looking down on everyone in the city.

∽

SOPHIE OPENED HER EYES, THE SOFT LIGHT FILTERING AROUND THE curtains telling her it was early morning. Scrubbing her hands over her face, she huffed out an annoyed breath. That dream had left her feeling greasy and soiled.

Cortez was right. What a bitch.

Snagging her dream journal off the nightstand, Sophie fluffed a pillow up behind her back and started documenting the dream.

As she finished the entry, Mac smacked his lips a couple of times, warning Sophie that he was starting to wake up.

"Soph?" he asked with a groan. "Did you have a dream?"

"Yeah. It was a Corporate Bitch dream."

"Do you want to talk about it?" Mac offered.

Sophie nodded and told Mac about the dream. As she finished the story, he got a thoughtful look on his face. Glancing at his watch, he confirmed, "It's six-thirty now. If it was around nine in the dream that means she's on the east coast."

"If she's real," Sophie felt the need to correct.

"True," Mac conceded. "But if she's real, it means we have the name of her ex-employee. We know that she's located in a city. And we know she works in a building tall enough to have a view. It's a place to start."

"Okay, but how many Gabriel Cortez's do you think there

might be on the east coast? It could be hundreds, if not thousands of people with that name."

"We'll make Larry track down all the Gabriel Cortez's," Mac said with an evil grin that made Sophie laugh.

Sophie tossed her journal aside, giving Mac a good morning kiss. "Sorry if me and my dreams woke you."

"Don't worry about it. It's about time I got up anyhow," Mac said around a yawn. "Speaking of dreams, we should see if Ruby had that dream too."

Reluctantly nodding in agreement, Sophie grabbed her phone and sent off a quick text to Ruby.

Hey, I just had a Corporate Bitch dream. Wanted to see if you had one too.

Her phone dinged in response before Sophie had even set it back down on the nightstand.

Poor Cortez! He's having a BAD day, huh? LOL

Sophie didn't respond, but just showed the text to Mac.

"Huh," was all he said. Sophie felt that summed it all up perfectly.

CHAPTER 14

*a*fter a week of primarily overcast days, the sun had come out for the final day of the Hunter's Moon Festival. It was one of those perfect days – warm, but with a taste of autumn in the air, an edge of the coming winter in the crisp breeze. The celebration had spread sometime during the night before and had spilled into the smaller lanes leading off Abernethy Street.

After a well-earned morning of sleeping in, Mac and Sophie had spent the day wandering the town. They'd sampled the food, purchased souvenirs, and spent time with their friends. It was the perfect reward for a job well done. They were to head home the next day, back to San Francisco and their ordinary lives.

Sophie steered Mac over to the pub as her feet had started to ache, and she wanted a beer.

The pub had set up several picnic tables in front of their store, taking over most of the sidewalk and spilling into the road. A large white tent spanning overhead and potted plants enclosing the area made Sophie feel like she was in a German-style beer garden. Luck had been with her and Mac when they'd found an empty space at one of the long tables. They offered the other half of their table to a family of cyclopes who looked ready to drop.

It had been a lovely morning, finally getting to relax and be the tourist she'd been pretending to be all week. Nothing was on her mind except ordering another beer and debating whether she had room for funnel cake.

The mother cyclops got up from the table, holding her baby, announcing that the infant needed a diaper change. That left the dad cyclops and his daughter. Sophie wondered what the child's age was, since she was the size of a pre-teen but her face had the chubbiness of a child still clinging to toddlerhood.

Her hulking parents were intimidatingly huge with hands the size of dinner plates. They looked like they could crush boulders with their bare hands and had shoulders that could block out the sun. But the little cyclops girl was adorable with her large, single green eye. She wore a grim reaper costume, but the hooded robe was blood-red instead of black. Since Halloween was coming up soon, it seemed like many of the local children had dressed up in their costumes for the event.

With her mother gone, the girl scooted closer to a spot directly across the table from Sophie and gazed at her with open curiosity.

"What're you dressed as?" Sophie asked, trying to engage the avidly staring girl.

She looked around and leaned closer as if sharing a secret, so Sophie leaned closer too.

"I'm an assassin," the girl whispered. "The most dangerous assassin in all the Faerie Realm."

"Terrifying," Sophie agreed, smiling when the child gave her a happy, gap-toothed grin.

Sophie waved her hand when Amira and Ace entered the tent, like they were looking for someone. When they spotted Sophie and Mac, they strode over.

"Is everything okay?" Sophie asked, already worried about what could be wrong.

"They're about to announce the winners of the pie contest. We should be there to support Fitz," Amira replied.

"Is he still freaking out?" Sophie asked, getting up from the table and quickly swallowing down the last dregs of her beer. When Sophie and Mac had finally wandered down from their room at almost eleven that morning, Ace had sent them to the inn's kitchen to try to calm Fitz down. He had been baking since before dawn and was on his fifth 'completely unacceptable disgrace of a pie'. It had taken all of the Odd Ones to get Fitz calmed down enough to just pick one of his pies to enter into the contest.

Fitz had been upset because the local store didn't have the brand of vinegar he needed for his pie crust. When Sophie had wrinkled her nose at the idea of vinegar in a dessert, he had explained that it helped tenderize pie dough by inhibiting gluten development. Letting him explain how his 'secret ingredient' allowed for a flakier and easier-to-work-with crust seemed to pull him out of the tailspin he had been in, so Sophie was happy to indulge him.

"Not as bad as this morning, but we should head over to support him," Amira said.

As the group exited the tent, Sophie looked back and waved to the cyclops child, who enthusiastically waved back.

They made their way down to the end of the street, where the pie contest winner was about to be announced. It was at the end of the road, almost precisely where Sophie had tackled Milford Bradley to the asphalt a few days earlier. Glancing over at Cordelia's Confectionary, she was glad to see it looking as if the attack had never happened.

Since the attack, Sophie had only been in the candy store once, but Ruby went almost every day to get a bag of homemade gummy bears or black licorice drops.

A long table covered in a checkboard tablecloth spanned the width of the road. More than a dozen pies lined the surface. A man with a rotund belly and a prominent bald spot with a microphone asked all the contestants to come forward. Sophie watched as Fitz stood at the table, his hands clasped behind his back and his jaw clenched in anticipation. He looked like he was heading to his own execution.

The man walked the table length, occasionally pausing for dramatic effect. By the time he finished his stroll, even Sophie was getting anxious. He then called out a few names of bakers that were honorable mentions.

"Now, for the real contest, I'd like to announce the baker whose pie came in third place," the man paused, looking up and down the contestants as if searching for the winner. "I'd like to congratulate Fitz Nilsen for placing third with his mixed berry pie."

Fitz came around the table, walking on stiff legs, and received his ribbon. He went on to politely applaud as the presenter announced the runner-up ribbon to Pam and the first prize ribbon to the candy store owner, Cordelia, but Sophie knew he had to be seething inside. He had wanted to win the contest so badly. He went over and shook Cordelia and Pam's hands, but the smile on his face looked forced and more like a baring of teeth than a genuine smile.

After the presentation of the first-place ribbon, Sophie and the rest of the friend group approached Fitz to congratulate him.

"I heard that Cordelia uses magic to get her pie crust flaky," Sophie whispered to Fitz as she gave him a hug.

"Figures." He scoffed and glanced over at Cordelia as she talked to a small crowd of well-wishers. He looked mollified by the rumor.

Pam headed over to give her congratulations to Fitz. Sophie knew he'd been to the bakery several times during the week, so they were on friendly terms. She tutted in sympathy when Fitz bemoaned about not finding his preferred vinegar at the small grocery store in town. She confided in him that she had begun to order her butter specially from a farm in Marin County because she could never get the quality of butter locally that she needed for her baked goods.

"Where's your dad?" Sophie asked Mac, looking around for him after realizing she had only seen him once, hours earlier. She'd expected him to be around, keeping an eye on the rowdy crowds. She'd seen Jameson and several other deputies throughout the day but not Carson.

"He's probably at the beach, keeping an eye on the vendors. That's where the real party happens."

"I love a good beach party!" Amira exclaimed. "I hope they have fireworks. Oh! And a bonfire."

"When does that start?" Sophie asked.

Mac checked his watch. "In a couple of hours, but we could head over sooner."

Sophie gave Mac a conspiratorial grin. "Nah. If we show up early, Carson will probably put us to work. Let's get some dinner first and then head out."

CHAPTER 15

⮷

*E*very restaurant on Abernethy Street had been filled to bursting with tourists, so the group agreed to meet back at Colpach Inn to get dinner. The dining room had been only half-filled with guests, so it had been the right move.

Sophie was sitting between Mac and Amira at the large round table in the center of the dining room. Ruby was almost directly across from her between Reggie and Ace. The three were laughing over something Ace said. Sophie was glad her friends had thawed toward Ruby after their initial chilly reception.

"She's not what I expected," Amira said quietly, following Sophie's gaze towards her sister.

"Yeah, I didn't want anything to do with her at first," Sophie admitted. "But now, I'm glad that Marcella forced us together for this assignment. I kind of like her. It helps that she's nothing like me. It'd be weirder to have a long-lost sister if we were spookily similar. Especially since she's technically a serial killer."

Amira gave her a long look.

"What?" Sophie asked.

"Well, sometimes you guys do and say things that are so alike that it's uncanny. You even make some of the same gestures."

"No, we don't. Flipping the bird doesn't count," Sophie protested. "She's bubbly and cheerful and talkative. And I'm, well, I'm just not any of those things."

"Okay, if you say so," Amira replied with a carefully neutral expression, turning her attention back to her plate of grouper.

Sophie looked back at Ruby as she rolled her eyes and then wrinkled her nose at something Ace said.

"Well, shit," Sophie griped under her breath.

∼

AFTER THE GROUP FINISHED EATING, EVERYONE PILED INTO different cars to drive to the parking area reserved for the beach party. Sophie, Ruby, and Ace got into Mac's rental for the drive to the beach.

They were supposed to park in a designated field and then trek just over a mile to Gold Bluffs Beach, where the festivities were being held. Mac was being very tight-lipped about the event, stating that it was a surprise every time Sophie tried to pry additional details from him.

There was a line of cars in front of and behind them on the way to the party. Mac said that most of the town would eventually show up by the time the moon started to rise, though many of the shifters would come in on foot rather than drive.

It must be nice to be able to run on four feet through the forest and skip the traffic, Sophie thought with a grin.

Following the line of cars, Mac turned onto a pitted dirt road that twisted and turned through the dense greenery. Branches and leaves brushed against the car's roof as he carefully wove along the forest road. Ace and Ruby cheered in the backseat as Mac bounced and splashed the vehicle over a small stream that bisected the road like they were on a roller coaster. Sophie yelped as they crossed the creek, water spraying out in a wave from the tires, worried that water would backwash into the vehicle.

177

They passed a sign stating they were entering the Prairie Creek Redwoods State Park. Not far past the sign was a cordoned-off field half-filled with vehicles. A man in a reflective vest waved them into an empty spot.

Piling out of the car, they waited for the rest of their friends to park.

The group, talking and laughing, followed a well-worn path into the woods. Sophie couldn't wait to get to the beach and put her toes in the freezing waters of the Pacific Ocean. It was time to let her hair down and party with her boyfriend.

"Come on," Sophie called out as Reggie and Grady fell behind, talking animatedly, at the rear of the pack.

The path through the redwood forest looked almost identical to all the other trails they had traversed since arriving in Cascadia. Not that it wasn't awe-inspiring, but the towering redwood forest had become a familiar sight to Sophie and had lost some of its initial reverence for her.

They followed a hiking trail through the woods. The canopy of trees overhead with their branches woven together turned the early evening into premature dusk. The trail disappeared around a bend in the path up ahead, where Sophie thought she could detect the sound of running water even over the noise of her boisterous friends.

As Sophie followed the twisty path, her feet halted when she turned the corner.

"Holy sh—" She glanced at Mac, whose face glowed with excitement.

Someone 'oofed' as they bumped into her back.

"Whooaa," Ruby said as she stepped around from where she ran into Sophie. A small sign to the right welcomed visitors to Fern Canyon.

Mac gave Sophie an I-told-you look. In front of them, the dirt path widened, turning into a stone-lined riverbed that transformed into a clear, shallow stream. But the real showstopper was the canyon walls rising on both sides of the path.

The lush walls of the gorge rose fifty feet on both sides, the walls shaggy with dripping ferns and moss. Water trickled and dripped down the canyon walls like a prehistoric rainforest. It felt like a place lost to the march of time. Sophie wouldn't be surprised if a dinosaur peeked its head through the ferns.

The path was twisty and winding ahead, so she could not see where the trail ended.

The setting sun flared orange through the canyon, reflecting beams of light off the burbling stream and making the damp walls rising on either side of the group glow. It was paradise.

"What is this place?" Sophie asked, straining her head back to see the ravine's top.

"I'm taking my shoes off," Ruby announced. The smooth stones lining the creek looked slippery, so Sophie decided her sister had the right idea. She also pulled her boots off and rolled her jeans to her knees.

Her first step into the water sent an icy shiver up her spine, making the air in Sophie's lungs wheeze out. Despite her best efforts, a girlish squeal escaped her lips. The creek was shallow but shockingly cold, streaming clear over a riverbed of smooth rocks.

Making it a game, Sophie hopped from rock to tree trunk to wooden footbridges like a kid pretending that the floor is lava. The group scrambled over and under a few fallen trees, their surfaces spongy and slick from years of moisture. A few footbridges were laid across the creek to help get them over the deeper areas of the stream.

The trail snaked its way through the canyon with fallen tree trunks occasionally blocking the path and forcing the group to slog through the stream. Mac helped Sophie scramble under and over ancient sodden logs worn smooth by the passage of many feet. The further they trekked into the canyon, the taller and narrower the walls became until the sun was blocked entirely from the tight space.

Towards the end of the path, water trickled down the lichen and moss-covered canyon wall in an ice-cold waterfall. Sophie cupped her hand, catching some of the frigid water and letting it trickle through her fingers. The ferns cascading down the ravine's walls bounced and danced as drips of water flowed over them.

After almost a mile, the canyon walls slowly widened and fell away, opening back up to the forest. Stepping out of Fern Canyon felt like emerging from a place of magic – a place lost to time. Sophie felt like she was waking up from a hazy dream.

She stopped and put her boots back on, giving Mac a happy smile. He pulled her up and into his arms. The rest of the group passed them by as they shared a kiss.

"Having fun, hellraiser?"

Sophie gave him another kiss as an answer. "Best day ever."

Sophie and Mac trailed after their friends, strolling down a narrow sandy path towards the beach. Now that they had left the protective walls of Fern Canyon, Sophie could hear the sounds of revelry in the distance.

The woods thinned out, morphing into tall grass interspersed with low bushes. As they emerged from the woods, Sophie noticed a herd of Roosevelt elk off to the right, silently weaving their way through the grass. She did a quick double-take when she realized that each animal had a bag slung around its neck.

As Sophie and Mac got close to the beach, out of the corner of her eye, she could see the elk transform into naked humans who were pulling clothes out of their bags and getting dressed right in the middle of the coastal grass and low bushes.

Topping the crest of a large dune, Gold Bluffs Beach spread out below them. The vast expanse of sand was filled with crowds of people spilling out of tents and surrounding various tables. In the center was an enormous unlit bonfire.

Sophie looked back at the way they'd come. In the distance behind them, golden-colored bluffs overlooked the beach. They were in a protected cove buffered from the wind by rolling, grass-covered dunes.

Despite the distance, Sophie instantly recognized Carson standing near the bonfire, with his arms crossed, watching over the crowd. Pointing him out to Mac, the two headed toward the sheriff.

"Hey, Dad," Mac greeted when they got close. "How's it going?"

"Other than needing to prevent the fire chief from getting into a fistfight with the chimeras when he saw the size of the woodpile they built for the bonfire? I'm doing just peachy."

"Same shit, different day," Mac suggested, making his dad laugh.

"You know it, kiddo."

"Any news on Boudreaux?" Mac asked, ignoring the kiddo comment.

"Not as much as I'd like. Magistrate Venturi called me earlier today to let me know that they were able to track Boudreaux to the San Francisco airport, where he boarded a flight to Atlanta the same day he left town. We have discovered that although Boudreaux has been visiting the area for years, his visits have ramped up. He's been here at least six times in the last four months. Jameson couldn't find any places he visited that seemed unusual, but she found a few people who had seen him in the company of an older man with a gray beard who usually wore a robe."

"Huh. Gray beard and wears a robe? Sounds like Bramwell," Sophie commented.

"Who is Bramwell?" Carson asked intently.

"He was a Fae that caused us some problems a couple of weeks ago. He's gone underground since, and no one's been able to find him," Mac replied. "I'll see if I can get a picture of him from Marcella. You can have Jameson pass his photo around and see if anyone recognizes him. It's probably not, though. I don't know if you've noticed, but many Mythicals like to wear robes." With a smirk, Mac pointed at a man just a few feet away wearing a tattered black robe.

"He's based out of Louisiana, right?" Mac asked. Carson nodded. "I wonder what he's doing in Atlanta. Is the New Orleans Conclave being cooperative and going to help Marcella to resolve this?"

"If they know what's good for them, they'll fall all over themselves to help the San Francisco Conclave capture Boudreaux. Marcella has the power and backing to make their lives completely miserable if they don't."

"We should check and see if any dead Fae has turned up in Georgia or Louisiana with mysterious bruises on their chests. Did Marcella know what Boudreaux's spell was trying to do?"

"Not yet, but what little they have figured out has them seriously concerned."

"What Mythical jurisdiction does Atlanta fall under?"

Carson looked thoughtful for a moment, then shrugged. "The Savannah Conclave, maybe? Thankfully, it's no longer my problem. I got my hands full enough with Murias and its residents."

"Alright, Dad. We're going to check out the party. Call me if you need anything."

Carson looked at the sky. "Looks like we might get lucky this year and have a clear sky for the Hunter's Moon. Most years, it's too cloudy to see clearly."

The party suddenly went quiet as a half-lion and half-dragon creature slowly stalked through the parting crowd towards the large stone-ringed pile of wood in the middle of the beach. Sophie spotted Ruby, and the rest of their friends gathered near the unlit bonfire.

"What is that?" Sophie whispered to Mac.

"A chimera," he whispered back. "Watch this."

The chimera took a deep, slow breath, held it for a minute, then blew a fireball at the wood. It went up in flame with a roaring whoosh. As the crowd screamed and cheered, the chimera took a bow and headed back the way it'd come.

"Shots! Shots! Shots!" Sophie could hear Ruby cheering over the crowd. She laughed as Ruby pulled Amira, Fitz, and Ace over to the alcohol and beer cart. As they got in line to order, Sophie watched as her sister looked around, searching for something. Turning in a circle, Ruby stopped when she caught Sophie watching her. "Come on, Sophie! Mac! The first round is on me," she yelled, waving at Sophie and Mac.

"Go on, you two. You've earned some fun," Carson said, nudging Mac towards the mobile bar.

CHAPTER 16

❦

*S*ophie was tipsy. But then again, so were almost all her friends.

It had been a fantastic night – the cherry on top of solving their case. They danced; they drank; they talked and laughed; Sophie and Mac kissed as the full moon rose over the ocean while everyone around them cheered, roared, howled, and screeched, ringing in the culmination of the Hunter's Moon Festival. It had been magical. The entire town of Murias had shown up to celebrate.

Even though the party still raged behind them, Sophie suggested they head back to the inn. They needed to go back to the city the next day, and she didn't want to be tired and hungover for the five-hour drive.

Sophie was toward the back of the group, smiling at her friends' antics as they walked the path through the woods in the dark. There was a shorter trail that skipped Fern Canyon they were taking, probably a good thing since Sophie figured she'd end up on her ass in the freezing cold creek if she'd tried to make her way over the slippery riverbed.

Ruby and Amira were clutching one another and giggling as

they wove their way drunkenly along the trail. Ace and Fitz were in a deep philosophical debate about the merits of rum versus vodka. As the designated drivers, Mac, Grady, and Reggie were at the back of the group, attempting to herd them toward the parking lot.

It was sometime in the wee hours of the night. Midnight had come and gone a while ago. In the pauses in conversation around her, Sophie could still hear the sounds of revelry filtering through the woods from the beach party.

Trees loomed over the dirt trail, blocking most of the star-filled sky. The beams of light from the full moon slipped through the foliage enough that Sophie could just make out the path in front of her feet. The leaves and trees gleamed silver in the dark. The hoot of a lone owl sounded from the trees to their left. Small nocturnal creatures scurried through the underbrush around them, quieting as the group neared their dens. A thin, watery fog clung to the boughs of the trees, giving the forest a fairytale-like feeling.

A break in the canopy allowed the moon to shine directly down on the group. Stopping, Sophie tilted her head back, letting the silver light fall on her face. Mac caught up to her, wrapping his arm around her waist and nudging her forward.

"The Hunter's Moon Festival is awesome. We should come back every year," Sophie suggested.

"Absolutely. I'm glad you had a good time. Hopefully, next time we won't—"

Mac suddenly stopped in his tracks, staring intently into the dark woods surrounding them.

"Wha—" Sophie started to ask, but Mac covered her mouth with his hand. She followed his gaze but couldn't make out anything in the darkness. The gloom seemed to stare back.

A low, warning growl issued from Mac's mouth, stopping the rest of the group who looked in the same direction he was intently staring into the dark, quiet forest. That's when Sophie realized she couldn't hear the usual sounds of nocturnal animals and insects. It was utterly silent and still. The hairs on Sophie's arms rose when a sense of menace washed over her, drying out her mouth. Squinting her eyes, she thought she saw a shadow shift in the darkness.

"Run!" Mac bellowed, pushing Sophie forward down the path. She followed his command and bolted toward her friends. Glancing over her shoulder, she watched as he transformed into his half-fox form, bursting through his shirt. Something large, dark, and furry leaped from the forest, tackling Mac and knocking him into the brush and out of sight.

"We're under attack," someone screamed. Snarls and growls sounded like they were coming from all directions. Sophie dropped down, trying to get her bearings and find her friends in the commotion.

"Get those bitches!" a deep, growling voice thundered from somewhere to the right.

As Sophie watched, wolf shifters broke from the tree line, rushing at the group; half of the attackers had transformed into their full wolf form and the other half into their half-human, half-wolf shape like something from one of those cheesy wolfman movies.

Still kneeling, Sophie pulled the knife from the calf sheath hidden beneath her jeans. She fished her taser out of her pocket when she stood back up. She didn't know what good it would do since she could barely make out anything in the dark. These were nocturnal predators on the attack, but it made her feel better to clutch her weapons.

Mac reappeared in the moonlight in the path in front of Sophie, blood dripping from his muzzle. He turned his head up to the sky and released a barking howl, a long and haunting cry. A moment later, an answering call came from the direction of the beach. *Oh, please let that be the cavalry.*

Sophie tried to reach Mac's side but had to duck as a shifter with shaggy black fur swiped his claws at her face. She backed up, trying to give herself room to maneuver. The shifter whirled back at her, swinging his arm wide, aiming for her face. Bringing her weapon up in a quick jab, Sophie caught the inside of the shifter's bicep with her knife. While the wolfman roared in rage and pain, she scuttled back, looking for an escape route. The shifter's muscles tensed and bunched as if he was about to leap at her. Sophie prepared herself to meet him head-on, distributing her weight evenly on her feet and keeping her muscles loose and ready.

The dark-furred wolf bared a mouth full of sharp teeth at Sophie, giving her a broad grin, confident and pleased at the look of fear she knew she had on her face. Sophie almost stumbled when a brown-furred face that looked like a hybrid between a bear and a badger suddenly appeared behind the shifter's back. The creature must've been seven feet tall to be able to loom over the wolf shifter. The badger-bear grabbed the sides of the wolf's head in its enormous, clawed paws before snapping the shifter's neck with a quick twist and crack. The wolfman was dropped carelessly on the ground.

"Ruby needs your help!" Grady's voice came from the monster's mouth, making Sophie gape in shock. *So that's what a wolverine looks like,* Sophie thought inanely as he raised a paw and pointed a long, sharp claw behind her.

Whirling on her heel, she spotted an armed Ruby trapped by two wolf shifters. Running on silent feet, Sophie sprinted, praying that she could reach them in time. Just as the one closest to her raised his clawed hand to strike at Ruby, Sophie leaped onto his back, sliding the knife across his throat. She stayed on his back as he toppled forward, riding him to the ground. Rolling to her feet, she watched helplessly as the other shifter back-handed Ruby, sending her sprawling into the brush off the path. The shifter took a threatening step in the direction Ruby had flown. Sophie saw him reach down and grasp her foot in his enormous clawed hand, pulling her back towards him. She couldn't tell if Ruby was conscious or not. Sophie was too far away to stop whatever was going to happen next.

"Hey, asshole!" Sophie screamed. The wolfman started to turn toward Sophie, Ruby's foot still gripped in its paw. As the shifter started to look in her direction, Sophie pulled her phone out of her pocket and chucked it at his head as hard as she could. It was the only thing she had handy to throw that wasn't her knife or her taser, and she certainly wasn't letting go of her weapons.

The phone pinged off the wolf's forehead, but he shook it off like swatting an annoying fly. However, he'd dropped Ruby's leg and turned towards Sophie. Snarling, he lowered his head, looking like he was about to charge. Sophie set her feet and watched as the shifter's muscles tensed for half a second before he lunged. For just a moment, as his furred arms were swung out for a killing blow, claws wide and extended, the shifter's chest was left open. On pure instinct, Sophie darted forward, right into that empty space. She pressed the taser to the wolf's side and deployed it. When the taser froze his muscles for a millisecond, she stabbed the knife into his chest, using her body weight and momentum to press it in as far as it would go. The blade ground jarringly against bones but, with a twist of her hand, she found space between the ribs and slid it into soft tissue.

The wolf made a noise of shock, air hissing between his teeth. As he staggered back, the knife slid free with a wet *schlick*. It took him a moment to recover, but the wolf shook his head and roared at Sophie.

Stepping closer, the shifter swung his arm, claws aimed right for her face. Sophie tried to jump back out of the way, bringing the knife up to defend herself, but he knocked the weapon out of her hand, scraping his claws down her arm. The knife skittered away, lost to the underbrush and darkness. Clutching her burning arm to her chest, Sophie took a step back as he loomed closer. The shifter looked down at the bleeding knife wound on his chest and then back at Sophie. There was death in his glare. All Sophie had left was a taser – it wouldn't be enough to stop him a second time. His lips pulled back from his fangs, and a long line of saliva dripped from his mouth.

"You bitch. You killed my brother, and you think I'm just going to let that go?" the shifter said on a low, rumbling growl.

Oh shit. It's Antonio, was the only thought in Sophie's head. Looking around her, she realized there wasn't anywhere to run. Wolf shifters were battling with her friends all around her, and she was pinned in.

A long warbling cry sounded behind Sophie, raising every hair on her body. It was the call of a monster on the hunt, a haunting cry warning of death. Dropping to the ground automatically, Sophie watched as a body covered in reddish fur sailed over her head like an avenging angel and tackled the shifter stalking her. Her rescuer hit Antonio like a cannonball, knocking both Mythicals off their feet. They tumbled, red fur and black fur flashing as they rolled, snarling and ripping into one another.

Scuttling away from the fight, Sophie tripped, falling on her ass in a dense patch of ferns and brush. Clawing her way back onto her feet, she watched as the two shifters grappled. They stumbled into a patch of moonlight, letting her see that it was a fox shifter that battled against Antonio. She couldn't tell if it was Mac or Carson in the dark. The shifters clashed, muscles bulging under fur, using their claws and teeth to tear into one another. The fox danced back, slashing with his claws as the wolf lunged forward. Sophie recognized the remnants of the shirt still clinging to the fox's torso. It was Mac.

She'd lost her taser in her fall, so she scrabbled her hand over the ground, hoping to find *something* to use as a weapon. Sophie wrapped her fingers around a jagged rock about the size of a fist. She jumped back to her feet, not wanting to just watch the battle. She needed to help.

With a roar, Mac threw himself at Antonio, digging his claws into his gut. With a strained grunt, he lifted the wolf shifter off his feet. Antonio made a gurgling cry, stuck on the claws of his enemy, quaking like a fish on a hook. Turning his upper body, Mac slammed the wolf alpha onto the ground, his claws buried under his ribcage. Antonio made a rattling noise in his throat before falling still. Mac stood up, shaking out his arms while Antonio slowly morphed back into his human form, his body crumpled and bloody in the ferns. Sophie knew that shifters returned to their human forms when they died.

"Mac," Sophie yelled, sprinting over to him. He tugged her to his side, standing protective and alert. They stood side by side, ready to defend themselves against the next attack.

With roars, hoots, screams, and haunting cackles, the townspeople of Murias burst from the forest. Every kind of creature from fairytale stories appeared, from goblins to nymphs to centaurs. They dove into the fight, hitting the wolf shifters in a stampede, rolling over them like a tidal wave. The wolf shifters were cut down without mercy or hesitation.

An enormous Roosevelt elk charged one of the wolves, gouging the shifter with its rack of sharp antlers. Tossing the wolf into the air, the elk stomped on the wolf when it hit the ground like Sophie once saw a horse crush a snake. The wolf shifter's bones snapped and cracked under the elk's hooves. The wolf shrieked an animal cry of pain and desperate fear before abruptly being silenced mid-howl. That shriek called to a primal place inside Sophie, a place where she was scared to die.

Sophie choked out a horrified, "What the *fuck?*" when the giant elk gave the corpse one last kick before stalking off into the forest, a long string of gore still hanging from an antler.

She didn't want to die. She didn't want her boyfriend or her friends to die.

She needed to fight.

Sophie and Mac braced themselves as another wolf shifter sprinted in their direction, feet flying over the dirt towards them. After witnessing the mass slaughter of his pack mates, the wolf's eyes were wild and feverish – the look of someone with nothing left to lose. "Sophie, get behind me," Mac commanded.

Sophie didn't even have time to scoff at that suggestion because the cyclops man from the pub earlier that day lunged out of the woods and snatched the wolf shifter up by his scruff like he was picking up a naughty puppy. The cyclops lifted the wolf high into the air, ignoring the shifter's snarls and flailing. Before Sophie could blink, he slammed the wolf down over his bent knee with a sickening crack. Sophie gaped as Cyclops Dad broke the shifter like a piece of kindling and then dropped them as if the shifter was a random piece of trash.

"Holy shit," Sophie gasped.

Cyclops Dad turned to Sophie and Mac with a concerned look in his single eye. "Are you two alright?" he asked.

"Yeah, um, yeah... we're good. Thanks for... that," Sophie responded slowly, pointing to the dead wolf. The cyclops waved away the thanks before turning and heading into the woods in search of more quarry.

Mac and Sophie stood back-to-back, watching the woods for any other attackers. Sophie raised her rock, ready to bash in some wolf shifters' skulls if they got within reach.

However, she never got a chance to use her rock weapon. Once the townspeople showed up, the fight was over in minutes. They streamed through the trees, attacking all the wolf shifters, picking them off one by one. A few tried to turn tail and escape, but they were quickly run down and dispatched. The smell of blood was thick in the air by the time the last wolf shifter was slain.

The sky was just starting to lighten to a pre-dawn gray, allowing Sophie to see the massacre around her. At least a dozen wolf shifters' broken bodies littered the forest floor within sight. If it hadn't been for the citizens of Murias's intervention, Sophie and her friends might not have made it through to see the sunrise.

Carson's voice could be heard over the milling pandemonium throughout the woods, calling everyone into order, organizing the chaos.

Dropping his defensive stance, Mac turned to Sophie and pulled her into his arms. She groaned when he pressed against the claw marks on her arm.

"Holy shit, Soph, your arm! You're bleeding," Mac exclaimed. He carefully lifted her arm to look over the wound from the wolf shifter's claws. Blood slid from the gashes and dripped wetly off her fingertips. *Maybe too much blood*, Sophie thought, suddenly woozy at the sight.

Seeing Sophie's eyes flutter, Mac practically carried her to a log to sit on while he yelled for a doctor. Blood was soaking through her sleeve, and the injuries were making themselves known now that the adrenaline of the fight had worn off.

Carefully rolling up Sophie's sleeve, Mac made a low noise in his throat. Four long jagged gashes were running down the length of her forearm. Three of them were somewhat superficial, but one was deep. The red of flesh and muscle and blood was evident even in the dim early morning light. "Are you injured anywhere else?" Mac asked, pulling off what remained of his shirt to press against the wounds. Sophie shook her head, watching as he wrapped the shirt around her arm. She hissed in pain when he tightened the dressing over the wound and pressed his hand against the cuts to stop the bleeding.

"I need a doctor!" Mac bellowed again. "Now!"

"I lost my knife," Sophie complained to Mac, who looked at her like she was losing her mind. "And my taser. And my phone."

It was easier to focus on her lost weapons than the fact that she'd killed someone.

"Don't worry about those things. We'll find them for you, or I'll get you new ones."

"I killed someone," she whispered to Mac. She looked down at her bloodied hands. They had started to shake and she couldn't get them to stop.

If Ruby touches me, she'll get a vision from now on.

It couldn't ever be erased or forgotten. She was a murderer.

"You did what you had to. They would have killed you or any one of our friends. I'm glad you killed the shifter. The world is a better place because you're in it. That doesn't change because you removed one asshole from the gene pool."

Mac pulled her into his arms. She nuzzled her nose into his red-furred neck and inhaled his scent.

Reggie came rushing over, still in his half-opossum form. Sophie bit her lip to keep from chuckling. There was something so incredibly adorable about seeing an opossum head on top of a human body in a button-up shirt and slacks that it made Sophie want to giggle. Happy for the distraction of his arrival, Sophie pushed all other thoughts away, choosing to focus on her amusement. He was so cute that she wanted to pet his rounded pink ears. Unlike some Mythicals, Reggie's shifted form wasn't much bigger or taller than his regular human body, so his clothes had remained intact. When he spotted Mac pressing the makeshift dressing to her arm, he hissed in distress, which Sophie found both charming and strange.

"I sent Grady to get the emergency first aid kit out of the car. He'll be back in a minute," Reggie told them.

"I'm fine," Sophie tried to reassure him, but one look at his face let her know he wasn't having it. "Have you seen Ruby? I think I saw her get knocked unconscious."

"I'll look for her," Mac promised. "You stay here with Reggie and wait for Grady." Reggie took Mac's place, pressing on Sophie's wound, while Mac hustled down the path, his fox muzzle turned up into the air as he sniffed for Ruby.

A moment later, Sophie heard Mac call out that he'd found her. She watched as he pulled Ruby out of a bush, scratched and dirty but whole. Sophie watched as he checked her over, finding an injury on the back of her head. Sophie could see Ruby's hair was matted with blood around her ear. She also looked a bit unsteady on her feet.

With a helping hand on her elbow, Mac led Ruby toward the log Sophie was sitting on. She was wobbling and looking groggy. "I've got this. Check on Ruby," Sophie ordered Reggie, replacing his hand with her own to apply pressure on her wound.

Reggie shuffled over to help Ruby sit down next to Sophie. He immediately homed in on a large cut over her right ear.

"You've got a nasty cut behind your ear," Reggie informed them. "Are you feeling nauseous? Or dizzy?" Ruby shook her head but then winced in pain at the motion.

"Just hold still for now," Reggie instructed, gently probing the area. He made a sympathetic hissing noise when she flinched. "I think you're going to need some stitches."

Back in his human form, Grady appeared with a medical case, opening it and handing supplies to Reggie. He also had a stack of spare clothes from his car. Sophie had learned that most shifters, especially the ones whose non-human forms were larger than their human side, kept spare clothes in easy access.

Grady turned to Sophie, pointing at her injured forearm. "Let me see."

Sophie held out her arm. Without letting up on the pressure, he carefully checked the wound. "Good news is that it looks like the bleeding is slowing. The bad news is that I believe you're gonna need stitches."

Sophie tried to pay attention to what Grady was saying, but Mac had transformed back from his half-fox form to human. Then he stripped out of what was left of his ruined clothing and into the sweatpants and t-shirt Grady brought. He had several long scratches all over his body, but they were already starting to seal. When he caught Sophie ogling him, he gave her an unabashed grin, mouthing the word 'later' at her. She rolled her eyes at him but could feel a blush staining her cheeks.

Sophie watched as Mac walked around, searching through the brush. After a few minutes, he seemed to find what he was looking for. He straightened up, triumphantly holding a phone in one hand and a bloody knife in the other.

Ambling over to Sophie, Mac gave her a pleased grin. He handed her the phone and promised to get the knife cleaned up and returned to her shortly.

Reggie checked Ruby's eyes with a pen light and proclaimed that she was lucky because she didn't appear to have a concussion. He wrapped gauze around her head, making her look like she was wearing an ugly '80s-style headband, but Reggie seemed pleased with the results.

Fitz came limping out of the forest with Ace's shoulder propping him up under his armpit, helping take some weight off his injured leg. Amira hovered anxiously behind them, her face drawn and worried.

"Are you guys okay?" Sophie called out, pulling everyone's attention to the threesome.

"Yes, I just twisted my ankle. It's fine," Fitz assured them.

"Ouch, that sucks. Come join us. There's room for one more on the injury log," Sophie teased, waving her hand at the downed tree she was sitting on, doing her best impression of a game show hostess.

Ace assisted Fitz to a bare spot on the log and lowered him to sit.

"It's not fair. At least you guys have claws and sharp teeth in your true form. My wings and beak are useless in a fight," Fitz complained as Reggie gently palpated his ankle. "If this keeps happening, I need to learn how to fight. Sophie, the Irish wolfhound that trains you – do you think he'd be up to taking on another student?"

"I'll ask Paddy when we get back to town," she said, watching as Reggie and Grady quickly wrapped Fitz's ankle with a compression bandage.

Sophie looked over her friends, most of whom were still in their shifter forms. All of them were dirty, disheveled, and bloodied. Her heart swelled with gratitude to her friends, but especially the townspeople who had put themselves between her and danger. If it hadn't been for them, Sophie knew, deep down, that she'd be mourning some, if not all, of her friends. That was if she hadn't been killed herself. It made her shudder to think how differently this morning could have turned out.

Sophie looked over at Antonio's discarded body. He was splayed on his back, naked and quickly cooling in the early morning mist. She had felt safe and removed from her troubles in San Francisco, but her problems found her hundreds of miles away from the city and the Sunset District pack.

"How?" Sophie asked suddenly, glancing over the wolf shifter bodies scattered across the ground. Each one had morphed back to their human forms and lay crumpled on the forest floor. Mac looked confused, so she continued, "How did the pack know where to find us? How did they even know we were here? Is there a mole in the Conclave or the police department? Marcella said that she wasn't going to tell anyone we were here. Dunham and Larry knew. But who else knew? Could it be someone local?"

The more Sophie threw out suggestions, the darker Mac's expression got.

"We're gonna find out," he replied, his voice tight and angry. "Are you okay here? I'm going to talk to Dad and get to the bottom of this. After that, let's go to the town clinic. Then we'll call Marcella and let her know what happened."

"Can we go to the coroner's office instead of the clinic? I'd rather have Grady and Reggie stitch us up there. I feel like the clinic's going to be super busy," Sophie suggested, nodding towards a couple of Mythicals that were nursing injuries.

Mac looked expectantly at Grady, who shrugged. "If you guys don't mind work that's not plastic-surgery worthy, I don't mind."

"That's fine with me. Reggie's stitched me up before," Sophie said, thinking of the time she accidentally cut her hand in the lunchroom when a knife slipped while cutting up an apple.

"Me neither. My hair will cover this scar," Ruby assured them, pointing at the still-bleeding cut on her scalp.

"Okay. I'll be right back, and then we'll go," Mac replied, getting up and stalking over to Carson.

Sophie watched as he talked to his dad. When Carson looked over at them in concern, she gave him what she hoped was a reassuring finger wave. Both men turned, heading to the group, heads close together in deep discussion.

With a chuffing grunt, a grizzly bear approached Grady, bumping him with its snout. Still kneeling at Fitz's feet, Grady turned and rubbed his forehead against the bear's. The creature had to be almost as tall as Sophie, standing on its four feet. She couldn't imagine how big and scary the bear would be if it raised itself on its hind legs. It had claws longer than Sophie's fingers and a hump across its shoulders that spoke of brute strength. There was blood on those claws, making Sophie vividly imagine exactly how the bear had used them.

"Do you have any injuries, Pam?" Grady asked, rubbing his fingers over one of the bear's cute round ears.

The bear made a huffing grunt that spoke of indignation, making him chuckle. With a final nuzzle, the bear turned and ambled back towards the beach.

"Wait…" Sophie said slowly. "Like sweet, friendly Pam from the bakery? Always-gives-me-a-free-scoop-of-ice-cream-on-my-pie Pam?"

Grady gave Sophie a look like she was a particularly dimwitted individual.

"Sorry, sometimes it's still a shock," she said with a shrug.

"I forget you humans aren't used to this," Grady reassured her, giving her a wink.

"Why didn't she say hi?" Ruby asked, her face a mixture of puzzled and indignant.

"I think she's self conscious about how deep her voice is in her bear form," Grady explained.

Sophie looked around, gazing at all the townspeople helping Carson clean up the mess left from the fight.

"They saved us. We would've died. I can't believe the whole town fought for us," Sophie whispered to herself, but Grady overheard and gave her hand a squeeze.

"Of course, they came. This town takes care of its own. I'm just glad they got here in time," he said.

Carson finished talking to a couple of kelpies before striding over. He knelt before Sophie and Ruby, checking them over like a worried dad. "Are you guys alright?" he asked.

"We're fine. They can't get rid of us that easily," Ruby boasted to him with a giggle.

Carson gave Sophie an intense look, so she held up her injured arm to show him. "I'm okay. It's just a scratch." Mac scoffed, letting his dad know that she was underplaying her injury.

"We're about to head to town and get the girls stitched up," Mac warned his dad. "You need any help before we head out?"

"Nah, I've got this well in hand. Now, as for how this happened... That's a different story. I will find out how these wolves got into my town and attacked you guys. And when I find out who is responsible, I'm going to make them wish they'd never been born. Someone had to have tipped them off. And no one arrives in this town without some busybody seeing and spreading gossip about it. Which means someone saw them arrive and didn't warn me. I'm not going to stop until I find it out."

"Do you need me to stay back and help?" Mac offered, looking like he hoped his dad would say no.

"No, I'd feel better if you were there to keep an eye on everyone. Keep 'em safe. All we've left to do here is make sure no one escaped, clean up the bodies, and investigate how this happened. I'm going to see if we can track where the wolf pack came through the forest. They must have vehicles hidden somewhere around here. They didn't run all the way from San Francisco. And if someone local was housing them, I will find out. You kids be careful, okay?"

Carson got up and headed back towards the beach, calling for Jameson.

"Let's get going so we can get you guys stitched up. I'm going to call Marcella on the drive," Mac said, carefully pulling Sophie to her feet. Fitz refused to be carried, so Grady and Ace helped him make his way to the cars, propping a shoulder under each armpit.

As the sun slowly rose over the horizon, the group hobbled their slow way to the field where they'd left their cars.

CHAPTER 17

$\mathcal{M}$ ac dialed Marcella's number almost as soon as he started the car. Marcella was furious that the wolf pack had attacked the sisters. It sounded like she was ready to kick ass and take names on Sophie and Ruby's behalf. Her outrage made Sophie feel infinitely better.

"I have no idea how Antonio could have found out about your whereabouts," Marcella said, her voice a razor's edge. "No one except myself, Chief Dunham, and Detective Turner have any idea you are in Cascadia. I'm going to bring Dunham and Turner in to see if there is any possibility that they leaked the information. However, I would be shocked if it was them. They are both very loyal to the Conclave, and I've found them to be men of the highest integrity. As soon as we hang up, I'm going to issue the order to lock down the Sunset District pack – what is left of them, that is – and have the remaining pack members put under temporary house arrest. Until we can place them in a new pack or put a new alpha in place, they are going to be under constant supervision by my people. I promise this is the last time you're going to have problems from them," Marcella reassured them over speaker phone.

"That guy Ziad also saw us here. Although we told him we were here as tourists," Sophie mentioned, remembering the smug Conclave representative.

"I would be surprised if Ziad had any interaction with the wolf shifters, but I'll make sure to check," Marcella replied.

"Any news on Boudreaux?" Mac asked.

"We know he landed in Atlanta, but we don't know if he's still there or what's he doing. It's certainly not on Conclave business – I double-checked to ensure there weren't any sanctioned operations. I also contacted the New Orleans Conclave, and they said he's not working for them on any assignments. Same for the Savannah Conclave."

"Do you trust them?"

"About this? Yes."

"Do you know if Bramwell and Boudreaux knew each other?" Sophie asked from the passenger seat, thinking of the Fae that had already caused her so much trouble. "Did they ever work together? Someone here in Murias said they saw him with an older man with a gray beard in a robe several times. It's probably a long shot, but I thought it was possible."

"Hmm. I'm not sure. I'll check. We've been unable to find a trace of Bramwell, so it would be good to know if he ever spent time in Cascadia," Marcella replied.

"Can Larry do a tracing spell on Boudreaux to see if he can locate him? My dad said that his hotel room was wiped clean of even a hair," Mac asked.

Marcella made a noise of doubt. "We can try. I'll see if the New Orleans Conclave will let us have something personal of Boudreaux's to do the trace. Even if they say yes, it will take time to get his personal effects sent to our office."

After promising to uncover how the wolf pack found them one final time, Marcella ended the call.

"Let's call Larry," Ruby suggested into the sudden quiet of the vehicle, quickly dialing his number on her phone and held the device up for everyone to listen.

The phone rang twice before Larry answered, his voice sleepy and warm, "Hey, sweetheart. You're up early. I didn't think you'd be calling until later."

Sophie turned to stare incredulously at her sister. Ruby's face flamed tomato red as she quickly let Larry know he was on speakerphone with Mac and Sophie listening in. Larry started to stutter an excuse, but Mac cut him off.

"Don't care what's happening between two consenting adults. And I don't want to know. Ever. However, we've had a situation here in Murias."

"Is he always so bossy?" Ruby stage whispered to Sophie, leaning forward and sticking her head between the car's front seats.

"It's part of his charm," Sophie replied, giving Mac a sugary-sweet smile. He looked like he was counting to ten in his head.

They caught Larry up on everything that had happened in Murias since they'd arrived. There was a moment of stunned silence before Larry promised to see what he could find out.

"Boudreaux has done work for the Conclave before. Have you ever worked with him?" Mac asked.

"Not really. I've heard that he's brilliant, but he's the type of warlock who will work for anyone given the right price. Not exactly the ethical type, if you know what I mean. I'm not totally surprised to hear that he was wrapped up in something corrupt. Plus, some of my spells are proprietary, and I didn't trust him not to steal my work, so I avoided him."

"Do you know if he knew Bramwell?"

"I have no idea. Sorry."

Ruby took him off speakerphone and was in the backseat having a giggling, flirty conversation with him. Sophie briefly considered plugging her ears with her fingers and humming loudly to block out the sound of her sister cooing at Larry the

Warlock. Mac gave her a commiserating look before turning the radio to an oldies station and turning up the volume.

They were pulling into the coroner's parking lot by the time Ruby was done talking to Larry. Sophie practically leaped out of the car to escape, pretending she was running for her life.

"You two are not funny," Ruby complained when she got out of the car.

"I'm not trying to be funny," Sophie said. "I don't want to listen to my sister trying to flirt. Gross."

"As if I don't have to listen to you two flirt all the time."

"What?! We do not flirt," Sophie said in outrage.

"Oh really? *You're such a dickhead, Mac,*" Ruby said in a high-pitched voice, making a kissy face. "*You're such a pain in the ass, hellraiser. C'mere and give me a kiss,*" Ruby continued in a deep voice, puffing up her chest, trying to look manly.

Sophie's mouth dropped open, but she couldn't think of a clever response. "I do not sound like that," she finally sputtered. She turned to Mac to get him to back her up, but he was too busy laughing his ass off.

"Ugh, you both suck," Sophie complained before stomping into the coroner's office, leaving them behind.

Sophie saw Ace, Fitz, and Amira had found a sofa in the tiny lobby and were sprawled in it. Amira's head rested on Ace's shoulder, and she looked almost asleep. Someone had managed to find a stool so Fitz could elevate his sprained ankle.

"Everyone okay?" Sophie whispered.

"Yeah, we're good. Reggie said to head on in, and he'd get you fixed up in no time," Ace murmured quietly, trying not to wake Amira.

"You guys don't have to wait here for us. I could get Mac to drive you to your hotel," Sophie offered.

"Nah, go get stitched up, and we'll all head back together. The Odd Ones stick together," Fitz replied with a sweet grin. "Maybe we could all get some breakfast when you're done?"

Feeling overwhelmed with gratitude, Sophie walked over and gave Fitz a kiss on his forehead. "Thanks, Fitz."

She found Reggie and Grady in the autopsy room, setting up a rolling tray with medical equipment. Sophie took one look at the long, curved needle she knew would be going into her skin momentarily and almost backed out of the room and ran for it.

She begrudgingly took a seat as Reggie rolled the cart over to her. When Ruby joined them, Grady had her sit in a chair a few feet away. Mac leaned against the door jamb, watching over everyone.

"Sorry, Ruby, but I have to shave a small area behind your ear. I'll make it as small as possible, and the rest of your hair should hide the spot," Grady apologized.

"That's okay. It'll grow back," Ruby replied in her usual chipper way.

Reggie cleaned the wound on Sophie's arm, then, thankfully, numbed the area. She determinedly looked away from her arm as he started to stitch her up. The stitches didn't hurt, but she could still feel the tugging of the needle as it pulled through her skin. It made her hiss in discomfort.

Turning to Mac, she commanded, "Talk to me. I need a distraction."

He started telling her about a funny arrest he made a few months ago when Grady made a slight noise of surprise. Sophie turned to look at him to see if there was a problem.

"Wow, Ruby. I didn't think you were the skull tattoo type. How very punk rock of you," Grady said, a teasing lilt to his voice.

"Yeah, right," Ruby guffawed. "I don't have any tattoos. You're funny, Grady."

Grady paused in his shaving of Ruby's skull, bewilderment painted across his face. Leaning closer to the back of Ruby's scalp, he tilted her head and started combing through her hair with his fingers.

"Uh, Ruby... I don't know if you're teasing me or not, but you absolutely have a tattoo on your head."

"I do not," Ruby argued loudly, looking angry as she pulled away from Grady to give him an incredulous stare. "This isn't funny anymore. I'd remember if I had a tattoo *on my head.*"

Ace appeared next to Mac in the doorway. "I heard yelling. Is everything okay?"

Mac leaned in and whispered something into Ace's ear. His eyes got comically weird, then he turned on his heel and headed back to the lobby. A moment later and he reappeared with Fitz and Amira in tow.

"Let me see," Sophie interrupted, trying to get up and walk over to her sister, but Reggie tugged her back down.

"I'm almost done," Reggie warned her. Once he finished tying off the final stitch, she leaped out of her chair and rushed to Ruby's side. Mac was already standing with Grady, both staring at her sister's head. Mac had a strange look on his face.

Grady showed Sophie the area he'd shaved, which revealed a portion of a black circle with a curlicue pattern inside it before disappearing into Ruby's black hair. Sophie gave Grady a silent questioning look, but he looked as confused as she felt. There was no question that she was looking at part of a tattoo, the majority of which was hidden by Ruby's hair.

Sophie reached out, using her hands to try and part her sister's hair. It was hard to tell how big the tattoo was, but it looked like it was at least the size of a golf ball.

"Uh, Ruby," Sophie said. "You definitely have a tattoo on your skull."

"Show me," Ruby demanded, panic and confusion flooding her voice.

"I'll take a picture," Sophie offered. Pulling out her phone, she took the photo and silently handed Ruby the device.

Ruby stared silently for a moment before looking up from the phone, her eyes lost and freaked out. "I don't understand."

"I don't either, but I think we need to see the whole thing. Ruby, can we shave the rest? I promise I'll only shave just enough to reveal the tattoo," Grady promised.

She agreed in a small voice.

Sophie backed up to give Grady room to shave the side of Ruby's head. She shared a concerned look with Reggie. Theories whirled through her mind, one tumbling over another. Could Ruby have been drugged, and someone put a tattoo on her? Who would do something like that? And more importantly, *why* would someone do that? Ruby seemed a bit crazy sometimes; could she have done this to herself and somehow forgotten or blocked it out? Nothing made sense.

A pit of dread opened in Sophie's gut. It didn't matter how Ruby managed to get a tattoo without knowing. This meant bad news. Really bad news. She was sure of it.

Grady finished shaving the section of Ruby's head and stood back, exchanging worried looks with Reggie and Mac.

"No one is saying anything. Why is no one saying anything? How bad is it?" Ruby said, panic making her voice loud and high-pitched.

Sophie pushed Mac aside so she could get a look at this tattoo that had everyone so concerned. She stared at the black ink of the tattoo in silence. It was a black circle about the size of a tangerine. A strange curving language, the symbols unfamiliar, ran along the inside of the ring. The inked lines of the words were neat and precise. Inside the circle was an image of a crown sitting on top of a pile of coins. Above the crown perched a bird and a squirrel. Despite the tattoo's small size, the animals' details were intricate and perfectly clear. Sophie took another picture for Ruby.

Ruby didn't say anything as she stared at Sophie's phone, but her shoulders rose and fell rapidly with gasping breaths. Sophie was worried that her sister was about to hyperventilate or have a panic attack, both of which Sophie thought were valid reactions to discovering having a tattoo that she was unaware of.

"That looks like a sigil tattoo," Sophie said slowly, looking at Mac for confirmation.

"Yeah, it does."

Sophie looked back at the tattoo. It was beautiful, done in crisp black lines; the artistry and craftsmanship were outstanding.

"But why would Ruby get a sigil tattoo? They don't work on humans."

"Soph," Mac started to say, but the words died on his lips. He gave her a helpless look that she couldn't interpret.

"What is a sigil tattoo?" Ruby interrupted. "Is it bad? It sounds bad."

"No, it's not bad," Sophie reassured her. "It's just a tattoo specifically for Mythicals. You need to have magic for the tattoo to work. Do you remember my friend Burg? The ogre? He has a tattoo that when he activates it, makes him look human. Otherwise, he is a giant ogre and couldn't live safely in this world. He says a special phrase, allowing him to appear completely human. Reggie has one that improves his eyesight. They don't work on humans like us because you must have magic to activate the tattoo. So, it's just a regular tattoo on you."

"Okay, but I *have* magic. I get those visions. Isn't that magic?" Ruby asked.

"But you're human, so it shouldn't work. Right?" Sophie asked, looking at each of her friends.

Mac exchanged a long look with Reggie and Grady before pulling Sophie to face him.

"Soph," Mac said, his words hesitant. Grabbing her hands in his, he rubbed soothing circles across her knuckles. "I think we need to consider the possibility that Ruby isn't human. That the sigil tattoo was put there to make her *appear* completely human.

And, if Ruby isn't human… Then that means you might not be either."

"No, that's not possible," Sophie said, incredulous. "How would I not know something like that? I *feel* human."

"I don't know. But… I promise you, we're gonna figure this out," he replied. He bit his lip, looking worried. "I think we need to check to see if you have a tattoo on your head as well."

"I almost don't want to know," Sophie confided in him, giving him a weak smile. Pushing out a deep breath, she turned, presenting Mac with the back of her head.

He tilted her head forward and started combing his fingers through her hair. It would have felt good if she hadn't been so freaked out. Sophie was concentrating so hard on his movements that she felt the moment that his fingers stalled and flexed against her scalp.

"You found one," she declared, knowing deep down that it was true.

"Yeah, it looks like the same design too," Mac confirmed. He turned her around and pulled her into his arms. "I'm sorry, Soph. I know you didn't want this," he whispered in her ear.

"I need… I need to sit down."

Mac led her to a chair, where she collapsed and dropped her head towards her knees, curling over in a protective ball.

Kneeling in front of her, Mac chafed her trembling hands. Sophie took a few minutes to calm down before sitting up and rolling her stiff shoulders. She still felt hollow and vaguely nauseous, but a meltdown wouldn't help anybody, even if it would feel good for a minute. The desire to throw a tantrum was strong. It would've felt amazing to kick over the medical tray or throw a computer monitor, but she wasn't going to put on a display. Sometimes being an adult sucked. When would the bullshit finally stop?

"Okay. Okay," Sophie repeated, rubbing her temples. "What do we do now?"

Mac pulled up a chair, sitting in front of her. "Now we try to figure out who put this tattoo on you and when it happened. I'm going to ask you some questions. Are you up for it? It's okay if you're not, because we don't need to do this now. There's no rush. Whatever we find out doesn't change anything. It doesn't change who you are or how I feel about you. Okay?"

"No. Let's do this now. I need to know."

"I'm going to ask both of you some questions, just to see if we can find any patterns or similar memories," Mac suggested. "Anything that can help us figure out what happened. I assume neither of you has any memory of getting that tattoo…."

Sophie exchanged a wary look with Ruby before they both shook their heads. Sophie veered her mind away from examining the thought that someone had done this to her. It made heat build behind her eyes if she dwelled on it for any length of time. It felt like a violation.

"Did either of your parents ever show any sign of magic? Even something small?" Mac asked. Sophie started to shake her head, but Mac held up a quelling hand. "Really think about it, Sophie. Was there ever anything strange about them? Anything at all? Or maybe another family member? A regular visitor when you were a kid that was different?"

"My parents were normal," Sophie asserted. "If they had any sort of magic, they never *ever* showed it. And I don't really know any of my other relatives. They weren't in our lives. There weren't any strange family friends or mysterious strangers hanging around when I was a kid."

"You didn't have any contact with family members like aunts, uncles, cousins, or grandparents?"

"Not really. I mean, I know I have some, but neither of my parents was close to their family as far as I know. We never spent any time with them. I don't have any memory of them."

"What about you, Ruby?" Mac asked.

"Uh, no, it was just my parents and me. They didn't have

siblings, and I believe my grandparents were gone before I was born," Ruby said slowly. "My parents were boringly normal, too. I had a completely unremarkable childhood."

Sophie and Ruby exchanged a concerned look.

"So, I'm probably adopted, right?" Ruby asked.

Sophie suddenly laughed out loud, a tinge of hysteria in her voice. "My god, what if we really are long-lost royalty?"

Ruby reached over and grabbed one of Sophie's hands in hers, giving it a squeeze. "We'd look amazing in tiaras." Sophie and Ruby dissolved into giggles. The laughter slowly died off, but Sophie felt a little better.

"Well, we've always known at least one of you had to be adopted. Maybe both of you were. Who knows, though? This whole thing is strange," Mac answered with a shrug.

"Do you think my parents knew about this?" Sophie asked, pointing at her head.

"I have no idea. Did they ever treat you like you were... different? Do you think *they* knew about the tattoo? Did they ever seem worried for your safety? Or were they overly concerned about strangers? Was there anything – anything at all – that makes you think they knew that you were different?"

"I don't think so," Sophie responded, her words slow and hesitant, processing all of Mac's questions.

When Mac asked the same questions of Ruby, she reiterated that she had a normal childhood.

"Well, either they adopted a baby without knowing about your powers or the sigil tattoo, or they knew, and you were given to them for a reason," Reggie theorized. "Whether to hide you or protect you or... who knows? I don't think we should try to guess because we just don't have enough information yet."

"Did you meet any strange people when you were teenagers? Or any time since? Any periods of time that you can't account for?" Mac asked. "Did anyone new suddenly appear in your life after your parents died?"

"No," Sophie said. "My parents died in a car crash shortly after I moved to San Francisco."

"How old were you when that happened?"

"I was twenty-two."

"Me too!" Ruby exclaimed.

"Hold up," Sophie replied, turning in her seat to face Ruby. "You were around twenty-two when your parents died? How did your parents die?"

"Also a car accident. They were killed by a drunk driver."

"Okay, the driver wasn't drunk in my case. It was just someone who ran a red light. But what are the odds?" Sophie asked, her voice rising and wavering. "What are the odds that both of our parents died in car wrecks in the same year?"

Sophie stood up from her chair, no longer able to sit still. Pacing around the room, biting her thumb nail, she tried to get her thoughts in order.

"Do you think that someone killed our parents?" Ruby said in a subdued voice.

"Let's not make any assumptions," Mac reiterated. "Marcella has someone looking into your pasts, and they haven't found anything unusual yet. But I think I'm going to start looking into your histories myself. Let's see what I can uncover before we jump to any conclusions. We can't rule out that it's just coincidence, even if it seems unlikely."

Sophie stopped her pacing and looked at all her friends. "Speaking of Marcella... Should we tell her about the tattoos?"

Everyone started arguing over whether to tell the head of the Conclave or keep it a secret. Reggie and Fitz were arguing to tell Marcella; Ace, Amira, and Grady were arguing against it. Mac, Ruby, and Sophie were silent, just watching the group volley pros and cons back and forth.

A stress headache started wrapping its fingers around Sophie's temples and squeezing just as the jingle of the bell on the coroner's front door silenced everyone.

"You guys here? I saw your rental was still out front, Mac. I have some news," a familiar voice called out from the lobby.

"Dad!" Mac yelled back. "Come on back here. We have some news too. And we could use your advice."

Mac looked at Sophie and Ruby. "Are you okay sharing this with my dad?"

"Of course," Sophie replied, which Ruby echoed.

Carson strolled into the autopsy room, looking around at everyone assembled around the room. His eyebrows rose at the looks of tension and concern on the group's face.

"You need some advice from dear old dad?" he asked. His teasing pulled a reluctant smile to Sophie's face, which he returned.

The smile quickly fell from Carson's face as they explained about the discovery of the sigil tattoos.

"Can I see them?" he asked, eyes blazing with intensity. Ruby got up from her chair and turned so he could see the shaved area. He stared intently for a minute before asking Sophie if he could look at hers as well.

It filled Sophie with a little smidge of relief that the tattoos bothered everyone else as much as it did her. It made her feel like she wasn't overreacting.

Carson made a low humming noise as he parted Sophie's hair and looked at the tattoo.

"I wish I knew what this language was. If we knew, it wouldn't be difficult to reveal your true form," Carson suggested.

"True form?" Sophie repeated, the realization hitting her like a tsunami. "Oh god, what if I'm a monster? What if I'm hideous?"

"You're not going to be hideous," Mac replied, giving Sophie an indulgent look that she wanted to slap off his face.

"You don't know that. I could be something disgusting. Something with slime."

"Here's something I don't understand," Ruby said, interrupting Sophie's meltdown. "Sophie said you have to say a phrase to activate the sigil tattoo... How do you know what to say? Is it always the same phrase?"

"Typically, the phrase is included in the tattoo," Carson explained. "It can be in any language. It will only work if the person who has the tattoo says the phrase. So, for example, if I said the phrase, it wouldn't have any effect on you. You have to be the one to say it. Whatever that sentence inside the sigil is, it is probably the phrase that will unlock your form."

"Well, that's easy," Ruby concluded. "Let's just say the phrase and find out what we are."

Carson took another look at Ruby's tattoo and shook his head. "But we don't know what language that is. It doesn't look like anything I've ever seen before. But I'm not exactly an expert on linguistics or sigil tattoos."

Sophie couldn't decide if she was relieved or not to have a reprieve from finding out what the tattoo was hiding.

"You know who we could go ask? Blathmac," Carson announced.

The name sounded familiar to Sophie, but she couldn't remember where she'd heard it.

Grady made a noise of agreement, so when Sophie looked at him, he explained, "He owns the Fae tattoo parlor on Abernethy. He should be home from the festival by now. He has an apartment above his studio."

"Okay. Let's go see Blathmac," Sophie agreed.

"Wait. What was your news, Dad?" Mac asked.

"Oh, yeah. I found out how the wolf pack knew you were all here. Deputy Jameson has a cousin in the Sunset District pack."

Jameson? But she seemed so nice, Sophie thought with dismay.

When Mac started to growl, Carson held up a hand. "She didn't know. She was talking to her cousin and mentioned that my son was in town for the festival – which was your official cover story. She had no idea that Antonio was after Sophie and Ruby. It appears that the alpha overheard the conversation and put two and two together and figured you guys were hiding out here. From what we can gather, he brought a large portion of the pack and was waiting for an opportunity to get you alone. When you left the beach party, that's when they attacked. I don't think they expected the town to come to your defense. When Jameson found out it was her fault that Antonio found you and attacked, she felt truly terrible."

At the look of anger on Mac's face, Sophie tugged on his elbow until he looked at her. "It's not Jameson's fault. How could she have known that Antonio was looking for us? The only person who deserves any blame is Antonio."

CHAPTER 18

*C*arson offered to drive, so Mac, Ruby, and Sophie piled into his car. Everyone else was in Reggie's car, right behind them. Sophie had considered asking them not to come, but she knew they would just worry about her. Plus, she might need their support if she found out she was something horrible, like a swamp monster or a creature with tentacles.

Sophie was silent during the car ride while Mac continued his questioning of Ruby's past.

"Before you moved to San Francisco, you lived in Los Angeles, right? And worked at Disneyland as a princess? Tell me about the first day on the job. Do you remember it well?"

"Yes, I remember it like it was yesterday. I was so scared that I would mess it all up, but as soon as I met my first visitor, it all clicked. This little girl lit up when she saw me in my Snow White costume. It was awesome."

"Any blank spots in your memory during that time?" When Ruby shook her head, he continued, "What about the job before that one?"

"Oh, I worked with this rinky-dink traveling acrobatics

troupe for a couple of years. We did small shows and carnivals. It was fun, but the money stank. Although I enjoyed the traveling."

"Did you have a lot of friends in the troupe?"

"Not really. They were nice enough, but I didn't mesh well with them. They were an existing group when I joined. They had a clique, and I was brand new, so I never found my place there. And I think they thought I was weird. I was friends with the lady who ran the troupe, though; she kind of watched over me. Her name was Moreen."

"Let's go over all your jobs, okay? Just for a few minutes."

"But why? How does this help us figure out how I got the tattoo?"

"Just trust me, okay? I'm just trying to piece it all together. I'm a trained detective after all," Mac said with a wink, making Ruby snort and relax a little. "Tell me the job that you had before the acrobatics troupe."

"There's not much to tell. It was boring, and I didn't work there for long. It gives me a headache to think about that job. It was at a mall retail store – just wasn't for me."

"Okay. Let's switch gears," Mac suggested. "Did you go to college?"

"No."

"How was high school? Were you popular?"

"It was fine. It was high school. I mean, I guess I was popular," Ruby said with a shrug. "I don't get what this has to do with the tattoo."

Mac waved away Ruby's concern and kept asking questions. "Were you in any sports in school? Were you a cheerleader?"

Ruby shook her head.

"Anything unusual ever happen in high school? Anyone strange in your life at that time?"

"High school was high school. I was a perfectly normal teenager, and nothing weird happened. Does anyone have a good time in high school? We're all angsty, trying to find ourselves and rebelling against our parents."

"We're here," Carson announced, turning off Abernethy to a small lane behind the stores lining the street. "We're going to park behind his place because I don't want anyone to see us. Not until we decide what to do with the information we've learned today."

"Thanks, Dad. We appreciate it," Mac replied.

Reggie's car pulled up next to them, parking in the last spot behind the tattoo parlor.

The back of the building was a lot more dilapidated than the front. A small dumpster sat next to a jumble of broken equipment. It was quite different from the front of the shop, which was clean and quaint. It complemented the aesthetic of the small town, but the back was dingy and run down.

When Carson and Mac got out of the car, Sophie and Ruby scrambled out after them. Reggie rolled down his window and let Sophie know they'd wait in the car for the moment until they were needed.

Carson walked up to the back entrance, pushing open a screen door that sagged sadly on its frame. He pounded on the backdoor loudly. "Blathmac! Open up." Carson waited a minute before pounding on the door again. Sophie could hear muffled words coming from the other side of the door. "It's the sheriff. I just have some questions. I need your expertise on something."

A man with short, disheveled brown hair stuck his head out of the door, closing one eye and squinting at Carson. He looked like they'd just woke him up, and he wasn't happy about it.

"Sheriff, I've only been home from the festival for a couple of hours. Could we do this later after I've had a little more sleep?"

The man glanced from Carson to Mac and then to Sophie and Ruby. He started to look past them to the car with Reggie when he did a double-take and looked back at Sophie. As he stared, the color drained from his face. A look of horror and dread washed over his features. Without a word, he turned and ran, leaving the door open behind him.

Carson made a noise of surprise. He looked back at Sophie and then into the back of the tattoo parlor.

"What the hell? Where the fuck does he think he's going? He's in his boxers," Carson exclaimed before darting into the parlor after the escaping tattoo artist.

Mac turned to Reggie and yelled, "He's making a run for it! Cut him off out front." Then he turned and ran after his father into the dim interior of the shop.

With squealing tires, Reggie reversed out of his parking spot, speeding around the corner and out of sight.

Sophie glanced at Ruby, trying to figure out what had just happened. From inside the shop, the sounds of breaking glass and cursing broke Sophie out of her shocked stupor. She ran into the shop with Ruby right on her heels.

She skidded to a stop when she found Mac and Carson piled on top of Blathmac as he flailed and fought, trying to escape.

"Blathmac!" Carson yelled. "Calm yourself! You're not in trouble. We just have a few questions."

"Don't let them hurt me! I didn't have a choice. I was just doing my job," Blathmac babbled, looking at Sophie and Ruby where they were frozen just inside the main room of the tattoo parlor.

Mac looked at Blathmac and then back at Sophie. The look on Mac's face turned into something ferocious. He turned and pressed a forearm across Blathmac's throat. "What did you do to them? Did you hurt them?"

Blathmac made a wheezing sound of pain.

"Mac!" Carson yelled, yanking on Mac's shoulder. "Let him go. We need to question him. We'll get to the bottom of this."

Movement outside the large front window caught Sophie's attention. Her friends crowded against the glass, trying to see inside the shop. "I'll... um... I'll let them in," Sophie said, swallowing thickly.

As she headed to the front door, Mac yanked Blathmac off the floor and tossed him into one of the leather tattoo chairs, looming over him menacingly. Sophie unlocked the door and let everyone in before locking it again.

"What happened? Why'd he run?" Amira asked, staring at the terrified man Mac had shoved into the tattoo chair.

"I don't know, but he took one look at me and panicked. He looked at me like I was a ghost. Or he thought I was going to kill him or something," Sophie explained.

"Do you know him?" Ace asked, giving the man a suspicious look.

"No, I've never seen him before," Sophie replied. She turned and looked at Ruby with raised eyebrows.

"No, I don't know him either," Ruby replied, staring at the man. "But he seems to know us."

With a determined step, Ruby approached the man. Sophie was impressed with how bold and put-together she seemed. Sophie was busy just trying not to faint or throw up. Grabbing the tattoo stool, Ruby rolled it up and sat near the man's feet. She sat silently, staring at Blathmac as he got more and more worried. He kept glancing at Carson like he was hoping the sheriff would rescue him.

When he tried to heave himself out of the chair, Carson pulled out his gun and cocked it. "How long have we known each other, Blathmac? At least seven years, yeah? You know I keep my promises. So, here's a promise for you – if you try to get out of that chair again, I will shoot you. Somewhere tender, got it? We've got some questions, and you will answer every single one. Do you understand?"

When Blathmac nodded like a bobblehead doll, wobbly and unsteady, Mac grabbed another stool and rolled up next to Ruby. Carson leaned against the wall, surrounded by framed examples of tattoo art. His arms were crossed over his chest with his gun resting against a forearm.

"Do you know me? Have we met before?" Ruby asked. Sophie shuffled closer, pressing against Mac's back, needing the touch for moral support.

"I thought you were here for revenge," Blathmac replied, his words rushed and frantic.

"Revenge? For what?"

"Um... Because you're a shard, and I was the one who did the sigil tattoo? But that's not my fault. I was only doing my job."

Shard? What the hell is that?

Sophie exchanged confused looks with everyone else, but then she glanced at Carson. He had gone preternaturally still.

"Did he just call us a *shart*?" Ruby exclaimed, disgust in her voice.

"When?" Carson demanded, ignoring Ruby's question. He pushed away from the wall and stood over Blathmac. "When did this happen?"

"I'm not sure. Like maybe four years ago? Possibly five."

"And you tattooed both of them? Who were they with?"

"There were five of them, actually. And it was a guy named Bramwell. He's the one that brings them to me," Blathmac explained.

"*Five?*" Carson repeated incredulously, his voice overly loud.

"*Bramwell?*" Sophie and Ruby yelled at the same time as Carson.

Mac held up his hand to silence everyone. He turned to his father with an intense stare. "Dad. What's a shard?"

Carson looked back at the group, his face unsure. His gaze settled on Sophie, and he gave her an apologetic look. "I've only heard rumors. If a Fae is deemed too dangerous or has displeased Queen Maeve, she has a way to split that person into pieces, like clones, or mitosis. She breaks them into fragments called shards. It's supposed to divide that person's power, making each shard less dangerous and powerful. Then she ousts them from the Fae realm and dumps them here. But this..." Carson gave Blathmac a dark look. "Tattooing them. Making them believe that they are human. Erasing their memories. That's... You're lucky I don't just shoot you here and now."

"Hey," Blathmac replied, raising his hands in surrender. "I didn't know about any of that! I didn't know their memories were wiped. I didn't know that they thought they were human. I just put the tattoo on them that makes them appear human. The rest of that is the Conclave's doing. I'm just a contractor."

"The San Francisco Conclave?" Sophie asked. She'd trusted Marcella. And she shouldn't have. Sophie felt like a fool. She *knew* Marcella was using her for her abilities, but still thought she could trust Marcella to look out for her best interests. But Marcella was only looking out for herself. It still shocked Sophie to realize that Marcella knew who and what she was and said nothing. It made Sophie want to hunt her down and make her suffer.

Mac took one look at Sophie's face and gave her hand a reassuring squeeze. "Hey, we don't know that Marcella or even the Conclave was behind this. Remember, Bramwell had been working behind her back to subvert the entire organization for some time."

"Tell us everything. Right now," Carson demanded, his teeth bared in threat.

"Okay, okay." Blathmac licked his lips nervously, looking over the faces in the room. "So, every couple of years, Bramwell brings me shards to tattoo. He works for the Conclave – or so I thought – so I never questioned it. The Conclave's already in charge of placing any Mythical who arrives from the Fae realm, so why would I think twice? He always told me they were dangerous or under the Conclave's protection. I was just doing my job. Usually, when Bramwell would bring shards, it was only two individuals. But when he brought them—" Blathmac indicated Sophie and Ruby "—there were five of them. I'd never seen more than three – and *that* was only once. They were fucking scary." Blathmac pointed at the sisters again. "Bramwell had them under his thrall, so they were quiet and compliant. But you could feel their power. They felt like death. They scared the shit out of me. So, I tattooed them like usual to make them appear human and to repress their powers even more. Then he took them away to wherever they go when I'm done with them. That was it."

Ruby kept repeating, "I don't understand," in a small, confused voice.

But Sophie understood. How many times had she felt lost and broken and incomplete over the last few years? She understood perfectly. She'd never been whole. She was just a broken piece. A leftover fragment from when they broke the original, a shard of glass recovered from a shattered bowl. Just an un-whole thing. She'd only recently started to feel normal and right. She'd just thought that's how everyone felt.

She looked at Ruby, and a feeling of revulsion washed over her. Did that mean that they were the same person? She didn't want to be a Ruby. Until this week, she hadn't even liked her. Frankly, she didn't want a serial killer – *vigilante*, whatever – to be the other half of her soul. Shit, the other fifth of her soul.

I don't want to be the same as her. I want to be my own person, not a part of her. I'm not a copy.

Ruby gave Sophie a look that told her that she felt the same.

Sophie had to clench her fists and lock her jaw before she started screaming. It wasn't fair.

"Hold on," Reggie said suddenly. "If the sigil tattoos repress their powers, how are they still able to access them? Both have abilities that a regular human doesn't have."

"Their powers must just be leaking through. You don't know what they felt like before. I can't even sense them now, so you're just getting a mere echo of their power."

"That doesn't matter. I want to know what the phrase is that unlocks our powers," Ruby said.

"I don't know," Blathmac replied.

"What? How do you not know what our tattoos say?" Ruby demanded.

"Bramwell only provided the text, and I inked it onto your skin. I don't have any idea what it says. I think it's in an old Fae language. I asked about it once, and Bramwell said that only Fae royalty even speaks it anymore. I know the rest of the design is Queen Maeve's crest."

"Well, that's not very convenient," Ruby griped. But Sophie kind of thought it was. She wasn't ready to find out more about her powers. She was perfectly fine with them just as they were. She wanted to be an ostrich and bury her head in the sand. She didn't want to be scary. She didn't want to frighten people with just her presence.

"Bramwell must have gotten them all to say the phrase in order to activate the tattoo. Do you remember any of it?" Carson asked.

"He made me leave the room before he had them activate the spell. I wasn't allowed to hear it. Every shard he's brought in has been under a spell that made them do whatever he said. They're like zombies when he brings them in. You were docile as lambs," Blathmac sneered at Sophie and Ruby.

And yet I still scared you, asshole.

Blathmac's jab seemed to jolt Ruby out of her bewilderment and tossed her right into pissed off. She gave Sophie an incredulous look, saying "Can you believe the balls on this asshole?". She turned back to Blathmac and gave him a long, considering look. Sophie almost felt bad for the man. Almost.

Ruby made a low *hmm* noise and drew out a knife from wherever she had it hidden on her body. The move was so quick and practiced that it almost looked like the blade appeared from nowhere. Blathmac blanched when he spotted the weapon in

Ruby's hand. He watched, mesmerized, as Ruby ran a slow thumb along the blade's edge like she was testing its sharpness. With a flick of her wrist, she flipped the knife in her hand before nonchalantly using the blade tip to clean under her nails.

"Do you know how many men I've killed?" she asked, looking up and giving him her signature sweet grin. It was so at odds with the menace of the knife and her movements that it even gave Sophie a shiver.

Blathmac glanced around the room, looking for help, but all he saw in return were hardened faces. He looked back at Ruby and shook his head.

"Twelve. Oh, wait, thirteen. I almost forgot to add the druid I killed last week in the sheriff's office. Now, now. Don't look so worried. Every one of them deserved it, I promise." Blathmac nodded, trying to placate Ruby, who winked at him. "You said that we were scary. And even without all our powers, I promise you, it's still very true. So, I would suggest you not be so rude to us. You need to answer all our questions, or I'm going to make you very, *very* sorry."

"You said we felt like death," Sophie piped up, stepping closer. "What did you mean?"

Blathmac shrugged but then gave Ruby a worried look, so he rushed to answer. "You felt like what I imagine meeting the grim reaper would feel like. All the life was sucked out of the room when you entered it. You felt like a grave."

Damn it. Sophie regretted asking.

"How many other shards have you tattooed?" Carson asked.

"Um, I'm not sure. Maybe ten groups of them?"

"When did you tattoo your first shard? Was it only Bramwell that brought them to you? How did you first get contracted to do this work?" Carson started peppering Blathmac with questions, but Sophie tuned it all out.

Backing away from the group, she found an empty tattoo chair hidden in a walled-off private cubicle. Curling up in the reclined leather seat, Sophie tried to ignore the interrogation happening less than ten feet away.

Mac popped his head around the partition wall, giving her a worried look. "Are you up for some company?"

"Aren't you needed for that?" Sophie asked, pointing in the direction of her other friends.

"Nah. Dad's got it under control."

"Then, yes. I'd like some company."

Mac entered the cubicle and picked her up in an impressive display of shifter strength. Climbing into the chair, he set her in his lap, tucking her head under his chin.

"I'm sorry about all this, Sophie," he whispered. "I can't imagine what you're going through right now."

"It sucks, and I'm pissed. But it also explains so much. Until recently, I'd always felt different. Incomplete. And it explains why I always avoid talking, and even thinking, about my past. It's because I don't have one."

"Technically, you do have a past. It's just not the one you remember."

"How is that possible? Did Bramwell implant false memories?"

"I believe so. Or someone did it for him. I noticed that you and Ruby often say that thinking about an old job or talking about high school gives you a headache. Then you change the subject." Mac hesitated for a moment.

"What?" Sophie prompted.

"Do you remember when we arrived at the border of Cascadia? How the geas made you want to turn away? It's set up so that people instinctively avoid it. I suspect that someone laid a geas on both of you so that you avoid thinking about your past. Otherwise, you might have noticed that your memories are incomplete or fuzzy."

"Is there a way to remove it?"

"I don't know, but we're going to find out. But now that you know it's there, maybe it's like the geas around Cascadia. Once you're aware of its presence, you can push past it," Mac suggested.

Sophie picked at her cuticle, rolling her new reality around in her head, trying to find a way to accept the situation. "Well, I don't have a choice, do I?"

Mac and Sophie settled back, snuggling, letting the murmur of voices wash over them.

∽

"SORRY TO INTERRUPT YOU TWO, BUT I NEED TO TAKE BLATHMAC down to the station," Carson announced, jolting Sophie from where she was drowsing against Mac's chest.

Climbing out of his lap, Sophie looked around, feeling disheartened. She was just about at her limit for bullshit for one night.

"I should go with Dad," Mac murmured to Sophie. "I'm sure it's fine, but I don't know if Blathmac is dangerous. I'd like to make sure Dad has someone watching his back." Mac took one look at Sophie's face, and he must have seen the dread there. "You don't have to come with us. I'm sure you've had enough of this."

"Sophie, Ruby, would you guys like to come to breakfast with us?" Grady offered.

Sophie gave Mac a hopeful look. "Are you sure you don't need my help?"

"No way. I'm going to help Dad get Blathmac locked up, and I'll meet you at the diner. How's that sound?"

"That sounds perfect. Thank you."

Mac tilted her chin up and gave Sophie a soft, lingering kiss. "Are you gonna be okay?" he whispered, his eyes filled with worry.

At that moment, Sophie knew everything was going to be okay. She had the best boyfriend in the whole world. Looking into his ice blue eyes, Sophie realized she might be in love with Malcolm Volpes.

Mac would be there for whatever came their way – murder, lost memories, mayhem. She'd be able to face it all because he'd be there to back her up.

"Yeah, I think it's all going to be okay," Sophie replied, pulling him into a tight hug. She looked up at him and gave him a reassuring smile. "I'll see you at breakfast, okay?"

Running a thumb along her jawline, he gave Sophie a probing stare before returning her smile. "Alright, hellraiser, order me some pancakes and bacon. Extra bacon. I'll be there soon."

Carson pulled off his cowboy hat and fit it over Ruby's head. "We need to ensure you keep that tattoo hidden until your hair grows in," he explained, chucking Ruby under her chin. It was a little big on her, but it would do.

"Thanks, Carson!" Ruby exclaimed.

Sophie and Ruby watched as Carson and Mac tossed Blathmac into the backseat and drove off, heading towards the sheriff's office.

As a group, they walked around the building to the main drag. A few early morning pedestrians strolled past. Mostly the streets were empty, more so than usual, even at the early hour.

As they walked past a ghoul, Ruby tipped Carson's hat like an old-timey cowboy. "Howdy," she crowed, then started laughing at her own joke. Sophie started to get annoyed at her apparent good mood. What was there to be happy about? Ruby was toxically chipper, and Sophie didn't even want her to be her sister, much less a former piece of her.

Sophie glanced at Ruby, and something of her thoughts must've shown on her face because Ruby recoiled from her. Ruby quickly turned her face away from Sophie's gaze, but she could see her shoulders were pulled high and tight to her ears like she was expecting to be attacked.

Damn it. I'm such an asshole.

Sophie was just looking for an excuse to be angry, and Ruby was the most convenient target for her ire. Ruby was a happy-go-lucky kind of person, which was actually a good trait. Sophie was just a grump and a brat.

"Hey guys," Sophie called out. Everyone stopped and looked at her. "I need a minute. I think that Ruby and I need to talk." Sophie turned and gave Ruby an apologetic look. "Would that be alright? I think we need to have a chat."

Ruby gave her a long look before slowly nodding. "Yeah. I think that's a good idea."

Sophie looked back down the street and spotted the pub. "Do you want to see if the pub is open? I could use a shot of tequila like you wouldn't believe," she said, trying to lighten the mood.

"Make it vodka, and you've got a deal," Ruby teased, making Sophie sag in relief.

"Hey guys, we'll meet you at the diner, okay? Save us some seats."

"Are you sure?" Reggie asked, looking worried.

"Yes. We're going to get one quick drink, and we'll be right there," Sophie assured him.

The group turned and headed toward the diner as Ruby and Sophie watched them walk away, an awkward silence between them.

"Come on. Let's get that drink."

When they got to the pub, Sophie tugged on the front door, but it was locked.

"Damn it," she cursed under her breath. She gave the door another shake, just out of annoyance at being denied the drink she so desperately deserved.

Standing outside the pub doors, the sky suddenly opened and it started to rain.

Well, that just figures, Sophie thought.

"Oh hey, look! It's Cordelia," Ruby exclaimed, pointing over Sophie's shoulder. Turning, she spotted the older woman unlocking the front door of her shop. "I know it's not tequila," Ruby continued, "but maybe we could talk her into letting us come in and get one of her sodas. They're so good."

Sophie knew how much Ruby loved sweets, so she agreed to go to the candy store.

"Cordelia!" Ruby yelled, waving her hand in the air. Cordelia stopped, looking around to see who was calling her name. When she spotted Ruby and Sophie, she waved back.

Sophie followed as Ruby scurried over to the shop owner, ducking down as the rain began to pelt against them. Cordelia opened her door and stood inside it, waving them inside.

"Ruby, dear, I heard you and your sister were attacked by wolf shifters at the Hunter's Moon Festival last night. Are you both okay?" Cordelia asked, looking them over carefully once she got the door closed behind them, blocking the rainfall.

"We're fine. We were very fortunate that a bunch of people from town came to our rescue," Ruby responded. "I know you don't open for a little bit, but do you think Sophie and I could come in? We really need someplace quiet to talk, and you know how much I love your candy. After last night, I could really use something sweet." Ruby gave Cordelia her purest, most innocent look. "I promise we won't make a mess."

"Oh, alright," Cordelia responded, giving Ruby an indulgent look. Sophie wanted to roll her eyes but managed to keep a straight face as the shop owner ushered them further inside.

They took a table near the front door, out of the way from where Cordelia worked behind the counter.

Sophie tapped her fingers against the tabletop, trying to figure out what she wanted to say. "I'm sorry about my attitude earlier. I'm just freaked out about the whole situation. I was just starting to get comfortable with the whole long-lost sister thing. So, to find out that we're just shards. It's just…"

"Right?" Ruby said when Sophie's words trailed off. "And

we're just sooo freaking different. How can we be parts of a single whole when we're nothing like one another? It's creepy."

Sophie was so relieved that Ruby wasn't as unbothered as she seemed about their new status as shards that she felt like an enormous weight had lifted from her shoulders. "What do we do now?"

"I don't know. What can we do?" Ruby said with a shrug.

"I mean about us. What does being a shard mean regarding us and our relationship?"

"Well... I think I'd like to just keep going as we are. I'd be okay being your sister, you know? Anything else doesn't feel right."

"Yes, I'd like that. I don't want us to be weird about it," Sophie thought about it for a moment more. "Yeah. I like having you as my sister."

Ruby gave Sophie a happy grin, already accepting and okay with everything that had happened. Sophie would take longer to get to a place of full acceptance, but she could see it all working out.

"I can't wait to get out of this town," Sophie announced.

"Really? I love it here."

"There's not really any reason for us to stay any longer. I want to get back to my apartment and my life in San Francisco. I can't wait to leave."

Cordelia happened to be carrying a box walking past them when Sophie said that. "Oh, are you guys leaving soon, now that the festival is over?"

Sophie didn't think she'd ever get used to how perfectly okay some people in Murias were about butting their noses into something that wasn't their business. She was comfortable laying heavy odds that everyone in Murias would know she wanted to leave town before the hour was up.

She turned in her seat and gave Cordelia a polite smile. "Yes, now that the festival is over, it's time for us to return to the city.

What an amazing time we've had, though. Murias really is such a lovely town."

"Oh, aren't you sweet? And here I'd heard that Ruby was the friendly one," Cordelia tittered at Sophie.

Only through the strength of sheer will did Sophie refrain from telling Cordelia where to shove it.

Look at me. Acting like a reasonable adult, she thought, not entirely joking.

She must not have been entirely successful in keeping her thoughts from showing on her face because Ruby was biting her lips to keep in her laughter.

A look of irritation passed over Cordelia's face so quickly that Sophie almost thought she might have imagined it. It was quickly replaced with an indulgent grandmother's sweet, plump-cheeked smile. "Well, if you're leaving Murias, I insist on treating you to my world-famous root beer float. I make the root beer myself."

When Sophie tried to offer to pay for it, Cordelia refused. "I won't hear of it. Not after the night you two have had. I want to make sure you have nothing but pleasant memories of Murias."

Fat chance, Sophie thought but plastered a smile of thanks on her face.

A few minutes later, Cordelia hustled out from behind the counter, a gorgeous root beer float in each hand. She placed one in front of each sister with a flourish.

"Go on," she prompted. "I know you've never had a root beer as good as mine."

She watched with an expectant look, so Sophie picked up her glass, clinked it against Ruby's, and took a big gulp.

Sophie had to admit that it was amazing. The root beer was tangy and biting, the ice cream creamy and sweet. It was delicious, and Sophie made sure to tell Cordelia so.

She took another big gulp, licking ice cream off her upper lip. It wasn't a shot of tequila, but somehow it soothed her nerves just the same. She exchanged a goofy grin with Ruby, who appeared to enjoy her float as much as Sophie. All the muscles in her shoulders finally started to release their tension. Taking another sip of her drink, Sophie tried to set it back on the table and almost missed.

"Watch out, dear," Cordelia said, helping Sophie set the glass on the table.

Sophie giggled, finding the fact that she was so worn out that she almost spilled her drink funny as hell. She looked at Ruby to make a joke about it, but her sister slid out of focus. Her head wobbling, and realization dawning, she turned to look at Cordelia.

"What did you do to us?" Sophie slurred.

Ruby slipped out of her chair and crashed onto the ground.

Sophie tried to surge up and attack Cordelia, but her legs buckled underneath her.

"The Conclave knows we're here," Sophie threatened, barely able to get the words out.

"Who do you think I work for, child?" was the last thing Sophie heard before the darkness swallowed her whole.

CHAPTER 19

*C*onsciousness returned to Sophie in small increments. At first, she was only vaguely aware of light. She wasn't able to keep her eyes open; everything was bleary and confusing. Despite her best efforts, her eyes kept sliding closed. In a deep part of herself, she knew something was wrong but couldn't seem to muster up the ability to think or move.

An indeterminable amount of time later, Sophie's eyes popped open. She was lying on her back on a hard, chilly surface. The first thing she saw was a familiar table displaying beakers, microscopes, and other equipment that looked like it belonged in a scientific laboratory.

With a gasp, she turned her head to take in the rest of the room. She immediately recognized the basement with its damp, concrete walls. This was the same room where Michael, the man found dead in the ocean, had met his end. When she tried to get up, Sophie realized she was tied down to the same metal table as Michael had been.

"Shit. Shit. Shit," Sophie chanted, her breath panting and gasping. Looking to her right, she saw Ruby strapped down to a metal table identical to hers.

"Ruby," she called, trying to keep her voice low.

Ruby groaned on the table next to her but otherwise remained unconscious.

"Ruby," she said again, a little louder. Shaking the table, she yanked her arms as hard as she could. The ropes bit into her wrists, but she didn't give a shit. She was not dying in this damn basement. She looked around the room to see if there was some way out. It was exactly the same as it had been in her vision, even down to the creepy cages lining the far corner. There was nothing within reach she could use to get out of her bindings.

She could still feel the knife sheath strapped to her leg, but it would do her no good unless she found a way to get a hand free.

"Sophie?" Ruby called out, her voice cracking with fear.

"Hey, I'm here," Sophie replied, looking away from her perusal of the room to stare at Ruby. Her eyes still looked glazed, but they were starting to clear and fill with fear. Sophie had never seen Ruby scared before. It drove home the seriousness of the situation like nothing else.

"What happened?" Ruby asked, looking around the room in a panic. Sophie could hear her gasping breaths as she tried to calm herself.

"That bitch Cordelia drugged us and brought us here. Ruby... I recognize this place from the death vision of that guy from the beach. This is where he died."

"Oh, shit."

Oh, shit was right.

"How did you not know that Cordelia was the killer?" Sophie asked, trying to keep the accusation out of her voice. "Didn't you touch her? You were at her shop practically every day."

"No. I never got a chance. She was always in the back, preparing for the pie contest. I touched all of her employees, but never her. And the time I got her out of the kitchen by pretending to have an allergy question, I couldn't get her to come out from behind the counter. I never got a chance to touch her. And once we found Boudreaux I stopped trying."

Ruby sounded so defensive that Sophie felt bad. "It's okay. You couldn't have known. It doesn't matter now anyhow. We need to get out of here before she comes back."

Ruby nodded and started pulling on the ropes tying her down. Sophie did the same.

The table rattled and groaned as Ruby yanked and flailed against her bindings, her breath labored as she struggled.

"What do we do?" Ruby pleaded, looking at Sophie with bleak eyes when the bindings didn't budge an inch.

"See if you can work the knots loose," Sophie replied, starting to twist her arms. The skin around her wrists was already beginning to burn, but she didn't care. If she needed to rub all the skin off her arms to escape, she would. "I just wish I could reach my knife."

Sophie felt her fingers along the table's lip, hoping to find a sharp edge somewhere. Her idea was to saw the rope back and forth across the edge to cut through.

Ruby paused in her struggle, giving Sophie an intense look. "Your knife is still in your leg sheath? Because I can feel that all my knives are gone. Cordelia must've missed your knife when she checked us over."

Biting her lip, Ruby gave a jolt on the table, throwing her body up, looking like an electrified fish. Sophie frowned in Ruby's direction. "What are you doing?"

"I'm trying to see if I can get this stupid table to move. If I can make my way down to your feet, maybe I can reach your knife."

Sophie was tied tightly to the table, spreadeagle, but she had enough maneuverability to wrap the tips of her fingers over the edge of the table.

"Let's do it. You try to shift your table down, and I'll go up. We'll see if we can get my knife to you. Deal?"

"Deal. I'm not dying for someone's bizarre science experiment. Let's do this."

Gripping the tabletop edge as tightly as possible, Sophie took a deep breath, she threw her body towards her head. The table made a terrible screeching noise but didn't move. Sophie stopped and held her breath, listening to see if she heard any movement from upstairs. Her ankles screamed in pain, and sweat gathered along her hairline and the small of her back. The screech was so loud that she feared someone would come to check on them. After a moment, when no one appeared, she decided to go all out.

Heaving, her body straining with exertion, Sophie threw her weight over and over again against her restraints. The ropes had tightened around her limbs from her struggles, making her toes start to go numb. The bindings had also dug deep into her flesh, and she could feel blood seeping from around them. But Sophie didn't care. None of it would matter in the end if she couldn't find a way to escape.

Finally, with a scream of a dying creature, the table jittered and shifted.

"Holy shit! It moved," Sophie exclaimed.

Ruby gave Sophie a look filled with fear and hope.

They both redoubled their efforts, fighting against their bindings. The breath sawed in and out of Sophie's lungs and her muscles burned as she repeatedly threw her body against the ropes holding her down. The tables made their slow way across the floor, inch by inch. Every tiny movement cost Sophie blood, sweat and pain as she tried to move her table.

Once Ruby had finally made her way even with Sophie's feet, they realized they were too far apart to reach one another.

"Okay, let's try to scoot closer," Sophie suggested.

Taking a deep, cleansing breath, Sophie willed herself to dig deeper. Then she started the process all over again, throwing her weight to the right instead. It was harder to get the tables to move laterally, but Sophie found if she rocked her body back and forth, she could build momentum to get the table to scuttle a little bit at a time.

A resounding boom rocked the building above them. The bare lightbulbs swayed above Sophie's head, swinging back and forth, casting strange shadows around the room.

"What the hell was that?" Ruby called out.

"I don't know, but let's not wait to find out. Keep going."

Sophie threw her body to the right, praying that Ruby could get a hold of her knife before Cordelia came looking for them. The table felt like it was about to tip over, so Sophie shifted all her weight to the left. The table hung on the cusp of falling over for a moment before the two legs hovering in the air landed back on the ground. Sophie gasped a relieved breath, her body vibrating with fear and adrenaline.

"Oh my god, I almost tipped over. Be careful," she warned Ruby.

Another boom hit the house, hard enough that dust rained down from the wooden ceiling. The lightbulbs danced above them again, swaying on their wires.

"I'm so close. I'm so close," Ruby said. "Keep going!"

Sophie could feel the brush of Ruby's fingertips as she tried to get a hold of the knife sheath. A soft sob came from the direction of Sophie's feet. "I can't reach," Ruby cried, despair filling her voice.

"It's okay. One more heave, and we've got it, okay? You just have to try again. You've got this," Sophie said, infusing confidence she didn't have into her voice. "Let's go on three."

"Okay," Ruby replied.

They counted down together. "Three. Two. One."

Sophie pushed past her lagging energy and dug for whatever strength she had left. This had to work. She threw the lower half of her body with all her might towards her sister.

The table skittered and almost tipped again, but it jumped another inch. A moment later, Sophie felt Ruby's fingers crawl their way under her pants leg. With a resounding, relief-inducing rip, the Velcro binding gave up its prize – the knife that Sophie vowed never to be without again.

"Cut your ropes and then get mine," Sophie called out, desperate but feeling hope start to fill her veins. They could do this. And Sophie planned to make Cordelia *very* sorry for her actions.

Above Sophie's head, a door banged open, slamming against the wall with a crash. She could hear unintelligible yelling from the floor above now.

The creak of a stair made Sophie freeze in a panic for a moment before she started twisting on the table, trying to contort herself so she could see who was coming down the stairs. She silently prayed for Ruby to hurry up and get loose.

Her view of the person was upside down, but it took only a second to recognize Marcella. Little bolts of lightning were flickering from her hands, and her silver hair was raised in a halo as if from static electricity.

Sophie felt a betrayal so deep she couldn't breathe. The hiss of shock near her feet made Sophie realize that Ruby was feeling the same way.

"I found them!" Marcella yelled, turning her head back to the open door at the top of the stairs.

As Mac's voice echoed from outside the door, relief swarmed Sophie. She could hear him roaring her name. Sophie lunged up from the table, wanting nothing more than to get to Mac, pulling at her restraints like a trapped animal. Mac appeared in the open door, eyes wild. His mouth dropped open in shock for barely a second when he spotted Sophie before he was clattering down the stairs, practically skipping three steps at a time.

Sophie didn't even realize she was calling his name until he skidded to a stop at her side, and he kept repeating, "I'm here. I'm here. You're okay now." He gently brushed her hair back from her forehead and pressed a kiss there. "I need a knife!" he bellowed.

"Here," Larry's familiar voice replied, handing Mac a knife. Her knife.

Looking over, Sophie saw Ruby crying in Larry's arms, the ropes that had restrained her gone, the cut ends frayed and tossed aside. After handing Mac the knife, Larry slid to the floor, pulling Ruby into his lap like she was a small child. She clung to the lapels of his suit jacket like she never wanted to let go.

Mac made quick work of the ropes, sawing through them efficiently. He hissed and cursed under his breath when he saw the state of Sophie's wrists and ankles. His face was haggard and filled with a murderous rage.

Helping Sophie sit up, Mac started checking her over. Something felt wrong with her left shoulder, and she couldn't seem to move that arm correctly. She suspected that it might be dislocated.

There was a part of Sophie that still couldn't believe that she'd been rescued. It all felt like an unreal dream. She'd thought she was going to die tied to a table in a grimy basement.

"Where are we? Are we under the candy shop?" Sophie asked.

"No. Do you remember the Butterfat Palace near Agate Beach?" When Sophie nodded, Mac explained, "That's where we're at. Well, underneath it, I suppose."

"How'd you find us?"

"Larry," Mac said, inclining his head towards the warlock who was still on the floor, sitting cross-legged and rocking Ruby. She was curled in his lap like she was trying to merge into his chest.

When Sophie wrinkled her eyebrows in confusion, Mac explained, "Reggie called me when you didn't show up at the diner. They waited for almost twenty minutes before getting worried. He thought you guys had a lot to discuss and didn't want to interrupt. When they couldn't find you, they called me. We checked the pub and the rest of Abernethy Street, but the rain had washed away your scent trail. I was freaking out, so Dad called Marcella to tell her that you were missing. She called in

Larry, who can do a tracing spell. He just needed something personal of yours to do the spell. Marcella brought Larry and half the Conclave's security team here on her personal jet. Larry used your hairbrush, and it led us right here."

"How long have we been missing?"

"Too long. I think I lost a few years of my life." Mac glanced at his watch. "Just under four hours."

Sophie repressed a shudder. Mac must've been losing his mind.

"Can we check you guys over?" a quiet voice asked. Sophie looked away from Mac to realize that Reggie and Grady were hovering nearby, wearing identical looks of worry on their faces. When Sophie nodded, Reggie approached her, and Grady veered off to check on Ruby.

A low murmuring drew her attention towards the basement entrance; Sophie could see most of her friends crowded at the top of the stairs. She gave them a thumbs up to let them know she was okay.

"Hey, Soph. Looks like you've had a hell of a day," Reggie murmured softly, making Sophie chuckle in a somewhat deranged way at the massive understatement.

He inspected her wrists and ankles, clucking at the damage. "Something's wrong with my left arm," Sophie informed him. The pain in her shoulder was starting to become unbearable. Agony shot from her shoulder in throbbing waves, cresting down her arm and making her fingers feel numb.

He gently palpated the area, giving Sophie a sympathetic look when she hissed in pain.

"She's dislocated her shoulder," Reggie said softly, his voice soothing like he was trying to keep from spooking a scared, wild animal. "We need to get her to the hospital. They'll be able to pop it back into place there."

Sophie didn't think she could wait that long. The pain was starting to make her head spin. She'd once heard that the pain would drastically reduce once the dislocated joint was back in its socket.

"Can you fix it now, Reg? I don't want to wait," Sophie asked.

"I can pop it back into place and then wrap it up. But maybe it would be better if we took you to the hospital," he suggested.

Sophie was already shaking her head before he'd finished making the suggestion.

"No. I trust you. I want *you* to fix it. Please?"

"I can put it back, but you'll still need to see a doctor. They'll need to x-ray the area to make sure you don't have damage to muscles, tendons, or ligaments. Promise me you'll go see a doctor after this?" Reggie demanded.

"I'll make sure she does," Mac promised. Sophie was too worn out, both physically and emotionally, to argue. She was sure that Reggie was right. Plus, she wouldn't want to walk away from this day with any permanent damage.

Reggie had Sophie lie back on the table that she'd hoped never to be near again. Reggie carefully cradled her arm in his, keeping it straight and level with her body, slowly moving it until it was at a ninety-degree angle from her side. "Hold her still," Reggie commanded Mac while he took a firm grip on her arm with both hands, careful not to touch the rope burns encircling her wrists. Reggie slowly started to pull on her arm with steady pressure, bringing it closer to her head and rotating slightly. Sophie gritted her teeth to lock away any sounds of pain that wanted to escape her throat. She felt the head of her humerus slide across the rim of her joint opening before it dropped into the socket with a *clunk*.

Despite Mac's tight hold on her, Sophie jolted off the table. She made an animal noise of pain despite her best efforts to remain stoic and silent. The agony was momentarily a bright and sharp thing, like being stabbed before it reduced to an aching throb.

Reggie brought her arm back to her torso, bending her elbow and laying her forearm gently across her belly.

"We're going to need to immobilize it. Have her hold it still while I look for something to make a sling," Reggie said.

"I'll get it," Fitz yelled from the stairs.

"Thank you, Reggie. It already feels so much better," Sophie said, reaching out with her good arm to clasp Reggie's hand in hers.

Reggie asked Ace and Amira to fetch his first aid kit. Out of the corner of her eye, she could see her friends scrambling away.

Fitz appeared only a few minutes later, ripping several long strips from what appeared to be expensive sheets.

"Where's your dad?" Sophie asked Mac, looking around and not seeing Carson.

"Oh, he's sitting on Cordelia upstairs."

"How pissed is he?" Sophie asked, picturing the sheriff in her head.

"I've *never* seen him this pissed. And I once snuck out of the house when I was grounded to go to a party and ended up wrecking his truck. She's lucky she's in one piece still. He's almost as pissed as I am." The look in Mac's eyes told Sophie that he was barely keeping his rage under control.

At Reggie's command, he had Mac help Sophie sit up. He carefully wrapped Sophie's arm to her torso and then used a second strip of bedsheet as a makeshift sling.

A few of Marcella's guards, looking suitably menacing and competent, were busy noting and cataloging everything in Cordelia's basement of horrors.

Ace and Amira clattered down the stairs, Ace holding Reggie's first aid kit in a tight grip. Sophie felt terrible because it was obvious that the kidnapping had terrified her friends. They were falling all over themselves to keep busy.

Opening the case, both Reggie and Grady pulled out bottles of antiseptic and bandages. They cleaned and bandaged the rope burns on Ruby and Sophie's wrists and ankles.

All the while the doctors worked, Marcella silently watched from across the room, her face unreadable. When Reggie finished wrapping the last wound, she floated over.

"We're about to question Cordelia. Would you like to observe? You've certainly earned the right to participate if you'd like," she offered.

"Yes, I would like to watch," Sophie confirmed. "By the way, right after she drugged us, she told me that she worked for the Conclave." She watched Marcella's face closely, wanting to know the truth. Marcella looked perplexed by this news, but Sophie figured that a seasoned politician like the Conclave Magistrate could easily fool someone like Sophie.

CHAPTER 20

⮽

*M*ac helped Sophie off the table and up the stairs with a hand on her good elbow. Walking through the basement door to the main house, Sophie was somehow both surprised and not by the tasteful elegance of the kitchen. It had the feeling of a French provincial cottage. A bowl of bright, cheerful lemons graced the center of a long trestle table that looked like it had hosted generations of families. Frilly curtains framed a window that looked out towards the craggy coastline of the Pacific Northwest.

The metaphor of rot hiding beneath a fancy façade wasn't lost on Sophie.

Walking through the house, she sensed that each piece of furniture had been picked with care to match the era and affluence of the home. She felt like she was walking through a magazine spread. It felt more like a museum display of the perfect Victorian house than a place where people lived and went about their daily lives. As Sophie walked past an overstuffed parlor set, facing a tiled fireplace, she nudged one of the seats off kilter. It was a small defiance, but it made her feel better.

More of Marcella's men in black were peppered throughout

the house, searching through Cordelia's belongings, looking for who knows what. Sophie decided she didn't really care. Her arm hurt, the rope burns felt like brands on her flesh, and she was hungry.

They entered one of those fancy dining rooms where a long wooden table dominated the space. The table was set as if waiting for a dinner party – ready to entertain at a moment's notice. Sophie would bet her salary that the cutlery was made of heavy polished silver and the plates were bone china.

Carson was leaning against a window framed by heavy brocade curtains in a rust red that looked out over an herb garden. It looked like someone had plucked an old-west cowboy and dropped him into Victorian England. His gun was again prominently displayed against his crossed arms, the barrel not-subtly pointed in Cordelia's direction.

Cordelia was sitting at the table across from Carson, looking timid. Mac pulled out a heavy wooden chair covered in the same silken material as the curtains for Sophie to sit in. He sat beside her, giving her thigh a reassuring squeeze.

A hard look passed over Cordelia's face when she spotted Sophie's sling made from her pretty French toile sheets. In a blink, the look disappeared, and Cordelia once again had her sweet granny façade back in place. She looked like a fairy godmother just hoping to get some poor teenage girl ready for the ball.

Sophie's friends, along with a small contingent of the Conclave's agents, spread throughout the room, filling the space.

Faced with a room full of pissed-off faces, Cordelia simpered, "I think this was all just a big misunderstanding."

To Sophie's left, Marcella sat. She leaned forward in her chair, looking like a raptor ready to strike its prey. "A misunderstanding," she repeated. "How exactly does kidnapping two employees of the Conclave, here in town conducting an investigation on my behalf, constitute a 'misunderstanding'?"

"I've been working with Bramwell for well over a decade," Cordelia said. Marcella's jaw clenched at the mention. "He is a well-known representative for the Conclave. I had no reason to doubt him."

Sophie felt like she'd heard that refrain a lot. What a cop-out.

"You've been killing people for Bramwell, and you didn't think to confirm that you weren't working for one of the bad guys?" Sophie scoffed.

"You're young, so it's understandable that you don't get how things work. You'll understand when you're older. But how naïve *are* you that you think the Conclave doesn't get its hands dirty?"

Sophie sputtered. "Understand what exactly? That it's okay to murder people for money? There's no justification you can possibly come up with that would excuse your actions. You're a fucking monster. And you were planning to murder me and my sister not an hour ago, so forgive me if I don't 'understand'."

"It was nothing personal, dear. It's just business." Cordelia gave Sophie a look of disdain that only an older woman could manage, both indulgent and condescending in equal measure.

Mac lunged at Cordelia, claws poking through his human fingers and outstretched for her throat, but his father managed to catch him by his nape and pull him back into his chair. Sophie placed her hand on top of his, running a soothing thumb over his knuckles while his claws slowly retracted back into his fingertips. A low, threatening growl rumbled from Mac's throat as he stared down at Cordelia.

Cordelia delicately cleared her throat, looking quite worried. She needed to be worried. "I wasn't going to murder you," she said. "I was just going to merge you both back together."

The table went silent at her proclamation.

Marcella leaned forward, her eyes blazing and intent on Cordelia. "Explain. What have you been doing here in Murias?"

Cordelia hesitated for a moment, but one look at Marcella's face, and she started talking. "Bramwell has been bringing shards to me for at least ten years. He brings them to me after they've been delivered through the Fae portal. Then he implants memories in them with my help. I also place a geas, so they don't look too closely at their history." Cordelia looked smug about her work, but hurried on when she realized that no one around the room appeared impressed. Quite a few looked positively murderous. "A couple of months ago, Bramwell approached me about a new project. He had found someone who had managed to put two shards back together. He wanted to recreate the magic, but with a few modifications. He had me work with Henri Boudreaux on a spell that would return the shards to their original form. He was especially interested in regaining the original's full magical ability. The first six experiments were complete disasters. The poor shards didn't survive the ritual. Some with truly disastrous results – what a mess!"

Sophie wanted to scream at Cordelia, who was so nonchalant about experimenting on people. She'd seen those 'disastrous results', and saying it was a mess didn't really convey the true horror of it.

"Well, we finally managed to merge two men back together," Cordelia continued, not swayed by the darkening expressions around her. "But then we found that because the shards had been living two separate lives with completely different personalities and memories, the men's minds couldn't handle being combined. We were going to see if we could remove one of the personalities, but he managed to escape before we could get started. I didn't realize he could teleport! Imagine my surprise when he appeared in town."

"Milford Bradley," Carson explained to Marcella. "We found him wandering, lost in the woods a few weeks ago. No wonder he could never remember if his name was Milford or Bradley. It was the names of two men, yes?"

Cordelia nodded her head. "And then he attacked my shop. What a dreadful incident."

"Yes, so dreadful." Ruby's deadpan voice seemed to go over Cordelia's head.

Sophie vividly remembered Milford standing on the sidewalk in pajamas, crying about noise while pointing at his temple.

A sudden thought popped into Sophie's head. "Two to one!" she exclaimed. "I thought he was saying numbers 'two two one'. But he was trying to tell us that he'd been turned from two to one."

Sophie had never wanted to hurt someone as much as she did Cordelia. Well, except maybe Bramwell.

"Then what happened?" Marcella asked, redirecting everyone back to the main issue.

"We realized that we would have to remove or supersede one of the shard's personalities for the ritual to work properly. Otherwise, the recombined shards would most likely go insane. The trick was to unite the bodies and power of both shards without the mind and memories of one. It took us a couple of tries, but we finally figured it out. We basically had to drain the power and lifeforce of one of the shards and put it into the other while leaving the mind behind. It was quite the success."

"What happened to that re-merged shard? The one that was a success?" Carson asked.

"Oh, Henri said he'd dispose of the body. Bramwell was clear that he wanted all loose ends tied up. Henri told me he took him out into the woods and shot him. Quite barbaric, I think, but Henri has his own methods. I'm not one to dictate how someone should conduct their business. I felt there were some bugs to work out in the ritual and told Bramwell as much, but Henri disagreed. He felt that the spell was good enough. He left town, but Bramwell gave me permission to continue my research. So, when I saw Ruby and Sophie in town, I assumed he had brought them here for me. I couldn't let them leave town when they mentioned returning to San Francisco this morning."

"Does Bramwell know that you kidnapped Sophie and Ruby?" Marcella asked.

"No, he doesn't know. I tried to call Bramwell and inform him, but he didn't answer."

There was a lull in the interrogation as everyone mulled over everything they had learned.

Sophie stared at Cordelia, trying to pull up a memory of her. But there was nothing but a blank in her mind. A headache started to form behind her eyes as she tried to remember.

"We've met before," Sophie clarified. "When Bramwell brought us to town to get us sigil tattoos. I have no memory of meeting you before this week, but we've met, right?" When Cordelia nodded but didn't elaborate, Sophie huffed an annoyed breath. "Tell us what happened when you met us."

"Bramwell brought the five of you here about five years ago. I'd never even heard of someone being fragmented into five pieces, so I found you very interesting. You'd already received your tattoos, so whatever power you had left was suppressed. I helped Bramwell insert your new memories and placed a geas on all of you. I was quite proud of that work. Doing five geases in one night is quite exhausting. It's delicate work, you know."

"I've looked into both of their histories. There is a paper trail supporting their implanted memories. How did you manage that?" Mac asked.

"I have no idea. It's not something I know anything about. Bramwell takes care of the paperwork."

There's paperwork? Sophie barely kept herself from rolling her eyes. This was all a bunch of bullshit.

"I want the geas spell removed," Sophie demanded.

"Me, too," Ruby agreed.

"I can remove the geas, but you'll still have your current memories that Bramwell implanted. I don't believe you can get your real memories back. He erased them," Cordelia explained.

"I don't care. I want it fixed now."

Marcella nodded to have Cordelia get started. Cordelia came around the table and began to reach for Sophie, but Ruby leaned across Sophie's lap and gave Cordelia a smile.

"If you do anything to hurt Sophie, or me, I will cut your throat," she warned. Ruby sat back in her chair, watching Cordelia with an unblinking stare.

Sophie heard Cordelia swallow before she placed her hand on Sophie's forehead. The witch said a phrase that sounded Italian or probably Latin, knowing how much Mythicals loved ancient languages. Sophie felt warmth spread out from Cordelia's palm, wrapping around her head. The heat lingered for a minute when the witch removed her hand before slowly dispersing.

Sophie watched as Cordelia went through the same process with Ruby.

As Cordelia returned to her seat, Sophie watched Ruby open her eyes. They stared at one another for a moment before Ruby asked, "Do you feel any different?"

"Not really. Although I can think about my parents now. You?"

"Same. I think I can feel the edge where the memories aren't as clear. My first truly clear memories were when I joined my first traveling acrobatics troupe. Everything before that is a blur. The further back I go, the fuzzier it all gets."

Sophie nodded in agreement. "Same."

Marcella cleared her throat. When Sophie and Ruby looked at her, she said, "So, you two are alright? No pain or discomfort?"

When they shook their heads, Marcella turned back to Cordelia. "Have you ever been a participant in the spell that creates the shards?" she asked.

"Never. From what Bramwell told me, only the Fae queen knows how to perform it."

Marcella nodded, a look of relief on her face. Sophie could guess that no one wanted that kind of spell to become common knowledge. If only one person knew how it worked, it would be easier to contain.

"Did you ever participate when Blathmac tattooed the shards?" Marcella asked.

"No. I've wondered if it was Blathmac who did the tattoos, but since he's the only local tattoo artist, it made sense that it was him."

It seemed like Bramwell kept each person working under him ignorant of the others. It was like trying to unravel a terrorist organization where each cell didn't know the identities of the others. Sophie was annoyed and worried that they'd never untangle Bramwell's scheme.

As Marcella started asking probing questions about the other shards, Sophie's attention began to drift off. She could feel the lack of sleep and food starting to catch up to her.

"I'd like to go home now," Sophie announced, her voice quiet but firm. She didn't care if she was acting childishly. She just wanted to go home, curl up in her bed and pretend none of this ever happened.

"Me, too, actually," Ruby agreed. "I mean, is there anything else we need to know here? Until Bramwell is tracked down, we're not going to learn anything else about ourselves. All we know is that we're shards. We don't know who we used to be or what we did to cause the Fae queen to split us up. Now, Bramwell is trying to put shards back together and is perfectly happy to kill a bunch of people to make that happen. We don't know why. We have repressed powers, but unless we can figure out a way to unlock our sigil tattoos, we can't access them." Ruby stopped and took a deep breath after her rambling monologue. She was sitting next to Sophie, across the table from Cordelia. Ruby gave Sophie a soft, sad look. "We have all these people getting hurt and killed. And we just want to live our lives as they are now. We've earned that right. And here is this bitch—" Ruby pointed an accusing finger at Cordelia "—acting like it's 'no biggie, just business' as if that makes what they've done to us and all the other shards okay."

Suddenly, Ruby lunged across the table and grabbed Cordelia's wrist in a tight grip. Then she started detailing Cordelia's many, *many* crimes. The witch tried to leap out of her chair and escape, but Ace and one of Marcella's minions pinned her back in her seat. By the time Ruby was done, everyone knew about the years and years of murders she'd committed in the name of 'business'.

Ruby got up from the table, dusting her hands off. Cordelia gave her a look of pure unadulterated hate. Ruby started to leave the room but turned and looked back at Cordelia like she was a piece of dog shit stuck to her shoe.

"Oh, by the way, Cordelia... Everyone in town knows you cheat and use magic to create your pie crusts. It's the only way you can beat Pam," Ruby announced, giving Cordelia a head-to-toe look of derision before she stalked out.

Getting up from her chair so quickly that it almost fell over, Sophie hurried to follow her sister. She didn't have Ruby's gift with words, so she gave Cordelia the middle finger as she left.

Sophie ran through a living room, dodging past Marcella's people, to catch up with Ruby and give her an approving look. "Damn, Ruby. Harsh. I like it," she teased, bumping her hip into Ruby's.

The sisters wandered past the men and women combing through Cordelia's house and out the front door. They sat, side by side, on the top of the steps leading from the expansive front porch to a circular gravel drive. The afternoon sun shone down on the rolling hills, making the entire area look like it was covered in a lush green blanket. Sophie could easily imagine children running through the tall grass, frolicking and playing tag. It should've felt magical. But Sophie couldn't enjoy the view. She felt hollow and sick to her stomach.

"Should we go back in?" Ruby asked, glancing back at the house with a look of dread in her eyes.

"And waste that epic walk-out? Nah. They'll tell us if they find out anything else important."

A few minutes later, Marcella showed up, sitting next to them on the step, which felt weird. Marcella didn't seem the type to risk soiling her expensive pantsuit, so Sophie appreciated her effort to put them at ease. Sophie assumed she was there to ensure the sisters weren't about to have a meltdown after the day's revelations. Or possibly go on a murder spree.

"Did you know about the shards?" Sophie asked. "The tattoo artist mentioned that they get dumped here by Queen Maeve, so they must pass through the Coit Tower portal, right? Isn't it your job to get the Mythicals ousted from the Fae realm settled in the community?"

"I've known about a few shards over the years," Marcella admitted. "But not you, and not any of the others that Bramwell's been experimenting on. I was always notified when they were being deported here, and my team fetched them from the portal. I personally got them settled in the city with new identities and jobs. But we *never* erased their memories or experimented on them. I don't know why Bramwell is doing all this, but it stops now."

Sophie shrugged. She didn't have complete faith that Marcella could keep that promise. She couldn't even locate Bramwell, so how was she supposed to stop his nefarious plans?

"Can I see your sigil tattoos?" Marcella requested.

Ruby turned her head, pushing her hair out of the way. Marcella leaned close, silently staring at the tattoo for a full minute.

"Well?" Ruby asked.

"That's Queen Maeve's crest, alright. She is certainly the one who did this to you."

"Can you read the phrase around the tattoo?" Ruby asked.

"No, I believe that is the lost language of the Fae. I'm not sure how, but we'll find a way to figure out how to unlock your sigil tattoo. There must be someone who knows the royal Fae language," Marcella said, probably just trying to soothe Sophie and Ruby's ruffled feathers. They had every right to be angry, and Marcella was the one who sent them directly into the path of danger. Although Sophie couldn't really hold a grudge – it's not like anyone could have guessed what would happen. *Marcella would probably love to have us at full strength and working for her.* She didn't trust anyone in a position of power to not use her and Ruby. And Marcella had always viewed them more as tools than people.

"I'm not sure I want our full powers back. Apparently, we were so scary – even after being fragmented – that the tattoo guy practically pissed himself at just seeing our faces again," Sophie replied. She found Ruby nodding in agreement.

"I understand that this investigation has turned into something quite traumatic. And I'm very sorry about that. However, I'm hoping you'll continue to work with the Conclave," Marcella said, becoming diplomatic once more. "Despite what Cordelia said, we are trying to do good. We just want a place where Mythicals can live in peace and thrive with humans. And I think you should consider the idea of accessing your full power. The fear of one man shouldn't keep you from your full potential. Weak men are often scared of powerful women."

Sophie appreciated the sentiment, but Marcella hadn't seen the look in Blathmac's eyes. This was more than simply a man intimidated by a strong woman.

Marcella fell silent after that suggestion, looking out over the rolling fields with a faraway look in her eyes.

"I'm going to be staying here in Murias for at least a few more days to see if we can uncover more about what's been happening here," she finally announced. "However, you are both free to use my jet to return home. I can understand if you'd like to get away from town for the time being. Take a few days to rest and recover, perhaps."

"Yes, I think I'd like to take you up on that offer. After the night I've just had, I'd really like to get back to my own bed," Sophie replied.

The sisters followed Marcella back into the mansion, trailing behind her into the dining room where everyone was waiting for them.

Marcella announced that Sophie and Ruby were leaving, and if anyone else wanted to accompany them, they were welcome to use her jet to return to San Francisco. Sophie saw Amira's eyes light up at the idea.

"What about our car rentals?" Reggie asked.

"My people will take care of it. Just tell them what you need," Marcella breezily informed them.

"It's good to be the Magistrate," Ruby whispered to Sophie with a smirk.

"We need to have Sophie's shoulder x-rayed at the clinic," Mac said; his face made it clear that it was a non-negotiable stop.

"Of course," one of Marcella's black-suited employees replied.

Cordelia watched with a sourpuss look as everyone got up from the table and started to shuffle out of the room with low murmurs. Before leaving, Sophie saw Marcella take a chair across from the disgraced witch, a deadly look in her eyes. Not that Sophie felt a single drop of sympathy for Cordelia. She was reaping what she'd sowed.

Sophie glanced around at her gathered friends. They looked like they'd been through the wringer. She felt bad; she'd brought them here and then repeatedly put them in danger. Sophie walked over and plucked a leaf out of Ace's hair. He laughed when he saw it, ruffling his fingers through his hair to dislodge any other forest detritus that might have been clinging to him.

Sophie looked over and spotted Larry and Ruby wrapped around one another like anacondas.

"I have to stay. I don't have a choice. Marcella needs me here," Larry softly told Ruby, who shook her head in denial. "I'll come to see you as soon as I get back into town."

Sophie quickly looked away to give them some privacy.

"I'll see you guys off, but there's work for me to come back to," Carson announced. "And I wanted to thank you for all you've done this week. I really appreciate everything."

Carson shook everyone's hands as they got into the car until only Sophie, Ruby, and Mac were left.

"Boy," Carson said, pulling Mac into a hug, clapping him roughly on the back. "I'm glad you came to visit. You should come by more often. And make sure you bring these fine young ladies with you."

"It's been a hell of a week, Dad. Thank you for everything."

"That's the understatement of the century," Carson said with a growl. "I can't believe all this has been happening in *my* town, right under my nose. Shards. Secret druid murder rituals. Unknown Fae turning up dead left and right. I'm ready to tear this town up by the foundation and root out all this corruption." Carson looked spitting mad and completely fed up. His jaw was clenched so tight that Sophie was concerned that he would crack a molar. But she also understood exactly how he felt.

Carson gave Sophie a big bone-cracking hug. "You come back and visit sometime, okay? Next time, there won't be any more trouble for you, I promise. You're welcome here anytime. Take care of yourself, okay?"

"I will," she replied, hoping she could keep that promise.

The drive back to Murias was quick and, thankfully, uneventful. After a quick stop for an x-ray, a real sling, and some pain pills, they finally turned down Abernethy Street. The town looked quiet for the first time since they'd arrived a week ago. Sophie assumed all the tourists in town for the Hunter's Moon Festival had left and returned to their regular lives, or were still sleeping in after the party.

Abernethy Street had returned to its sleepy small-town feel. It was quaint, pretty, and a nostalgic throwback to a simpler time. And if Sophie never saw it again, she wouldn't exactly be heartbroken. She would, however, miss many of the townsfolk, who'd fed her, welcomed her, and in the end, fought for her – especially Carson and Grady.

They turned at the end of the street, heading to drop off Grady back at the coroner's office. Everyone spilled out of the SUVs to say goodbye to him. Sophie waited patiently for her turn to hug the coroner she'd become so fond of. He had seamlessly integrated into Sophie's collection of odd friends as if he'd always been a part of the group.

"I hope you come visit again. Things are never boring when you two are around," Grady teased, pulling Ruby into his arms, squishing her against Sophie's side in a group hug. She still felt uncomfortable around her sister since the reveal of their true nature. But she knew she needed to push past the feeling – it's not like it was Ruby's fault that they were shards.

As Grady and Reggie shook hands, Sophie gave them a fond look. Despite how rough the week had been, Sophie was glad that the two doctors met and had a chance to become fast friends.

CHAPTER 21

As the plane picked up speed, the tree-lined airstrip
became a blur outside the window. As the jet took off,
Sophie's stomach felt weightless for a moment before settling
back inside her body. The town of Murias quickly shrank until it
was swallowed by the surrounding forests. Beneath their wings,
all Sophie could see was a vast dark green forest spreading until
it hit the ocean in one direction and disappeared over the curved
horizon to the east. Sophie was glad to leave Murias behind.

All she wanted was her bed in Brown Betty.

Sitting back, Sophie closed her eyes and took a deep,
cleansing breath. The upholstery was a butter-soft white leather,
cool and plush beneath her. Mac threaded her fingers with his. It
anchored her in a way she desperately needed. And the pain pills
were giving her some much-needed relief from the ache in her
shoulder.

Reclining the seat back, Sophie was cupped in its luxurious
hold. She immediately felt herself start to relax and deflate like an
old balloon.

The plaintive cry of the tea kettle pulled her from her book. Dog-earing the page, she got up from her reading chair and headed into the kitchen. A fluffy orange cat jumped onto the counter as she poured the steaming hot water into her favorite mug.

"Obie," she remonstrated. "You know you're not allowed on the counter. Naughty boy."

She scooped up the feline and deposited him back on the tiled floor.

A small black cat came running into the room, sliding to a stop next to Obie and giving a pathetic mewl.

"Dinner isn't for another hour, Titania. You don't need a snack."

A chime sounded from her office, informing her that one of her sensors had been disturbed. Heading that way with her two cats twining about her feet, attempting to trip her, she entered the room. A wall of monitors greeted her. Looking closer, she located what had set the alarm off: a delivery man in a brown uniform was dropping off a box at her front door. She watched as the delivery man walked back down her sidewalk, letting himself out of her front gate.

The long drooping palm tree fronds by the gate started waving in the wind, heralding a late afternoon storm.

~

Sophie opened her eyes. Above her head was an unfamiliar ceiling, futuristic and smooth. It took a moment for her to remember that she was in Marcella's plane.

"Did you have a good nap?" Mac asked. She looked over to find him watching her with a small smile.

"I did. How long was I out?"

"Less than an hour. We're going to be landing soon," Mac said.

Suddenly Sophie remembered the dream.

"Oh! I think I saw one of the shards," Sophie said, excitement churning in her stomach.

"The Corporate Bitch?" Mac asked.

"No, I think it was a different one."

CHAPTER 22

✺

*A*fter arriving back at Brown Betty, Sophie slept for fifteen hours straight. If she'd had any dreams during that time, she didn't remember them, and that was absolutely okay with her.

She wandered out of her bedroom, finding Mac in her kitchen, putting together a meal with the meager offerings from her pantry. His hair was still wet from a recent shower, and he wore a pair of faded jeans and a t-shirt. He'd never looked better in Sophie's eyes.

Mac carried bowls of oatmeal and some oranges to the kitchen table while Sophie grabbed their coffees.

"I need to head into the station," Mac said apologetically. "There are a bunch of cases I need to catch up on. And I'm sure the chief wants an update about Murias." He pressed a kiss to Sophie's forehead. "Oh, by the way, Reggie sent a text and said you didn't need to go into the morgue tonight if you need some time off."

Sophie shook her head. "I think it'll be good for me to get back to normal. How long do you have before you need to head in?" She gave him a carefully nonchalant look.

He must've guessed Sophie's thoughts because Mac gave her a lascivious grin. "I've got some time."

Sophie pointed her spoon at his bowl. "Well, eat up. You're gonna need your strength."

~

AFTER MAC LEFT FOR WORK, SOPHIE SHOWERED AND HEADED TO Birdie's apartment. She needed the normalcy of daytime TV with her best friend.

Birdie opened her door. "I didn't realize you were back. Why didn't you call me?" Birdie asked, clucking her tongue. With one fist propped on her hip and the other hand shaking a disapproving finger at Sophie, Birdie was the perfect picture of a sassy old lady. "I would've—Wait... Something's wrong. What happened?"

And just like that, Sophie inexplicably started crying.

Birdie ushered Sophie into her living room and steered Sophie towards her floral sofa with a firm hand, letting her cry on her shoulder. She made soft shushing noises and patted her hair. It took a few minutes to get herself back under control, but Sophie's tears finally ran out. She extracted herself from Birdie's arms, trying to get her watery sniffles under control.

"Do you want to talk about it?" Birdie asked, fetching a tissue box from the bathroom.

Sophie blew her nose, then staring unseeingly at the crumpled tissue in her hand, she started talking. The whole story poured out, the words tumbling out of her mouth almost feverishly.

Ginsberg, who was not usually one to tolerate being held for more than a minute, crept into her lap and let Sophie snuggle him under her chin the whole time. Maybe he sensed how badly Sophie needed the additional comfort.

"And then Marcella let us use her fancy jet to fly us home,"

Sophie finished lamely. She raised her eyes slowly from her tissue to look at Birdie's shocked face.

"Well, damn, girl. That's a lot. No wonder you're so distraught."

"I killed someone less than forty-eight hours ago. And I'm not as upset by it as I should be. I think that's what freaks me out. I should feel bad and I don't. I don't even know who I killed. There were bodies everywhere and I don't even know which one I murdered. It makes me feel like a bad person."

Birdie clucked her tongue in disagreement. "I think you need to give yourself a break. You were in a life or death situation and you chose life. There is nothing wrong with that. You protected yourself and your friends. You didn't start that fight so I don't believe you should feel a single moment of sadness over the choices those shifters forced you to make."

Sophie wasn't sure it was as cut and dried as Birdie described it, but she knew deep down that if she could go back in time, she would make the exact same choice to kill that shifter. Whether that made her a bad person or not mattered very little.

Birdie made some tea while Sophie traced her finger around one of the orange flowers decorating the sofa cushion.

Accepting her mug of tea, Sophie confessed, "I think what bothers me the most is that I don't even know who I am. I'm not even a whole person."

"The hell you aren't," Birdie replied, looking indignant.

"I'm one-fifth of a person," Sophie argued. "And no one else seems to care. Ruby already seems back to normal, like it doesn't even faze her. She was on the plane, sharing expensive champagne with Amira like she didn't have a care in the world. I mean, Ruby's different, so I don't expect her to react like someone normal. She's a bounce-back kinda person. But no one else besides me seems concerned that I'm broken."

"Sophie," Birdie said, her face stern. She sat down and grabbed both of Sophie's hands in hers. "I want you to listen to me. I've been around a very long time. I've met plenty of broken, incomplete people. And you're not one of them. Maybe when that asshole wizard fellow split you apart you were... Who knows? But whoever you used to be, whatever you used to be, you're whole now just as you are. I've watched you grow and make a place for yourself in this world. You're not one-fifth of a person. You're Sophie Feegle, and you're my friend."

Sophie felt tears flood her eyes. Maybe Birdie was right. Maybe who she was in the past didn't matter as much as who she was now.

"Also, don't assume Ruby is as unaffected as she appears. I suspect that girl is hiding her hurt behind a cheerful façade," Birdie said.

"You might be right. Maybe I should check in on her later."

Sophie knew that a looming cloud of problems awaited her, hovering in the future. She needed to find the other three shards, she wanted to help stop Boudreaux and Bramwell, and she needed to start school. But at the moment, she had her best friend, some tea, and daytime TV to enjoy. The rest was coming whether she wanted it to or not, so she needed to just embrace the joy of the moment.

"Isn't it almost time for *The Bold and the Beautiful?*" she asked, smiling slightly.

ACKNOWLEDGMENTS

I'd like to thank my beta readers for all their help. Their assistance is invaluable. Thank you, David, Jessica, Joanne, Karen, Paige, Pam, Tina, Rachel, and Susan! I'd like to thank my editor, Arundhati Subhedar. I'd also like to thank Rebecacovers for another beautiful book cover.

Lastly, I need to thank my husband. Without his encouragement and support, these books would not exist – and not just because he was the one who encouraged me to write in the first place. He is my soundboard and my support system. Seriously, every time I get stuck, I'm like 'Hooonnneeey, I can't figure this out'. And then he sits with me and brainstorms until we figure out the issue – and he usually comes up with something completely brilliant. So, thank you, thank you, thank you, babe.

You may have noticed that we have temporarily left my beloved San Francisco behind for this book. Odd Times for Sophie Feegle visited the northern edge of California for this story. I loved this area of California (and Oregon) when I lived in SF. The soaring Redwoods, the tiny mountain towns, the craggy coastline. Ugh, all gorgeous. If you're ever on the west coast, visiting the Redwood National and State Parks is well worth the trip.

I think part of the reason that I loved living in San Francisco so much was that such a huge variety of climates and landscapes were within a few hours drive of the city – beaches, mountains, deserts, rainforests. Now I live in Florida, where if you drive for five hours, you're still in Florida!

I based Murias off a couple of towns in California, mostly

Ferndale and Eureka. They have the most Butterfat Palaces for me to draw my inspiration from. In Irish mythology, four magical treasures of the Tuatha Dè Dannan came from each of the island cities (you know I love my Irish mythology). Those cities were named Gorias in the east; Finias in the south; Murias in the west and Falias in the north. Well, I had to pick the western city.

The Colpach Inn was based off the Carson Mansion in Eureka. It is one of the most photographed Victorian houses in America. It's now a private club, so plebeians like us can't get inside anymore. You can, however, take a virtual tour online. Fun fact: they based the train station at Disneyland after this building.

Fern Canyon is real, and it is worth the trek to get to it. Fair warning, it is slippery to walk through – and cold. Ask me how I know! I landed on my ass in that ice-cold water in front of my entire family. All of whom took delight in laughing at me! Rotten bunch.

Gold Bluffs Beach and Agate Beach are both stunning beaches. I vividly remember following the path to get to Gold Bluffs Beach and coming across a herd of Roosevelt Elk. Holy cow – they're huge! Also, you can camp on the beach itself there. I never got a chance to do so, but wish I had. What a way to wake up.

Lastly, Cascadia is real. Well, sorta. They have a flag, so good enough for me. It's a bioregion that covers Washington, Oregon, British Columbia, and parts of California and Alaska. From what I can understand, the Cascadians believe they should be an independent nation because the Cascadia bioregion should not be divided between several states and countries. They want to govern themselves and 'increase the independence and autonomy of our bioregion, reverse harmful colonial mindsets and policies, and grow a network of bioregional movements around the world.' I'm not one to debate the politics – I just thought it was an interesting idea to weave into the book.

Thank you for reading Odd Times for Sophie Feegle! I hope you enjoyed the book. If you did, please leave a review on Amazon – it really helps indie writers like me!

Please visit my website at www.gwendemarco.com or send me an email at gwen@gwendemarco.com.

ABOUT THE AUTHOR

Gwen DeMarco is an avid reader, wine & coffee drinker, gardener and a lover of all things nerdy. Gwen loves to write paranormal romance novels with a focus on the weird and wonderful. She loves to write a good snarky heroine and a grumpy male lead. Sophie Feegle is her first foray into the world of shifters, fae, ogres and vampires.

Gwen is happily married to her high school sweetheart and has two teenage children. She can often be found with her nose in a book and a glass of wine or mug of coffee in her hand.

To learn more, please visit my website and sign up for my mailing list to receive updates at www.GwenDeMarco.com

Made in the USA
Columbia, SC
03 April 2024